Praise for *Lessons in Faking*

"Athalia and McCarthy deliver peak enemies-to-lovers perfection. They're chaotic, complicated, and completely compelling. *Lessons in Faking* had me flying through the pages and grinning the whole time."

—Hailey Almsted, @haileyalmsted

"That slow burn? Torture, in the best way. I was hanging on every moment until it finally lit up, and wow, it delivered."

—Dana, @thesmallestbookclub

"This fake-dating situationship will have you kicking your feet as you wait to see what happens next between Athalia and McCarthy. A great first installment from Selina Mae!"

—Katie Gia, @thegiacobra

"Oh. My. God. This was so cute and so good. If you love Ali Hazelwood's *Deep End* and Elle Kennedy's college hockey series, this one is for you!"

—MacKenzie Wilcox, @bookskenziereads

"The banter was to die for!! I'm obsessed with Athalia and McCarthy's dynamic. If you love enemies to lovers and fake-dating, then you will fall in love with this book!!!"

—Brianna Whitman, @briannasreadingnook

"I absolutely adored this book. I read it so fast and loved it so much!"

—Abby Roth, @reviewbookswithabby

"The banter?? The tension?? The contracted fake dates that spiral into real feelings?? I was HERE for it."

—Allison, @allisonbookish

"This book had me swooning, crying, laughing, and feeling every emotion."

—Gabriella Tilaj, @gabbydoesreading

"A super cute and funny college romance that's full of yearning, tension, witty banter, and yummy chemistry. Throw in the fake dating trope with a snarky FMC and a charismatic, arrogant MMC, and I am completely SAT!"

—Jess Kaige, @jess.fantasybookshelf

"Fake-dating, spicy study sessions, & the TENSION! Selina Mae is spoiling us with these two!"

—Shay Franklin, @shayreads

LESSONS IN FALLING

By Selina Mae

Hall Beck University

Lessons in Faking
Lessons in Forgiving
Lessons in Falling

LESSONS IN FALLING

A NOVEL

SELINA MAE

An imprint of Authors Equity

Authors Equity
1123 Broadway, Suite 1008
New York, New York 10010

Cover design © Jeannine Schmelzer, Bastei Lübbe AG, and © Guter Punkt, Munich. Illustration © fjordwind. Motifs from Shutterstock (© Bobnevv; © Giuseppe_R; Platon Anton; Miloje)
Book design by Scribe Inc.

First published in Germany in 2025 by LYX, an imprint of Bastei Lübbe.
First published in the United States in 2026 by LYX, an imprint of Authors Equity.

Library of Congress Control Number: 2025948421
Print ISBN 9798893311631
Ebook ISBN 9798893311693

Printed in Canada
First printing

www.lyxbooks.com
www.authorsequity.com

This book contains explicit content. For more detailed information, please see page 379.

Disclaimer: The content warning includes spoilers for the entire book!

We wish you the best possible reading experience.

Love,

Selina & LYX

To those who love others much more than themselves.

Thank you, but it's time to think about you.

LESSONS IN FALLING

CHAPTER 1

VALENTINA

Fuck. Fuck, fuck, fuck, fuck.

I didn't speed often, really. Usually, I followed rules and drove the speed limit—and I was quite proud of the fact that I'd never been pulled over by the cops before. I was a good driver, and not much would make me jeopardize my reputation as one. But (accidentally) drifting around corners and squeaking to a stop almost with emergency-break swiftness didn't scream *safety* to me, so maybe I had changed.

I was late, though. For the best day of the year, no less.

Bottomless margaritas. Karaoke performances that became progressively worse the longer the night went on. Sandy feet, the sound of waves rolling against the beach in the near distance. My friends. A shabby bar on Oakport Island on the first weekend of July—where we'd stay for the rest of summer break.

Two months in which I didn't have to worry about my sister (impossible), my mom (always did), or the burden of upholding my imperfectly perfect college life for the sake of my family's validation. Two months in which, for the first time, I wanted to think about myself. Sometimes, at least.

So: Late. Drifting. Screeching to a stop in front of the gray colonial-style house I could almost call home. The blue shutters by the windows were open—probably hadn't been closed since the house had been built ten years ago. I could see the window to my room and already had the sheets of the upper bunk in my head.

Bunk, because I'd always stayed in the kids' room by myself, while my best friends were split into the other bedrooms that had a much more grown-up, *no-bunk-bed* feel to them.

All three of them stood on the curb now, performatively tapping one foot against the pavement and checking the time on the nonexistent watch around their wrists. Synchronized.

My windows were rolled all the way down, so I heard when one of them yelled "You're late!" just in case I hadn't realized. Iris grinned widely, gap between her two front teeth on full display when she emphasized, "I don't think I've ever seen you late for anything."

Alfie—his red hair wild from the coastal winds—nodded, then dramatically narrowed his eyes when our gazes met. "The invite says eight, and Valentina Rhodes will be on frat row at eight on the dot. It's an unwritten law."

"But here she is. Our favorite honors student," Anni jumped in, her German accent, as always, heavier after the month she'd spent back home. "Late. For the best day of the year."

Shutting the car door behind me, I tried to glare at them. Really, really hard.

And failed.

The corners of my mouth lifted, and everything that was happening—the deep, goofy smile on my lips; the way my cheeks hurt; the sparkle in my eyes; and the way my arms opened widely—was beyond my control. Like my body had a natural reaction to seeing my best friends and there was nothing I could do about it.

Our group hug (more of a tackle, really) was inevitable. Anni squealed first. She broke formation to jump those four steps toward me, her blonde hair whipping in every possible direction when she collapsed into me. The rest followed.

It had only been a month—one month and eight days, to be exact—since we'd last seen one another. Since Anni had flown to Stuttgart, Iris had gone back to her family in California, before they took off for a dream vacation to Cancún (which I'd not only been forced to follow on social media but received at least a thousand texts about, including beach and sea and pool pictures). Alfie had been *here:* his family's summer home on Oakport Island. And the rest of the Dunbridges—Mom, Dad, two younger brothers—had left yesterday.

"I missed the ferry," I mumbled my explanation into . . . somebody's hair. "They switched ours with the pedestrian one and let it go early. For reasons unknown." Iris pulled back, and I finally knew it was Alfie's wild, naturally red hair that had been tickling my nose, because Iris's *unnaturally* red hair followed with her. A color she'd said she'd picked to match his . . . gingerness. Only that it had turned out far more orange-pink-looking on her first dye job two years ago, and she'd stuck with the pastel color since.

When I first dyed my hair a week later, I'd kind of done it for the bit. Same as Iris, though I'd stuck with the cherry red. Her brown eyes were scrutinizing me now, narrowing and assessing. "You're usually an hour early to departure anyway. What—?"

"Mom."

There was no need to explain that my mom had been out all night and hadn't come home until an hour *after* I'd wanted to get going—even less that I couldn't leave my sister without knowing if she'd come home at all. Because my best friend closed her mouth and gave a single understanding nod, without my having to spell it out. "Ah."

I expected a moment to breathe when the rest started to untangle from me. Some time to take in the hydrangeas around the house, always at their best right after Alfie's family left. When we'd come here in the spring or autumn, sometimes over winter break, they did not look . . . well. But I had no time to marvel at their colors or hurl my luggage into the house or text Mom that I'd arrived (not that she'd care, necessarily), because Iris glanced at her phone, presumably saw the time, and zeroed in on me.

"Now *we're* late!" she screeched, and I barely had time to lock my car—still half-heartedly parked on the curb—before she dragged me toward her mint-green Bronco in front of the garage. The first time she'd rented it, our first summer here after our first year of college together, she'd said affectionately, *"One day I will buy you,"* and then kissed its hood goodbye.

For now, she'd opted for renting it every time we were here and insisting she always drive to make sure she spent "as much time with her as possible." *Her* being the car.

It must've been less than a minute before all four of us sat in Iris's beloved Bronco, and I didn't even attempt to request getting my luggage inside or having a glass of water or generally just a moment to breathe before we took off again. Alfie and I sat in the back while Anni got comfortable in the passenger seat. Iris glanced at me through the rearview mirror as she reversed out of the driveway. "I cannot believe you were late," she teased.

"The ferry was *early*."

With a cruel smile, her eyes went back to the road. "Because the ferry was early," she repeated pointedly, still smirking in that loving, know-it-all way of hers, "we're close to missing Chester's opening performance."

"And we cannot start our summer without a seventy-something guy singing 'Dancing Queen' to us!" Anni cried in agreement, and Iris sped up.

Our first weekend on the island always looked the same. Friday night was karaoke and margaritas, and Chester always opened the stage at 8:30 with the same song. Saturday morning was always full of regrets: a big hangover breakfast assembled from whatever Alfie's family had left behind before we stumbled into town, sometimes still half drunk (Alfie had thrown up on the twenty-minute trek at least twice already), to eat ice cream, window-shop, and eventually get another alcoholic drink once the Friday-night margaritas had settled.

We'd walk back slightly buzzed, sun burning, the breeze never breezy enough to feel relieving. Anni would be slightly sunburnt by then. Alfie as red as a lobster. And despite the inevitable nausea, I'd be the happiest I'd been in a long time. Sundays—Mom used to say, "*like God intended*"—we'd rest. Read books, swim in the pool or ocean, or take long, cold showers to cool down, depending on how warm the respective bodies of water would be.

It was 8:31 when we rolled into the parking lot of Blitz. "If we miss even a note of 'Dancing Queen,' I'm blaming Valentina!" Iris yelled, already halfway to the bar's entrance.

Alfie was, apparently, less worried about missing something. No urgency in either of our strides, we strolled up to the wooden door, its blue paint chipped by the salty sea. "You know," he said with a snicker, "you could've taken that pedestrian ferry, if you'd stop insisting on driving all the way down here with a vehicle that's not guaranteed to make the two-hundred-mile trip. Rent a car here that *doesn't* break down twice a month."

I would've also made it if I'd just stop insisting on cleaning up messes that, technically, weren't mine to begin with. Though minding your own business became a lot harder when it was your mother's mess, and you'd been growing up doing nothing but trying to please her.

I snorted, something between a laugh and a cackle as I shook my head. "Instead of eating when I get back to Hall Beck for grad school, right?"

"I'd take care of it."

"The eating part? Or the car-renting part?"

"Either." Alfie shrugged. "Both."

But he always did. It was half the issue. Feeling like I was inconveniencing my friends when they got me gifts or paid for stuff or went out of their way to do something nice for me, without expecting anything in return. It kind of just felt like they'd get tired of . . . providing eventually, and I'd lose them. Which was something I couldn't afford, ever.

"You know I don't want you to. It's enough you've been bringing us here for the past four years. Free of charge, by the way." I leveled the ginger with a look, pushing the creaky door to Blitz open.

The chatter was loud inside. Someone shouting orders at the pretty woman behind the bar, every kind of alcohol imaginable illuminated on the wall behind her. The stools were all filled, and she gracefully maneuvered from one paying customer to the other. The booths were strung along the walls, some of the red leather seats torn—but never enough to justify replacing them. Most of them were full, but I spotted Anni and Iris in the one closest to the stage, set up on the left, opposite the large French doors leading to the patio and beach.

My gaze snapped back to my friends, their full attention on Chester, taking up the entire stage with his presence. A maximum of ten gray hairs on his head, big nose, small glasses, wearing a flannel and shorts and Birkenstocks, he spotted us at the door, and at 8:33, his first "Ooh!" barreled through the bar's speakers. The crowd went wild.

*

I was on my second margarita (frozen, watermelon) when I noticed Anni's boyfriend was missing. He'd been a pleasant addition to our trips since last year, which meant he'd experienced a summer, winter, and spring on Oakport and had become an official part of the group in March. "Where's Mike?"

For a dreadful second, I feared they might've broken up. Then thought, *There's no way Annika Schmidt would go through a crisis like that without alerting the group chat.* The way she carelessly shook her head—a tipsy, endearing smile on her face—confirmed that and threw the rest of my worries out the window. Her lips pursed; she was probably about to say something like *Late* or *Waiting at the house* (becoming an official part of the group also meant knowing where the spare keys were hidden).

Instead, Iris leaned across the booth. Her arms sprawled over the table, fingers curling around the opposite side. "Mike!" she drawled, then sipped on her fourth margarita.

It took her five tries to get that straw into her mouth before she distractedly went on: "Even if we'd all been friends with him before, I might've still been fine with you two, you know?"

Alfie, beside Iris on the other side, gasped. "Despite the No-Fraternization Rule?" he whisper-shouted, and on the other side of Blitz, someone howled the high notes of "My Heart Will Go On" into the microphone.

"Despite the No-Fraternization Rule," she agreed. "And despite the fact I'm not particularly fond of men right now."

The No-Fraternization Rule.

Something that had started as somewhat of an inside joke four years ago and had turned into a solid ground rule between all of us since. We'd met through a happy coincidence called *free booze and no one to share it with* at a freshers' party. Around an illegal bonfire in somebody's backyard, for the sake of keeping our conversation going, Iris talked—and cried and shouted to us—about the ugly breakup she'd been going through.

That she'd lost her entire friend group because it'd been his friends too, and he must've been cooler, apparently, because they'd all *stayed* his friends and quite quickly—and unanimously—agreed not to give Iris the same courtesy. She'd lost her boyfriend, her friends, and her entire support system in the blink of an eye, and we'd been the strangers she could let it all out to.

We'd grasped almost immediately that we wouldn't stay strangers, though, and Iris had made it official thirty minutes later. She'd looked all of us in the eyes—Anni first, then Alfie, and me before she said, *"No dating within this friend group. We'll only adopt new people into it if none of us want to sleep with them."*

Four years later, it was still just us: something that would make it seem like we were a bunch of horny twenty-somethings, unable to find people we wanted to be our friends, without the desire to sleep with them coming up.

Not the case.

I'd had a handful of hookups since—something I had my physics major to thank for, among other things (I was much more likely to fuck up my sleep schedule with studying than another person)—and exactly one of them had been memorable. So the problem wasn't having too much sex to find other friends. The problem—and it wasn't really one—was, simply put: We didn't need anyone else.

Probably didn't *want* anyone else.

So the No-Fraternization Rule (NFR, for short) had never been a problem. Anni started dating Mike—Hall Beck University's soccer captain, very far removed from our social circle—and he started coming to Oakport as Anni's plus-one a year later. He seamlessly became a part of our *Us* because we really, truly loved him for her. He also got us into great parties, invited us for pizza after games, snuck us alcohol when we'd still been underage, and was incredibly fun to be around (when the soccer team was doing well and none of his guys were getting into trouble).

The latter was rare, the former much less so.

Then there was the fact that my one memorable hookup had been thanks to him—some guy on his team—which awarded Mike some more brownie points.

"Wow, Iris," Anni gushed, endearingly rolling her eyes, smiling brightly. "Thank God we have your blessing!" Then she looked back at me to answer the initial question. "He wouldn't have made it here on time. Said that if he wouldn't catch Chester's performance, 'what's the point, babe?'" Her voice pitched three octaves lower when she imitated him impressively well. "He's waiting at home."

And the word brought that familiar, fuzzy warmth back into the pit of my stomach—the one I'd been searching for since I'd been a child. That made me feel safe and accepted and like I belonged. *Home:* a feeling more so than a place.

So while Anni's boyfriend waited for us to get home, we demolished a last round of margaritas—on the house, courtesy of Iris's shrill, out-of-tune, but very passionate performance of "What Makes You Beautiful." At this point, Alfie struggled to get the straw into his mouth as well. Iris was ready for another rendition of an iconic 2010s song. Anni kept her from going back up to the mic, almost falling out of the booth, laughing and squealing. And all three of them had to keep me from texting my favorite Oakport fling so I wouldn't seem *desperate*, laughing and throwing my phone around the table to keep it away from my very desperate hands.

I couldn't have seen it coming: how big of a turn the night was about to take the second I'd get home.

CHAPTER 2

CADEN

I'd always thought of Valentina Rhodes as this whimsical, perfect figment of my imagination. Don't get me wrong, I knew she was real, and I was about . . . 90 percent sure that what had happened between us had been real too, but the second I'd laid eyes on her four months ago, she'd seemed a little impossible.

Her cherry-red hair, big brown eyes, round, rosy cheeks. The way she'd timidly sipped on her drink, smiled at me from across the bar—and the fact that she'd clearly had no idea that the way she walked and talked and danced had affected me so wholly.

That when she'd asked, after an hour of talking in some secluded corner of the party we'd been at, *"Are we leaving together, Callahan?"* I'd nearly combusted. And that sometimes, when I'd had a particularly bad day, I'd replay the way she'd said my name.

But because I hadn't heard from her since, I'd convinced myself I must've conjured her up. Ten percent of me, at least, believed I had imagined the whole thing.

Until now.

Four months later, a little past midnight too—but without a smile on her lips. Without that palpable tension between us, the need for more than flirty nothings exchanged in a loud college bar radiating off her. Because I was in her room, and judging by the scowl on her face, she had not expected me here.

In my defense: When Mike had warned me that I'd be sharing a room with one of his friends, the last person I'd expected to walk through the door was Valentina. Then again, when I'd walked through that door of our shared room a few hours earlier, the last thing I'd expected to find there was a bunk bed.

I'd been thinking about her a lot since we'd first (and last) seen each other four months ago, and still nothing could've prepared me for the visceral reaction I had when our eyes reconnected for the first time.

Like something had been unleashed, a sense of awareness that flooded through me. Reminded me of every single perfect thing about her—and why I hadn't been able to stop thinking about her. She'd been breathtaking then, in my mind, where I'd redrawn her from memory more often than I'd like to admit, but she'd still exceeded expectations. Somehow.

"What . . . ?" Her eyebrows drew together, as if she wasn't quite sure how to react to my presence. Fair enough, honestly. A (somewhat) strange man in my bed wouldn't exactly elicit a different response from me.

Valentina blinked rapidly, round eyes narrowing as she searched for the right words. Going by what I'd learned about her in those few hours months ago, I expected a *What are you doing here?* Maybe a *What is happening?*

Clearly, I did not know her half as well as I'd liked to.

"What the fuck?" The words basically flew out of her mouth, and at least she seemed a little surprised by them as well. Then she caught herself—planted one hand on her hip while the other pointed an accusatory finger at me. "*What the fuck* are you doing here?"

Did she remember? The way she'd whimpered my name, then cuddled into my chest like we'd been married for years? Then left before I'd woken up? It had only been a few minutes, but the fact that she hadn't acknowledged what had been the highlight of my fucking year . . . pissed me off.

I sat up straight, almost hit my head on the ceiling, and promptly remembered why I hadn't done that before. "Valentina, you wound me," I pouted. She narrowed her eyes—I wasn't even sure if she could still see me. "I missed you so much, I simply had to break into your room and ruin your summer."

The fact that I knew I wasn't being fair kind of made this worse. Obviously she deserved to know *what the fuck* I was doing in her room—I owed her an explanation, almost as much as her friends owed her an apology for the missing warning.

A simple *Hey, you'll have a bunkmate this summer* would've done the trick.

"Cut the shit, Callahan." Finally, Valentina stepped into our room. She forgot her suitcase in the hallway and swayed with each step until she could hold on to the dresser against the wall, to her right. She was clearly plastered. Drunk off her ass. Would probably not remember this conversation tomorrow. But all I could focus on was my name coming out of her mouth.

That despite the fact that there was nothing flirtatious in her tone, it still sounded just as beautiful as it had the last time.

So she did remember.

The satisfaction uncurling in the pit of my stomach was almost embarrassing—the urge to ask *Why didn't you call?* even worse. Juvenile, petty, not at all me. *I* was supposed to be the one who didn't call. The one who didn't care. *I* wanted no strings attached, and Valentina had done me a favor by leaving.

If I repeated it often enough, maybe I'd actually start believing it.

The women I hooked up with weren't usually this averse to seeing me again either. Mad because I hadn't called, maybe. Or shy because I *had* called, and they hoped I'd be trying to make whatever thing between us more than casual sex—which I never would and had made abundantly clear from the beginning. But neither of those seemed to be the case for Valentina. She seemed annoyed by my presence, not by the fact that I hadn't called. And there was nothing shy about her.

"Maybe you should ask your friends." The words were out before I could stop myself, and for a second, I wondered if *I'd* been the one who'd had too much to drink tonight. It would explain the way none of my bodily functions were under my own control and that I was still thinking about why she hadn't called. Or that it annoyed me way too much.

Unfortunately, I was not drunk. That captain spot waiting for me two months down the line made sure of it.

"They're not here, are they?" She crossed her arms, leaned against the dresser to face me on the top bunk. At this point, it seemed kind of ridiculous to still be up here. But getting down would feel too much like defeat. "Why would I go into their room when you're here—in mine?"

And she couldn't have given me a better in. I smiled. "*Ours.*"

She blinked at me. The silence between us felt louder than most stadiums and the next moment more crucial than a penalty shot. Like she was about to set our dynamic for the rest of the summer into stone.

Valentina burst out laughing.

She literally bent over, hands on her knees, and laughed so hard, she lost balance for a dreadful second. Her entire body was still shaking when I seriously thought she'd hit her head on the dresser behind her, sprinkling the white wood crimson. I didn't even realize getting off the bed, all traces of my own amusement wiped away, until I stood right in front of her.

She must've caught herself, though, because she slid down to the ground, back against the dresser, and there was no visible sign of a laceration, and no blood on the wood. She was still laughing, and my heart was still beating twice as fast, for some reason.

I did not need my new roommate to bleed out ten minutes after she got here.

"You okay?" I asked unnecessarily, crouching to her level. She was okay. Clearly. Smiling up at me, round eyes wide, *still* visibly amused.

Valentina snorted. "All that bleach must've gone to your head, Callahan," she said—*slurred*, really—one hand driving across my platinum-blond buzzcut.

I didn't think she meant for the touch to be as electrifying as it was. I think it was meant to be condescending. Her gaze held mine when her hand fell back into her lap, and I could breathe again. "If you think I'm sharing a room—*a bed* with you for eight weeks."

"Really?" My lips quirked. "You didn't seem to mind the last time we shared a bed. In fact, I remember you were sound asleep when I was barely out of you."

The reminder shot color into her cheeks, and she scrambled off the floor to gain some semblance of control over the situation. Meanwhile, the words directed blood into a completely different part of my body. Any and every thought about that night did, really.

Valentina shook her head, and I straightened back up to my full height with her. I could tell she tried not to let her eyes wander . . . up my chest, across my shoulders, all the way to the smirk on my lips. She was obviously failing. Her eyes were glued to them right up until they flicked upward to meet mine. "Why are you here, Caden?"

And I swear, I would've given her a proper answer this time. That I wasn't quite sure myself. That this was my first vacation in . . . ever, probably. That, when Mike had asked during penalty practice if I'd wanted to join him and his friends, the *no* before I scored had been an automatic response. I hadn't even thought about it.

"Come on, man," he'd said, walking to the other corner of the goal to get the ball. *"You could use a vacation."*

"Are you trying to tell me I look like I could use some rest and relaxation?" I'd asked, but the bags under my eyes probably answered for me. *"How dare you!"*

Mike had snickered, but the look my captain pinned me with said he hadn't been joking. *"The dark circles under your eyes have dark circles, dude. You missed four out of five penalties today. You're supposed to take over this team, and you need to be back on your A game by then. Two months on Oakport, and we can get you there. You want to be captain, right?"*

His question had been rhetorical, which was why I'd lied. *"Of course,"* I'd said—but that was just the thing, though. I didn't *want* to be captain. I wasn't even sure if I still wanted to be on the team. After winning the NCAA championship, one would think the school might take it easy on us, that there'd be less pressure. After all, we'd won them a trophy. What more could they expect? Not all of us could be Henry Pressleys, going pro and earning millions.

Turned out: a lot. To defend that title, for example. Apparently, for me to carry the team that was supposed to defend that title. Which came with a truckload of pressure and expectations I hadn't anticipated and had made enjoying the game significantly harder.

So Mike had been right that day. The circles under my eyes were beginning to look criminal. I had not been playing as well as I could have. And there was at least one person that did deserve my best.

Valentina didn't give me the chance to say any of that—at least a shorter, less whiny version. Because right after the words left her lips, her gaze diverted. Like she'd forgotten she'd asked me a question in the first place, her eyes darted through the room, looking for something she clearly couldn't find. She twisted and turned, walked from one side of the room to the other, and only remembered I was there when I said, "Outside."

Her eyes latched onto me, and I couldn't help my chuckle—although I did try to hide it with a cough. "Your suitcase," I elaborated. "It's by the door."

"That's not what I'm looking for." But she went out into the hallway anyway. Her head still shook in denial when she rolled the thing back into our room and closed the door behind her.

Our room.

It sounded more intimate than I'd like—as if there was more than that bunk bed we shared about our lives. As if we'd made a conscious decision to be here together and *liked* the fact that we were. Which was very obviously not the case.

I watched Valentina roll her suitcase through the room before I answered her earlier question. "Mike invited me. That's why I'm here."

Which wasn't all that much more revealing than my previous cryptic answers.

She groaned, but I wasn't sure if it was in response to my bullshit (yes, I could admit to that much) or the fact that she'd discovered my clothes in the top two drawers. Which, judging by the noise, she must've wanted for herself. Probably a combination of both.

"Your things are in my drawers," she confirmed. "You are in my room. In my bed." Valentina took a deep breath before she turned back, finding me leaning against the ladder of our bunk bed. "And I'm so drunk, I'm not even sure if I'm just imagining you. I mean, what are the odds? I let myself think about you once, and—" She shook her head again, turned back around like I might really just be a hallucination. Like she could get rid of me by simply focusing on something else.

Which was taking my clothes out of the top two drawers and moving them to the bottom ones. With no regard to how neatly they'd been folded, she threw them into their new home.

I thought she might be more careful with her own things when she began unpacking, but nope. She just threw those in as well. And I couldn't care less. "You were thinking about me?"

For a brief second, she stopped unpacking. Froze mid-motion, with her back still toward me. I tried not to let my eyes wander to the underwear bunched up in her hand, on their way into the drawer, but I did wonder if she'd brought the lacy pair she'd been wearing at my place that night.

Another rush of blood where it shouldn't be going forced me to shove all thoughts of her in those panties—of me, sliding them down her soft thighs—into the furthest corner of my mind. *Jesus*, I was worse than a teenage boy.

Valentina cleared her throat, threw her underwear into the drawer and closed it, too forcefully to be casual. When she turned, her cheeks still seemed a little warmer.

She shook her head. "Briefly," she confessed. "I don't make a habit of thinking about you, if that's what you're getting at."

I do, I thought. *Getting you out of my head has been a problem, and I don't know why.*

"Good enough for me."

She huffed, and I think she was giving up. Her shoulders sagged, and she leaned back against the dresser, crossing her arms lazily as her features relaxed.

And God, she really was beautiful. Even now, frustrated, flustered, and defeated. It felt appropriate to thank some higher power for making me come here, for making our paths cross again, and for making me realize that if there was one thing I wanted more than getting back my A game, it was having her again.

"Well." Valentina swallowed thickly before she pushed herself off the wooden dresser. And for a second, I truly thought my silent prayer was about to get answered and my wish granted—mere seconds after thinking it up. With the way she stopped only a foot short of where I was standing, I seriously considered finding my way back to God.

I looked down at her, our eyes connected, and I could swear everything that swam between us the last time we'd met—lust, awe, anticipation—was there again. For a very brief, very beautiful second. Her lips quirked before she burst that bubble of mine when she simply said, "The top bunk is mine."

CHAPTER 3

VALENTINA

I woke up where I always did in July. On the top bunk, in the guest room, in Alfie's summerhouse. On Oakport Island. I felt the way I always did, too: violently hungover.

And although never here, I'd had the occasional dream about Caden as well. Just never a bad one before.

When I usually thought of him, it would be with his hands on me, his body between my legs, and it always ended in an amazing orgasm. Then I'd remember that he'd given me three of those when I couldn't have known him for longer than a few hours and wistfully fell asleep.

So maybe it wouldn't have been all that bad if he'd actually been here—if only because I could finally thank him for whatever he'd done to me that night. Changed my perception of what sex could be, maybe. That men were actually capable of getting you off, and you didn't have to fake every orgasm when you wanted them to finish. It was a glorious discovery.

Disoriented, I glanced around the room. There was no sign of him, nothing that could hint at the possibility of last night being anything *but* a dream. Which was . . . relieving. Otherwise I'd feel bad for being rude and snarky and—dare I say—an asshole for so long, it would get exhausting even for me.

Because if Valentina was one thing, it was nice. Easy and accommodating. Thinking about being anything else made me feel physically sick, although that could just be the alcohol still swimming around in my system.

Getting off the top bunk still a little drunk, without falling off or throwing up, was significantly harder than I remembered, but I managed. My suitcase, half unpacked in front of the dresser, made me wonder what ghost of productivity had possessed me to unpack last night and why it hadn't made me finish the job.

I fished the T-shirt I'd originally packed to sleep in out of my suitcase, which drunk-me had clearly seen no benefit in doing. She'd thought climbing into bed in our sweaty, *drenched-in-margarita-spill* clothes from last night was a good idea. It was not.

I shrugged out of them, then into the oversized shirt, and continued my first full day the way I always did: heading downstairs, rummaging through cupboards for leftovers, trying to prepare breakfast with whatever I could get my hands on. As the first one up, that burden always fell on me.

Although, honestly, I hardly saw it as one. Being able to maneuver around a kitchen like this—with its long counters and professional equipment and the massive island in the middle—felt like a small blessing in itself. And after weeks spent at Mom's, cooking meals for three with one working burner and unsure if we'd still have electricity by the time we'd get to eat, I appreciated it just a little more. This one, though, was spacious—and we definitely didn't need to worry about the Dunbridges' energy bill.

The kitchen was an extension of the living room, in a big alcove to the left. Gold handles, white marbled counters, blue cupboards matching the window shutters outside. The theme extended into the rest of the house, too. The couch was white, the pillows dark blue, the vases and lights with golden accents. The TV hung above a fireplace, opposite the couch, which the dining table stood behind.

I looked around, letting the feeling of *Home* settle, and got started. After three glasses of water that were needed before feeling physically able to scramble the eggs I'd found in the fridge. Then another glass before I trusted myself with a sharp knife to cut up some of the fruit basket's contents. When I heard shuffling from upstairs, sounds that gradually turned into groans and curses, I toasted the bread and cracked the last two eggs into the pan—Iris preferred hers sunny-side up.

My best friend staggered into view a second later. Still groaning and cursing, she came up behind me, slung her arms around my torso, and whispered, "You're an angel" right as I plated her eggs. "I love you. How do you think my future husband will react when I tell him our wedding day could never live up to the moment of waking up on Oakport Island, violently hungover, not sure if you'll survive, only to see Valentina Rhodes behind the stove when you get downstairs?"

"How do you think *my* husband will react when I tell him the exact same thing?" Alfie materialized in the doorway, throwing another compliment at me before I could even soak up the first one.

The smile on my lips was too wide—my cheeks hurt. And no matter how hard I tried to play it cool (rolling my eyes, shaking my head, waving them off), how much I enjoyed all of this was apparent. Being showered in the loving-kindness my family never really gave me. A thanks here and there, sure . . . but I couldn't remember the last time they'd truly appreciated me or any of the things I'd done or accomplished.

Graduating summa cum laude from Hall Beck University got me nothing but a disinterested nod, paired with: "Cool. Congrats."

But this—my friends' smiling faces, their laughs and words of *actual* appreciation—almost made me remember why I'd craved the exact thing from Mom and my sister for so long. It also reminded me of why I needed to stop. Why I'd come up with a stupid plan to hopefully help me get there.

I had people who loved me, and that *should* be enough to keep me from seeking validation elsewhere. In a perfect world, they'd be enough, and in an even better scenario, appreciating *myself* would be all I'd need. Standing up for myself. Doing things for myself.

Unfortunately, I'd never been the selfish type.

Anni kissed my cheek when she joined us, snapping me out of my spiraling thoughts by taking Iris's plate out of my hand to give to her. "We can ask what *my* future husband will think when I tell him." She snickered in amusement at our synchronized eye rolls. As we carried plates, cutlery, and food to the outside dining area, she explained, "Him and Caden should be back any second. Think they went for a run."

I halted. So abruptly, Iris walked straight into me. Thank God she'd only had the bread in her hand, because she balanced the full basket like a pro (after a shrill, high-pitched gasp at my sudden stop) and sidestepped me to get outside.

I still hadn't moved an inch. Still stood in front of the sliding doors leading into the backyard. I could feel the light summer breeze, smell the salt in the air—but I could not move.

"Who?"

It was unnecessary to ask. Everything I'd chalked up to a funny nightmare suddenly felt paralyzingly real. Our entire conversation flooded back to me in one giant wave of regret.

Details I'd struck up as trivial (because they'd only been a dream) suddenly seemed life-changingly important (because they'd not been a dream). The way I'd barged into that room so drunk, I could barely keep upright. Then the way I'd unpacked my underwear like he couldn't see those lacy things in my hand.

If I remember correctly, you were sound asleep when I was barely out of you.

And my cheeks burned bright red even before he was just suddenly *there*. Like it was the most natural thing in the world, Mike and Caden jogged around the corner of the house, through the yard, and slowed when they approached the laid table.

Caden wore a cap, backward, that he adjusted as he came to a stop. Black shorts, gray shirt I couldn't see a drop of sweat through, despite the fact that they'd clearly been working out. His usual blond buzzcut was hidden, but that only left me focusing on his face more. A face that, unfortunately, was just as handsome as it had been four months ago. Just as carved and defined and unique as it had been last night.

Our eyes met, and the piercing blue of his finally snapped me out of my stupor—if only to get away from his gaze.

Fuck. He's real.

If possible, my cheeks turned an even darker shade of red as I sat down and continued remembering every single awful thing that had been said last night. That none of it had been a dream and all of it had actually happened. To distract myself (or try, at least), my eyes flickered across my friends so fast, I felt dizzy again.

None of them seemed surprised by his presence at all, though.

"Oh," Iris said when she looked at him, and I thought, *Finally.* Finally, someone would say *What the fuck?* in the same way I had last night. Ask why he was here so that I didn't have to.

Her gaze jumped back and forth between us, and she pointed her fork first at him, then me. "How's the roommate situation working out for you guys?"

All I could do was blink at her. Like a deer in headlights, mouth open. "What?"

Iris, full fork now on its way to her mouth, looked at me like *I* was the one losing it. "You guys are bunking together, no?" she asked, too casually for my liking. "How. Is. That. Working. Out?" Around a full mouth, she annunciated every word loudly and slowly, like I might actually be hard of hearing.

What the fuck is going on?

My eyes flew around the table again, quite manically. Caden, of course, had taken a seat opposite me. Mike and Anni sat next to him on the bench, Iris and Alfie on my side of the table. None of them made it seem like my confusion was justified.

Caden cleared his throat, and I made a point of not looking at him when he broke the silence between us. "It would've probably gone better," he said, reaching for a piece of bread. "If she'd been warned about the roommate beforehand."

Alfie gasped. Anni honest to God shrieked.

Iris, as always, said what the rest of them were probably thinking. "We forgot!"

"Oh my God," Anni said. "Oh my God. We didn't tell you. We forgot to tell you. Oh my God."

It seemed my friends could interpret the look on my face correctly, because they all wanted to explain—and started with a different part of the story, at the same time, making it an unintelligible mess for anyone who wasn't used to it.

"Because you were late—" Iris began.

"It must've been during that power outage at your mom's—" Anni said over her.

While Alfie was already thinking out loud, "You missed that weekly FaceTime call once, could it be—?"

I glanced at Mike and Caden. Unfamiliar with our group's dynamic, they were probably two seconds away from giving up on us. But there was a subtle smile on Caden's full lips when his gaze flicked between my friends, and Mike was just listening to his girlfriend talk, *I love you* written in the blue of his eyes.

"This is so fucked," Alfie concluded their rendition of Why We Didn't Tell You You're Sharing a Bed with a Stranger.

A quick summary: Two weeks ago, there'd been a power outage in Mom's neighborhood. It had been around six when the light in the oven turned off and ruined my dinner plans. When I'd grabbed my phone to tell Mom and Lisa, it was dead. I couldn't charge it and therefore had no way of telling my little sister "Get something on the way home." And no way to tell Mom "Have dinner at the bar."

So instead of the lasagna baking in the oven while I caught up with my friends on FaceTime, I drove across half the city (which, granted, wasn't very big) to blow some of my savings on takeout Chinese. *Lisa and Mom wouldn't be happy*, I thought—and they hadn't been. But it was all I could do to avoid how a lot of my childhood meals had looked: empty table, a shrug from Mom in front of the TV, who'd probably been too high or too depressed to feel any hunger in the first place. And had probably forgotten that just because she wasn't hungry, didn't mean we weren't.

Anyway, that night must've been when my friends conspired to put a near-stranger in my room. When I'd gotten power back the next day, there were over three hundred new messages in the group chat, and when I asked if I'd missed anything important, they'd moved through five other topics and had landed on Sophia Fischer's new hairstyle (which they weren't fans of). Their earlier question ("Hey, Val, Mike wants to bring a friend to Oakport. Is it fine if you guys share a room?") had been completely forgotten.

Which was how we'd ended up here.

Alfie shook his head. "We can put him in the room above the garage—no offense, mate." He seemed to realize as his head cocked toward Caden. "The bed is just a mattress on the floor. And we'd still need to buy that mattress. But it's got a private bath—"

"If you like your water pressure reminding you of a calm, trickling creek," Iris threw in.

"And I'm not quite sure if we fixed the plumbing . . ." Alfie muttered, then glanced back at the guy. "Anyway, I don't mean to kick you out, but if Valentina—"

Before I could help it, I heard myself say, "It's fine."

And immediately regretted it.

But I couldn't tell if Alfie felt guiltier for forgetting to tell me or having to put Caden into . . . well, a glorified attic space without a bed or working plumbing. And this was much less about Caden's comfort than not wanting Alfie—or any of my friends, for that matter—to feel bad. So . . .

"Don't worry, it's fine," I repeated. "A heads-up would've been great, but it's all good. We actually hit it off last night." My fingers crossed when I said, "*This* close to best friends."

Caden looked at me like I'd just committed a crime—or like he was trying to figure out *if* I had. Eyes narrowed, brows furrowed, lips a thin line. Probably because our encounter had been anything but buddy-buddy. Thanks to me, and that fourth margarita that had given me the rest.

I needed to apologize for that. Not for the alcohol—but maybe that, too?—but for how rude I'd been. After breakfast, when we'd be trapped in the same room, anyway, I'd apologize, beg him to forget last night ever happened, and turn over a new leaf. One in which the only time we'd met was when he'd given me three great orgasms before letting me fall asleep against his chest.

And if there was no bad blood between us, would he still flirt the way he had last night? Look at me that way, too? Would there be anything to stop us from falling into habits we'd created in the few dark hours we'd had together?

The thought—of the way he'd touched me and the way his body had felt beneath my fingers—kind of made me want to apologize faster.

Like a friendly reminder (that Valentina Rhodes rarely ever got what she wanted), Iris guffawed across the table. At something Caden had said, presumably, because she was pointing at him, still laughing.

I must've been so occupied thinking about him that I missed whatever incredible joke he'd just made, and I had no time to ask about it. Iris, still cackling, said, "You fit right in, Callahan. Like a part of the group we didn't know we were missing!"

They all hummed and snickered in agreement, jokingly raised their glasses of orange juice in a toast of initiation as conversations continued animatedly. My glass was up there with theirs, but my thoughts had gone somewhere else entirely.

Part of the group.

My eyes met Caden's blue ones, and for a brief second, I mourned that I'd never see them up close again. Wouldn't feel his soft lips against various parts of my body. Would never again hear that guttural "Fuck" he'd groaned against my skin when he'd finally pushed into me.

Because there'd be no apology. No friendly smiles and flirty banter. No *fraternizing.*

Not now, after Iris had ambitiously declared him part of our group. Not now, when sleeping with him could cost me the greatest people I'd ever met.

We'd never discussed what would happen if someone broke the NFR—I could only assume exile.

Alfie leaned toward me, asked in a low voice, "I'm really sorry, Val. Are you sure this is okay? The garage unit would work—"

And my eyes were still locked with Caden's across from me when I cheerily said, "Of course. Don't worry, Alfie. Really."

But my smile dropped, and it seemed the man opposite me knew exactly what it meant.

CHAPTER 4

CADEN

Valentina had excused herself from breakfast after a single piece of bread and a forkful of eggs. *The hangover*, she'd said, but it was obviously not the alcohol that had spoiled her appetite.

It was me, and whatever silent conversation had happened between us beforehand. Whatever had been going through her beautiful head, right before the corners of her lips fell back into a straight line. Right after she'd lied to her friends and told them my presence was *fine*.

They must've had no reason to assume otherwise, which led to my observation: "You didn't tell them."

"What?" she asked, distractedly rummaging through a tote bag on the windowsill. She'd showered and gotten dressed in the meantime. Her cherry-red hair was still wet, and she was wearing more than that fucking T-shirt she'd walked around the house in earlier.

I cleared my throat to steer away from the image; stay clear of anything that could make this conversation very awkward, very fast.

A boner, for example.

"You didn't tell your friends," I repeated. "About us."

What us, *asshole?* a voice in my head screamed. It damn-near pleaded with me to get a fucking grip. But, in the past twelve hours I'd found out that every time I looked at her, reason went out the window. Her brown eyes met mine, and all I could think of was the way she'd looked up at me when I'd been buried deep inside of her. That it had been four months since then, and I desperately needed to see her that way again.

She finally turned around, and a zing of awareness shot from the tip of my toes to the crown of my head when our eyes connected. *Embarrassing*, I thought, *how predictable the effect she had on me was.*

"About us?" She repeated my words slowly, maybe because she was just as confused about my desperation. Maybe because she took pity on me. "I'd never have taken you for the kind of guy who'd care about whether I did or did not tell my friends about . . . *us*."

And usually, that would be spot on.

I was not the kind who cared. In fact, I was the guy who appreciated his business not being spammed across various group chats and close-friend stories. But alas, here I was. Caring, for some reason. Kind of annoyed that she hadn't told them, for another one altogether.

"You'd be right," I confirmed, although reluctantly. "I just thought that's what girls did after—" I hesitated, unsure whether I should've led the conversation where I just had. The sun was out, it was barely noon, and I was about to bring up the way I'd fucked her. It seemed tactless.

"After?"

"After great sex." I crossed my arms, satisfied with the blush across her cheeks. Maybe I did still have an effect on her, no matter how hard she tried to play it off.

Valentina swallowed thickly, but to give credit where it was due, she maintained eye contact. "Was that what we were having?" she asked, batting her eyes innocently. "Great sex?"

It was a cruel attempt at riling me up—in every sense of the word. Her teasing voice, her long lashes, and the way she tilted her head, just slightly, like she was deliberately trying to draw my attention to the spot she had wanted my lips and teeth that night.

"You'd disagree?" I asked, only to be saying something.

I knew she wouldn't, but I was still relieved when she shook her head. Her gaze fell down my body once, quickly, like a silent invitation.

Which was what my legs took it for, anyway. They moved without asking my brain for permission first—knowing it would've said, *Don't you dare.* But everything seemed like an age-old instinct I couldn't turn off when it came to her.

The way I stepped closer, almost crowding her against the windowsill. The way my eyes flicked to her lips. Over and over again.

At least she couldn't help her body's reaction to mine, either. Like they'd been waiting to be back in each other's orbit for months.

"No," she confirmed. "But I don't kiss and tell, Callahan."

I shook my head, wanted to roll my eyes. There was a smile on my lips, and I had no idea where it came from. "You guys don't seem like the type of friends to keep anything from each other." It wasn't hard to grasp; a second with all four of them in a room and you could tell.

Valentina thought for a moment, then huffed—still so close I could feel her breath against my skin when she did. "We're not." Her eyes flicked across my face, considering me. "Not that it's any of your business," she prefaced, "but the guy Iris was dating ended things out of the blue. Because he didn't 'want a relationship.'" She put air quotes around the statement, then rolled her eyes. "Two weeks later, he had a girlfriend. I'd gotten home, and she just found out. It seemed rude to brag about the life-altering one-night stand I just had. So, no, I didn't tell them."

I couldn't help the sound that squeezed past my lips. A deep, satisfied hum of approval.

Life-altering.

Still, I managed enough restraint to dismiss the thought and say, "That sucks. About Iris."

And I meant it, but my sincerity was hard to portray when the words *life-altering one-night stand* still floated around my head and when it took everything in me not to push that damp strand of hair behind her ear after she shook her head.

"Just so we're clear, though. I wish I *could* disagree," she added, circling back. "I wish you'd been terrible, and I wish I wasn't still thinking about it every time I look at you."

The honesty in her words surprised the shit out of me. I almost choked on my own spit, that's how much it threw me off.

When we'd first met, Valentina had been polite but playful. Charming, but never too much so. She'd been eager to please me, and I'd been dying to please her. She was still all of those things—but less of them.

Last night, she'd been outright the opposite. Rude, unapologetic, and it didn't seem like she cared about what I thought of her at all. Sure, the alcohol had played a significant role in that, and the fact that she'd found a near-stranger in her room as well—but still. I wasn't sure which version I preferred. And I could only guess which one was real.

The version I was just getting to know seemed brutally honest, too, because she did not seem embarrassed by her admission.

Meanwhile, I needed a second to process it. The fact that I wasn't the only one playing that night on a loop in my head whenever we locked eyes. Like now, gazes holding because I was unable—*literally not capable* of looking away from her.

I needed her, I realized. The way I'd needed her that night, just a million times more desperately. It'd been too long since my fingers had danced across her skin, and I'd swallowed every sweet sound of hers with my mouth.

"That was months ago," I finally choked out. Again, my brain was not consulted before I said, "I could refresh your memory, Valentina."

No matter how pathetic, she seemed to like my pleading ways. Her breath shallowed, her bottom lip caught between her teeth, and her eyes batted open—jumping from my lips back to my eyes.

She was right there, so close, I would've bet my entire savings account on the fact that she was about to kiss me, and I hadn't touched that in seven years.

A good thing, apparently, because I would've lost it all.

Valentina shook her head, took a step back, hit the windowsill, and turned around. "No," she said, resuming the search in her tote bag for fuck knows what. It seemed she needed a distraction more than whatever she was looking for. "I can't," she continued lowly. "I want to—I want you to. But I can't." She shook her head again, as if to set the decision in stone. As if the gesture was more for herself than for me.

I took a step back, and her body went from completely rigid to only slightly stiff. The only sound was her deep inhale, exhale. I still hadn't said anything.

"Caden." She spoke toward the window, eyes probably roaming the front yard and the single road that passed Alfie Dunbridge's summerhouse. Gone was the airy tone in her voice, the teasing lightness of it. "I'm only going to say this once, and I want you to know that I mean it."

Nothing good ever followed a statement like that, but I put on my best smirk, took another step back, and leaned my forearm against the top bunk. "I'm all ears."

"I told my friends this is okay because I love them, and I don't want them to feel bad. But I'd like to make this perfectly clear—I don't want you here."

Right. Cool.

Whiplash was an understatement. Two minutes ago, we'd been standing so close, her breath had mingled with mine, her eyes had continuously flicked to my lips, and she'd undoubtedly considered the possibility of kissing me. I had already come to terms with the fact that she would—that's how sure I'd been. That's how wrong I'd been.

"It's funny." I snickered. "You want me here so little, yet you can't say it to my face. What's so interesting out there, Rhodes?"

My words did exactly what they were supposed to. It only took a couple of seconds before she turned on her heels, strode over to me, and left us standing as close as we'd been three minutes ago.

Her eyes narrowed in sync with mine, and she brought her finger up to my chest. Poked it between each word as she repeated herself. "I. Don't. Want. You. Here."

But the tremble in her voice said otherwise. The way she sucked in a breath when I inched closer did, too. My lips were a hair's breadth away from hers when I whispered, "I'll get over it."

CHAPTER 5

VALENTINA

Despite the way I'd fled our last encounter (back into the bathroom until I was sure he'd left again), there was a net positive to Caden's appearance. When, an hour later, we trekked into town—a walk on which I was usually either still drunk from the night before or sober enough to be violently hungover—I felt fine. No headache, no sickness, and no whiny *I'll never drink again*.

At least from me. Iris, for example, was still whining plenty.

My shower had definitely helped, and the rest of the alcohol's effects had to make way for whatever argument Caden and I had had—*if* one could call anything with that amount of sexual tension arguing. Every now and then, it had felt like prolonged foreplay.

But no matter how spectacular the tension, Caden was a blindingly bright neon sign that spelled, in capital letters and with an exclamation mark behind it, "NO!"

There was exactly one rule to my guy choosing, and it was usually easy enough to follow: He can't be friends with my friends.

Unfortunately, judging by the way Iris had locked her arm with his, laughing at something he'd said to Alfie, Caden had infiltrated my circle in less than twelve hours.

And had unknowingly become off-limits.

Plus, I had other things to focus on this summer. Things that didn't have piercing blue eyes, a bleach-blond buzzcut, and incredibly skilled fingers.

My summer bucket list rested peacefully in the pages of an otherwise empty journal, at the bottom of my tote bag.

I hadn't told my friends about my plan yet—mostly because the majority of items on there didn't seem like their kind of thing, and I didn't need to push my plans onto them when we'd been perfectly content with theirs for years—but I did have one.

Eight items on a list that had been angrily scribbled into the book. After I'd come home from college, handed Mom my degree, and gotten a *disinterested nod* in response. A *well done* before she'd asked me to cook or clean or fix something broken in the house. After I'd busted my ass for four years studying physics, sacrificing a college life that could've been much more fun and much less studying, only to not get what I'd wanted out of it: my family to be proud of me. At least happy or excited about something I'd done.

Nobody had given a shit.

And after twenty-two years of exactly that, something had snapped. Not in the way that would get me on national news but in its more introspective, self-aware counterpart. Where I had taken not a knife but a pen. Where I hadn't violently lashed out but instead asked myself, *What the fuck am I doing all this for?* And the answer hadn't been me.

I'd never really done anything for myself. For Mom, yes, because life had seemed so hard on her after Dad left, she'd barely noticed how hard it had been for me, *the child*. For my little sister, yes, because she shouldn't have had to suffer the consequences of constantly fighting parents, an absent father, and an emotionally unavailable mother.

I had tried to keep that household from collapsing for so long—distract the people inside of it from the fact that it was—I'd just been chasing *some* kind of appreciation.

At that point, it hadn't mattered for what. Keeping my mom alive or being a mom for my sister or getting good grades in school. Anything would've done. And that realization was so sad, so depressing, it had been like a slap in the face. Something needed to change.

Do something for yourself, Valentina. It hadn't been my voice that said it, but it *had* been in my head. So I'd written that stupid, trivial bucket list. And that alone had made me feel . . . better. Like I was finally doing something right.

Having this tiny little thing to myself. Living out what should've been part of my teenage years but never finding enough space between running a household and going to school, raising my sister, and working enough part-time jobs to keep us afloat.

My priorities had been elsewhere, and at the time, it had been fine. But I was almost a graduate student—and

I had a whole two months on Oakport Island in which I didn't have to worry about my family (as much).

Why not make use of that?

sleep outside
go for a run
full-moon walk
skinny-dipping
break a law
watch the sunrise
sex on the beach (not the drink)
play pool

By the end of August, I'd be a changed woman. Or at least a woman who'd been skinny-dipping and had sex on the beach.

Technically, I'd broken a law already. Yesterday, when I was rushing to get here and went ten miles over the speed limit. I was still debating whether I'd let it count.

So between finding a way to break the law and the courage to go into the ocean completely—never mind the fact that I wanted to do it naked—I was busy enough this summer. Focusing on myself, I think?

I didn't need to think about a problem named Caden Callahan as well.

My eyes slid back to him, his animated conversation with Mike and my friends, and I couldn't help but sigh. In annoyance, perhaps, that he'd shown up here. Then that I hadn't told my friends about . . . us (if that's what he wanted it to be—an *us*), because Iris would've never let him join if she'd known we had history. Even less if she'd known it was good. Good enough that, for just a second, I wondered if he could be the rule I'd break.

I dismissed the thought—didn't even let myself entertain it—when the familiar clock tower of Oakport's biggest town (which was still quite small) announced our almost-arrival. Everyone still suffering from last night's antics groaned in sweet relief.

East Isleton had a single road running in and out of it. Winding through white, modern storefronts and paint-chipped restaurants, past the well-cared-for hydrangeas blooming in various colors and the American flags flying high beside most buildings. The redbrick sidewalk was appreciated after walking two miles on the side of the road, in constant fear of being run over.

The sight was as familiar as the view from the roof of my house had been growing up, and that distinct feeling of *Coming Home* settled in my stomach again. *Quiet. Peaceful. Completely and utterly content.*

"Remind me again why we think this whole walking-into-town thing is a good idea?" Iris muttered, slinging her arm across my shoulder (and leaning very heavily on me for support). She and Alfie had abandoned Caden to walk with me—which, yes, gave me *some* satisfaction. Sure. "Every year, we make the same mistake."

"Of walking?" Alfie asked, amused. "Or drinking until we don't know our own names anymore?"

"Both," we said in unison. Iris nodded so grandly, she immediately stopped short, both hands coming up to her mouth. I'd been surprised she hadn't thrown up on the way here—the quick motion must've finally done it for her. "Definitely both," she confirmed. "I'm gonna have to sit, guys. The only thing that can save me now is a scoop of lemon ice cream."

Behind us, Anni gave a sound of approval. "Last one to Charlie's is a lazy egg!" She started running, barely made it past us, and stopped. Which must've been around the same time she remembered that she was hungover, too. "Okay, no. Never mind. Forget I said anything."

"She means rotten egg, right?" Alfie whispered conspiratorially, both of us still focusing on Anni and the way she held her throbbing head, regret written all over her face as she clung to her boyfriend for support, more mental than otherwise. "That's how the saying goes? *Last one there's a rotten egg?*" Alfie seemed like he might not actually be sure.

"Oh, shut up, Alfie." The blonde threw an amused glare over her shoulder despite the headache. "It's the same in German, alright? Lazy and rotten both mean *faul.* Come on, repeat after me. F-a-u-l."

All of us muttered some variation of "Here we go," rolling our eyes and laughing and giving Anni *that* look as we walked into Isleton.

It's the one thing she loved teasing us about: that she spoke a second language, while we felt lucky to know one well enough to communicate with each other.

"Okay, we get it—you speak two languages, oh superior being that you are. Why don't you try running to Charlie's again? Last one there's a *faul* egg, right?" Alfie shot back, to which Anni simply held up her middle finger. They both laughed. A cackle that felt so synchronized, I wasn't quite sure which belonged to whom as he skipped a few steps over to walk beside her.

Then regretted his skipping in a wave of nausea.

It was hard to explain, sometimes, that my friends' bickering felt more like home than my childhood bedroom. That I could probably discern the pattern of their footsteps from that of a thousand others, that their laughter mixing with the touristy bustle of the boardwalk was more familiar than the tone of my mother's voice. That the way Iris locked her arm with mine was the most normal thing in the world and that I'd probably die without it.

"I have a confession to make," she said bluntly, the way she did anything, and half of her weight rested on me as we continued walking, a few feet behind the rest. "I feel awful. And I can't go another second without telling you. Don't be mad at me," she prefaced.

Immediately, I was on high alert. Because of what my best friend was about to tell me, sure. But more so because it immediately reminded me of my own confession—that I should feel awful and that I shouldn't be able to go another second without telling her about Caden, either.

My eyes flicked to him, walking ahead, when I snickered and then said, "What did you do?"

"Promise you won't be mad," she repeated, lifted her head from my shoulder to narrow her gaze at me. "Swear it."

My eyes rolled, and I crossed my fingers in the air with a laugh. It took a lot to keep up the playful act when I honestly felt a little sick by now. I hated lying to begin with; doing it to my friends felt objectively worse. Like treason. "I swear I will not be mad at you. Now what did you do?"

One word was enough. She winced even before she said, "Jason."

The smile on my face fell, my eyes narrowed, and at least I didn't have to fake any more emotions. It couldn't get more honest than this: "Iris—" I began, disappointment, annoyance, disbelief in my tone.

In defense, she whisper-shouted, "You promised not to be mad!"

Scum-of-the-earth-Jason, as we'd affectionately nicknamed him, had given Iris the world, then, on a random Saturday night, told her he wasn't ready for a relationship, wasn't ready to be a boyfriend—when he'd been boyfriending for a whole two months beforehand. To make matters worse, he'd gotten into a relationship two weeks later.

Knowing Athalia Pressley had slashed his tires after they'd broken up years ago should've been enough reason for Iris to stay away from the guy. But alas.

That had been four months ago, on the day I should've told my friends about Caden. Iris's heartbreak took priority over my sex life, though, which was why I'd kept my mouth shut. For a little too long.

"We've just been talking," she confessed. "He texted me a few days after they broke up. Apologized, asked if we could see each other—"

"To which you should've said, *Fuck you*. I thought you blocked him!" I cried.

She gave me an apologetic smile, pearly teeth and gap between them on full display. "I did not. I'm sorry!"

I sighed. In defeat and acceptance, I think. "And now what?"

Iris shook her head. "Nothing." She shrugged. "Going in with no expectations. We've been texting, that's all. Although it's been a little quiet since we left campus. But that makes sense—" She hesitated. "Right?"

I kept from rolling my eyes and agreed, only not to make her feel worse. "Sure."

"I'm sorry I didn't tell you earlier!" she repeated. "I just wanted to see what he wanted before you steal my phone, block him, and delete his number for good. Otherwise, I would've told you right away. The urge was very strong."

And there it was again: guilt. Running from the tip of my toes to the top of my head, heating my blood and making me blush with . . . shame, probably.

Tell her, tell her, tell her.

"It's fine, really." I gave a weak smile. "Sometimes we think keeping something to ourselves is the better option, right?" I tried to test the waters and wasn't surprised when I got scalded with her next words.

"Nah." Iris snickered, then nudged my shoulder in amusement. "It was stupid. You tell me everything, I tell you everything. That's how it's supposed to be."

Fuck. Was someone giving her a script of exactly what to say to make me feel worse? If they were, it was working.

I faked another laugh, and something finally snapped. "Speaking of—" *Telling each other everything*, I wanted to say. *I might've omitted a small detail about Caden and me. We aren't just sharing a room; we shared drinks, then personal space, then saliva.*

I'd been this close to laying it all on the table, but Alfie ruined it. Because just five feet away from us, he barfed into a trash can.

Which made Iris beside me squeal in disgust, then gag. "Dude!" she cried.

It kind of ruined the moment. Another time, then. I'd tell her, just not now.

"Sorry, sorry. I'm fine." Alfie waved it off but looked the opposite. "Just need—" His hand came up to his mouth. "Ice cream. To cleanse my palate."

At this point, Alfie throwing up on the way here was a common enough occurrence not to fuss over it more than Iris's squeal had. Usually, it just happened way earlier. Not on the boardwalk, busy with people who'd decided to keep a safe distance from us now, sidestepping with worried glances.

I sighed. "You guys go ahead. I'll meet you at Charlie's." Alfie's face had almost gone back to its normal color. "For ice cream," I emphasized. *And to get my guilty conscience back under control.*

Caden hadn't said much in the past fifteen minutes, probably lost in thought, maybe wondering what he'd done to me (nothing) and when I'd turned into such an asshole (out of necessity, I'm sorry!), and he hadn't once looked back. Not for Anni's and Alfie's arguing, not when Iris had complained or when Alfie had thrown up. Now though, his eyes flicked to mine, and something inside of me reacted. Bad sign.

Before he could say anything, Iris, having overcome her own nausea, guessed, "Boardwalk Books?"

And I nodded.

The white color of the inconspicuous little bookstore by the water had become so worn over time, only flecks of it were left, leaving the wooden building looking tattered. Some (me) would call it charming.

And while my degree had kept me busy during the semester, these two months on Oakport were the only time I could catch up on my books for the year. Ninety percent of my reading happened here, with books from this exact shop.

On good days, the owner, Anthony, would lend me some, if I promised not to break the spine and bring them back. Other times, copies I'd swooned over all week magically appeared on my desk the next day, and Alfie always swore he had nothing to do with it. Shame he's an awful liar.

"I'd love to." Iris winced before she even said the next words. "But I really need to sit down. Just thinking about the stuffy air in there—" She cut herself off with another gag. Alfie nodded vehemently.

"Iris," I said with a snicker, "I will survive a bookstore by myself. Like I said, you guys go ahead."

That way, at least I didn't have to worry about how much time I'd spend reading blurbs, admiring covers, and getting lost in first chapters. A win-win situation in my book.

Just not in my friends'.

Iris snorted, as if the suggestion in itself had been ridiculous. Alfie, almost fully recovered, carefully shook his head like I should've known better. And Anni, the only one who understood where I was coming from, simply shrugged. She knew there'd be nothing I could do about what would happen, and her look told me to just give up now.

My suggestion wasn't dignified with a response; instead, Iris asked, "Who here is still either drunk or hungover?" Her own, Alfie's, and Anni's hands shot up. "And who here will die if they are separated from Annika?" Which was when Mike's hand went up, too, a sheepish smile on his lips. Iris cleared her throat. "Settled, then. Caden's staying with Valentina. Do you read, Caden?"

My gaze shot in his direction, and I slowly, gently shook my head. To signal, *No, you don't read. In fact, you have deep-rooted issues keeping you from ever entering a bookstore again.*

His smile was so big, I'm sure it was meant to piss me off. "Love it."

Unfortunately, I still had to match it when every single pair of eyes shifted back to me. "No, really. He doesn't have to." I looked back at him, emphasizing, "You don't have to."

"No, no, no!" Iris intervened, knowing grimace on her face. "Don't fall victim to Valentina's puppy eyes. She'll look at you, big, sad eyes, and suddenly you're prone to do whatever she wants. Don't fall for it, Caden."

Intrigue and amusement glimmered in his gaze. He wasn't even looking at my best friend when he said, eyes still locked with mine, "I'll try my best."

"It's all anyone can do with this one," Alfie noted.

I tried to reason, saying, "I don't know what you guys are talking about—" but I didn't get very far. All four of them started walking backward, keeping their eyes on us to make sure Caden and I wouldn't separate. But seeing their proud, mischievous smiles, I could only sigh. In defeat and amusement and annoyance.

I loved these guys so much, even when they left me with the one person I shouldn't—*and didn't want to*—be left behind with, I couldn't be mad at them.

Even when I was drowning in guilt, I couldn't help but smile.

The second they turned around and disappeared into the familiar bustle of the Isleton boardwalk on a Sunday afternoon, the corners of my mouth dropped, though. "Thanks for . . . literally nothing." I glanced at the man beside me, shoving my guilty conscience into my back pocket.

Caden held the door to the shop open, waited until I stepped inside, and followed. "Can you blame a man who loves books for wanting to go to a bookstore?" he asked, the bell above the door ringing a second time. "And can you blame any man at all for wanting to spend time with you?"

I snickered but gave Anthony behind the counter a warm smile. My voice lowered when I hissed in Caden's direction, "Yes. If the man knows I'm not going to sleep with him."

Which made him snicker. "Contrary to popular belief, Valentina, I am capable of being friends with the opposite gender. Do you need references to believe me? I could give you their numbers—I'm sure they'd love to tell you all about it. *Caden Callahan is an amazing friend and has never tried to sleep with me. Ten out of ten. Great company, too.*"

"And that's what you want us to be?" I asked, raising a skeptical eyebrow as I disappeared into an aisle. He followed. "Friends?"

Caden tilted his head, and I used the few seconds of silence between us to look at him, sun peeking through the dusty windows of the shop behind him. His blond buzzcut, blue eyes, cheeks and nose a little reddened from the sun. "Not necessarily," he said honestly and not at all embarrassed about it. The nonchalance in his voice made *me* blush, for some reason. "But I respect your boundaries. And we *are* sharing a room for a considerable amount of time. So, yes, maybe I think we should be friends. It's the very least we should be. For the sake of this trip." He blinked at me. "For the sake of anyone else on this trip *with* us."

Of course, he couldn't know *everyone else on this trip with us* was the reason I was acting this unreasonably in the first place. That I didn't think I could do the whole friends thing with Caden without eventually wanting to do the whole benefits thing, too.

Which I couldn't do without breaking the one rule my best friend cared about.

All I had to remember was Iris's face when she'd told us about what had happened with her ex and their friends. How almost four years ago, we'd sat around a bonfire, and she'd told us the tragic tale: her high school sweetheart breaking up with her. Their friends, slowly drawing away from her. Telling her they were busy when she was heart-broken and grieving, then seeing all of them hanging out together, including her ex.

How she had lost not just the love of her life (who'd turned out to be a loser) that day but all of her friends, too.

The No-Fraternization Rule wasn't just a stupid inside joke to Iris. It meant something to her, and so it meant something to me. And surely I could avoid some guy I seemed to have spectacular chemistry with if it meant not breaking my best friend's trust—even if said spectacular-chemistry-guy and I shared a room.

Caden and I *couldn't* be friends. Ironically, that had been off the table the second Iris had ceremoniously declared him our friend over breakfast. He just didn't know that.

Standing at the other end of the short aisle, books left and right of us, he honest to God looked a little hopeful. Like he'd finally found a way to bury the hatchet I'd put between us. I felt bad—not just a little—when I simply turned around and disappeared into the romance section, leaving him standing somewhere between self-help and cookbooks without an answer.

I had never been in the position to make someone dislike me before. Usually, I worked overtime to get every single person in my vicinity to love me. But if Caden wanted to be my friend so badly, I'd simply have to convince him otherwise.

Show him my worst side: the one that didn't put others' feelings before her own, didn't always smile to keep up the mood, didn't sacrifice her own plans to make sure everyone else was enjoying themselves, and didn't always give and give and give.

Coincidentally, that had been the plan for the summer, anyway. And this way, Caden could simply be my guinea pig; I'd get to be selfish around him, put myself first the way my bucket list intended, and I didn't even need to be worried about repercussions because I didn't want him to like me in the first place.

It was perfect.

A sense of peace settled as my plan fell into place. Like I'd averted a crisis before it had fully turned into one. By day three, at the latest, he'd be fed up with my act enough to leave me alone of his own accord—move into the attic by his own free will, only to escape me.

No one really stuck around if you didn't give them your best, right? Best grades, prettiest smile, funniest jokes.

So as I traced the pastel-colored spines in the romance section—some books I'd read, others I'd been dying to—studied blurbs of mysteries, and marveled at fantasy covers, I tried my very hardest not to think about Caden waiting on me to finish.

That's what I'd just decided on, right? Putting myself first.

But despite my incessant need to ignore him, he was like a lingering shadow. Didn't speak, didn't even hover close by, but I could feel him—around the corner or behind the shelves, head buried in a novel. Every now and then, my gaze unexpectedly met his, and he'd give me a small smile before turning his attention back to the book in his hand.

And something plummeted into the pit of my stomach every time.

CHAPTER 6

CADEN

If there was one thing I'd be impressed with by the end of this trip, it would be this group's tolerance for alcohol. While they'd still been wildly complaining about their throbbing head and toe-curling nausea five hours ago, they now sat by the pool with a glass of white wine in hand.

Alfie's skin was almost as red as his hair at this point, despite the layers of sunscreen I'd seen him slap on this morning. *"It's fine, though,"* he assured me. *"It'll turn into a tan in no time."*

It seemed impossible, but Valentina's red-and-white-checkered bikini was already showing off her tan lines impressively well. Which were obviously the only things I was admiring. The tan lines. Not her curves. Not her breasts. Definitely not her—

"You want her." Beside me, Mike sat and slipped his feet into the pool. My thoughts were cut short, and I should probably thank him for that.

The little gratitude I could muster was the only reason I dignified his assessment with a lazy, "What?"

But my eyes didn't shift away from the girl. Valentina sat with the rest of them on the other side of the pool, sharing a lounge chair with Iris, head on her lap. She was the only one without a glass—or entire bottle, in Alfie's case.

"You want her. Valentina," Mike clarified.

I almost snapped back that I've *had* her. That this unnatural pining wasn't all that pathetic because I knew she'd been attracted to me, too. At some point, at least.

But there must've been a reason why Valentina still hadn't told her friends about us, even when bad timing and Iris's breakup were no longer viable excuses. And if I'd told Mike about us now, it would take an hour until Annika knew, tops. Then an hour and two minutes until the rest of them would, too.

So I kept my mouth shut. Grunted in response and hoped he'd leave the subject alone. But I wouldn't be sitting next to Mike Thatcher if he had.

"Listen, she's a great girl. I get it," Mike drawled on. "It makes sense. You're sharing a room—"

I doubted he could imagine my dilemma at all. Knowing she was right above me, sleeping in an oversized shirt and nothing more. Knowing what she felt and tasted like and knowing I could not have it again.

"A bunk bed," I corrected. "We're sharing a fucking bed, Thatcher. It's torture."

I could feel his gaze on me, but I only caught a glimpse of his eye roll when I finally took my full attention off Valentina. "It's been one night. How torturous could it have been?"

More so than he could imagine, I'm sure. It had been worse than I'd imagined, and from the second she'd stumbled into our room, I'd expected it to be bad.

Last night, I think Valentina had fallen asleep before her head had even hit the pillow. Her even breaths had filled the otherwise silent room and managed to creep into every corner of my mind. I'd been counting them like I was seven years old and they were sheep in my fucking head.

Five minutes after she'd told me the upper bunk was hers and after I'd given it up without a fight, she was sound asleep above me. Meanwhile, every time she'd turned from one side to the other—and she did that a lot—I held my breath. For God knows what reason. I certainly couldn't tell you.

Needless to say, I had not slept well. Valentina's presence made me restless, apparently.

Probably because for the life of me, I couldn't figure out what I'd done for her to despise me this much. She'd been the one to leave that night—without so much as her phone number on the back of my hand or a piece of paper. She hadn't even given me the chance to play avoidant asshole because she'd taken on that role herself.

And I wondered if she had more compelling reasons than I did for not letting people close. Seeing her around her friends, though, I doubted that—close was an understatement for them.

"Believe me," I finally huffed in response, "it's worse than you think."

The feet he'd previously been sloshing around the water stilled. "Holy shit," he gasped. So loud, everyone's head shot in our direction. Valentina's brows furrowed; I could see the crease between them from here.

Great. Now she probably thought I was spilling our little secret to the chattiest guy on the HBU soccer team, and she'd probably hate me more. We'd move further away from potential friends and closer toward reluctant enemies.

Beside me, Mike shook his head, waved the group off—unsuccessfully. They were still watching us suspiciously. Valentina's features morphed into dread.

Did you? she mouthed.

No.

"Sorry!" Mike's voice boomed across the backyard again. "Please, get back to what you were doing, girls!"

Alfie raised his bottle in our direction. "No worries!" he shouted back, then took a big sip.

More mindful of his surroundings, Mike repeated himself. "Holy shit," he whisper-shouted. "Holy shit, dude. You don't want her. You *like* her."

"Don't be a fucking idiot, Mike." *I didn't like her. I barely knew her.* "I met the girl all of—" Four months ago, actually. Then spent the time since wondering if I'd see her again. "All of twenty hours ago. Eight of those she was sleeping."

His eyes narrowed as he assessed the sincerity of my words. His blue eyes flicked across my face until he gave up. "Caden." He sighed. "Valentina's great. If you don't like her, don't fuck her up the way you do every other girl you get involved with."

"I don't—"

"Sarah, study group. She seemed like the most mentally balanced psych major I can think of, and she turned up to training with a carton of eggs and started throwing them. In broad daylight."

"That's not—"

"Lacy Halloway published an entire article on how damaging college hookup culture was because you didn't want to go out with her—I *know* you didn't sleep with her. That makes it worse, dude."

I let my head fall back with a groan, hands placed on the pool deck behind me. "How does that make it worse?"

"I don't know what you do to these girls," he continued, completely ignoring my valid comment. "But I don't think Valentina is the casual type. Please don't sell her this Caden-fantasy bullshit, only for you to rip it away once you've slept with her."

I was starting to get offended here. I didn't sell . . . *fantasies* to anyone. I didn't trick or deceive or play an act to get what I wanted. That's not who I was at all, and that's not who I'd been when I hooked up with Valentina either.

And yet she seemed plenty interested in casual—contrary to Mike's belief.

I shook my head regardless. "There's no need for you to worry. She's not going to sleep with me."

She'd cut my dick off before ever considering the possibility again.

CHAPTER 7

VALENTINA

Number one: sleep outside.

It was an easy enough objective to tick off the list. Something to get the ball rolling, start building momentum for the more courageous items like skinny-dipping or breaking a law (I'd decided the speeding did not count).

And now it came with the added bonus of avoiding Caden.

When I got back to our room—it must've been around eleven—he'd been in the shower. The water was running, steam escaped from below the door of the adjacent bathroom, and my first thought had involved me in there *with* him. Which catapulted me toward my decision to sleep outside. Away from him, and my thoughts, and any more temptations.

I'd changed into my warmest pajamas, grabbed my blanket, and was about to take my bucket-list notebook (that was literally blank, save for the list), but the bathroom door unlocked, and I froze.

Damn it. I hadn't even noticed the water stopped running.

There was a click that made me unwillingly straighten, very—*too*—aware of myself and the situation he was about to find me in. Me, on the ladder of our bed, blanket bunched up in my arms. Before Caden could even say anything, I warned, "Don't."

I really tried not to look at him, but five seconds and one glance later, I'd failed. Caden leaned against the dresser by the bathroom door, arms crossed in front of his bare chest, dark-blue towel hanging dangerously low on his waist. Failed *spectacularly*, judging by the way I had to *force* my gaze off him. It snapped back to the blanket, which I pressed closer against me, and carefully climbed (alright, ungracefully jumped) off the ladder.

My plan was simple: head low, avoid eye contact, and escape this situation without saying another word to him.

"Sharing a room with me cannot seriously be this bad," he said, amused. The corner of his lip tipped up farther—and I'd already failed steps one and two of my plan because I was looking right at him again. "Where are you going to sleep? On the couch? Above the garage?" he guessed. "Are you going to squeeze between Annika and Mike tonight?"

And step three followed: "None of your business."

My tone wasn't snappy, per se, but it was . . . careless, in a way. Maybe because I actually was. Because there was no need to put up an act and convince him of how great Valentina Rhodes was. For the first time, I didn't have *Please, love me* written on my forehead and the desperation that came with it.

Caden should've taken offense at my tone, the dismissiveness in my voice. He did not. "It's not," he agreed instead. Nodding pretend-thoughtfully as he went to grab something out of the drawer. Underwear, I realized. My gaze darted away from him, back to the blue blanket in my arms. "And yet when your friends find out I made you flee the comforts of your own bed, it'll be my head on a spike. Not yours."

I snickered. "There will be no heads on spikes," I assured. "They won't even know—or care enough. Just Valentina being Valentina . . ." I trailed off, but the look on his face made me do a double take.

Incredulously, he huffed, "I don't know if you've noticed, but these people would die for you." The way he said it was very . . . matter of fact. Not a single trace of humor in his tone, which was rare. The sincerity in his gaze made me uncomfortable. Made me want to run the other way only to get away from it—in the best of cases, before I could read more into it.

I tried my best to laugh it off. "Great. Thanks for the pep talk." Then fled the room.

Unfortunately, PJs on, nothing but a thick blanket in my arms, it took about thirty seconds to decide this had been a terrible idea. I hadn't even made it outside, and already I regretted the entire plan—*maybe the entire list.*

I didn't have a pillow, I forgot to bring mosquito spray, and—I stopped. In my tracks, at the bottom of the staircase I'd been . . . swiftly walking down.

Fuck. The notebook.

Resting on top of my mattress, exposed for all the world to see. Which was, primarily, the guy tall enough to easily peek at the top bunk. Something told me Caden was the nosy type.

My cheeks were a blotchy, embarrassing red even before I'd made it back to the room, and that couldn't have taken longer than fifteen seconds, because I'd sprinted. Back up the stairs, around the corner, toward the first door on the right. I was panting when I basically threw myself against it.

Despite my efforts, I was still too late. I could tell.

By the way he leaned against the ladder of the bed, smile on his lips like he'd known I'd be back and like he'd been waiting for me, wondering just how long it would take to realize my mistake. Turned out: one minute. His hands were clasped behind his back, and I could only guess what he held in them.

My mind took stock of every single embarrassing thing I'd put on that list. Skinny-dipping. *Sex on the beach.* If possible, the color in my cheeks got worse.

I kept my mouth shut when I dumped my blanket and closed the door. And I did not take my eyes off him when I took a single step into the room. I hoped it was at least a little intimidating. I don't think it was. The smile on his lips grew, like he'd just been let in on a secret. Then, from behind his back, he held the book out to me. "Forgot something?" he asked sweetly, tilting his head. Inviting me in, to come and get what was rightfully mine.

I wish I could say I didn't fall for it.

My strides were forceful and long, and it barely took five until I stood right in front of him, once again way too close for comfort, a situation we kept finding ourselves in. Unfortunately, the second I reached for the notebook, the hand holding it stretched upward, casually keeping it out of reach.

Bastard, I thought. Then realized I could say it, too, and did. Caden only snickered, half amused, half surprised. "Tell me, Valentina," he drawled, and my stomach dropped. Another rush of heat climbed up my spine when I was sure he was going to bring up item number seven: the sex thing.

But he did not.

"I know what moonwalking is. But what the fuck is *full* moonwalking?" He pulled a face. "Is it like an extra step only real Michael Jackson fans know? Which would lead to my next question: Are *you* a real Michael Jackson fan? Are you trying to become one? Why?"

I blinked at him. Why on earth was he talking about Michael Jackson? "What?"

"It says right here," he explained. Above his head, he opened the notebook onto the first page (in hindsight I should've put the list somewhere in the middle of it) and tapped on item number three. I wondered if he might've been so baffled by what he'd interpreted as a dance move on my list that he didn't even read the points below it. It was some glimmer of hope I held on to as he continued. "Full. Moon. Walk," he read slowly.

Despite the precarious situation I'd found myself in (being this close to him again, detecting the fresh scent of his body wash, noticing the single drop of water running down his chest, which was still bare), I laughed. Or, well, snorted loudly in amusement—which was almost the same thing.

He seemed offended. "What?!"

"It's not—" I shook my head with another laugh. "A walk. During a full moon," I explained. His confusion was kind of . . . endearing, I guess? At least it was something other than that mask of confidence he wore. "What about that list made you think my priority this summer would be learning how to *moonwalk*?"

"Literally nothing." Caden's blue eyes narrowed before something in his expression lightened, and I was back on high alert. "It did seem weird. Imitating Michael Jackson on the same list as sex on the beach."

So he had read the whole list—*great.* Whatever trace of amusement in my features was gone. "I liked that you specified, by the way. In case you forget you didn't mean ordering a cocktail."

Which was exactly when I gave up. The tension in my body dissipated, and I deflated like an old balloon. "Alright, fun's over," I deadpanned. "You can give it back now." My eyes flicked from his face to the notebook high up in the air above us. Wasn't his arm starting to hurt?

"Aw," he cooed. "Already?" He did not lower the book, and I didn't feel like humiliating myself further by trying to reach it. I wasn't necessarily short, but he *was* tall.

I sighed, and a note of warning lingered in my voice when I said, "Caden."

His smile deepened. "*Valentina*," he singsonged.

My groan was loud and unapologetic—and made him smile even wider.

I could abandon the notebook, if I had to. Copy the list to my phone and never again think of the fact that Caden had the original. But abandoning the first thing I'd done for myself felt objectively wrong, so I heard myself ask, "What do you want?"

"For this?" he waved the book around, and the sound of his playful hum filled the room. It seemed awfully clear he'd had something in mind way before I'd actually asked, so I didn't know why he bothered pretending to think about it. "How about," he finally said, "you tell me what your problem is? What did I do to make you hate me?"

What I really hated was how sincere he sounded. Like he'd been dying to ask and dying to know.

I considered Caden in the low light of the room. His pink lips, dark eyebrows drawn together just slightly. Those blue eyes resting patiently on me, blinking slowly as he waited for an answer I knew wouldn't come.

If I confessed that all that was keeping me away from him was a flimsy pact made years ago, I doubted he'd hold back his advances as much as he had been. I doubted he'd understand that it wasn't just a stupid rule and that for Iris, there was trauma and feelings attached to the entire ordeal.

Then, if he wasn't holding back, I'd give myself a week before *I* couldn't hold back anymore either. It was already hard enough now.

When he was standing as close as this. Arm stretched upward, defined muscles strained. His bare chest almost touching mine. It was probably delusion, but I felt the air radiating off him. The smell of his shampoo lingered between us and almost made me want to throw the NFR to hell.

And the way he was still patiently looking at me gave me the rest, I think.

I abandoned the notebook. I left Caden standing there, arm in the air, and turned on my heels. Gathered my blanket into my arms again, held it tightly against my chest, and made a run for it. Or tried to, at least.

"What makes you think I'm going to let you sleep outside by yourself?"

I guess, after reading the list, he interpreted my exit correctly.

My brows furrowed. At the playful tone that contrasted the genuine concern in his words. "What makes you think I need your permission to do anything?"

Caden huffed. "You don't," he agreed. "But may I remind you about my head on a spike? Something happens to you, I find myself in the same scenario."

I rolled my eyes as I fled toward the door. Just before closing it behind me, I poked my head into the room again and pinned him with a look. "Do not follow me."

CHAPTER 8

CADEN

I followed her.

It barely took five minutes of silent debate in my head before I threw her notebook back onto her bed, grabbed my blanket and pillow, then *her* pillow, and followed downstairs.

I'd have done it for any girl, I kept telling myself. What kind of person would let her sleep outside in the middle of nowhere? By herself? Not even her worst enemy—which, at the moment, seemed to be me.

So I'd tiptoed through the house, slipped out the back, and spotted Valentina on one of the lounge chairs overlooking the ocean from the edge of the Dunbridges' property. She seemed to have just gotten comfortable. Her blanket spilled over the edges; she turned from one side to the other, shifting and moving until she found a comfortable position. Or a position considered comfortable for the situation she'd found herself in.

I felt kind of bad when I stopped by her side, still undetected, and said quietly, trying my best not to scare her, "Anybody missing a pillow?"

She shrieked like I'd just rammed a knife into her chest regardless, hands clenched into fists in front of her. I kind of liked that she seemed *ready* to fight, at the very least.

"Caden!" she gasped when she finally spotted me, and it was hard to focus on anything but the way she said my name. The panic in her voice raised it a few octaves, and it paired beautifully with the relief in her tone. "What the fuck is wrong with you? You go on this whole tangent that I'm not safe out here, then you decide to sneak up on me? Are you trying to give me a heart attack—*why* are you smiling?"

I wish I knew.

"Sorry," I apologized. At least partly for the smile I still couldn't do anything about. "In my defense, I wasn't trying to scare you. But the waves do cancel out most noises around you. Another reason why being—*sleeping* out here by yourself isn't the . . . safest option." I held the pillow out to her, and she took it without comment.

Valentina must've calmed down enough to really look at me. Her eyes had probably adjusted to the darkness around us better than mine had by now, and I was more than just a threatening dark shadow. Unfortunately, that drew her attention to the rest of me. "Is that a blanket?" she asked, right as it dawned on her. "Oh, no." Her head shook. "You're not—"

My pillow and blanket landed on the next lounge chair over, in sync with the way she collapsed back into her bed for the night.

"I came here to get away from you!" she groaned, then went completely rigid the next second. Like she hadn't meant for the confession to be . . . confessed.

"Interesting." I slipped onto the chair, under my blanket, and turned toward her. "I thought it was for that bucket list of yours." She did not meet my eyes, even when I mindlessly continued, "Now, why would you need to get away from me, if not—"

If not for the fact that she felt this gravitational pull toward me, too. If not for the fact that I *wasn't* misinterpreting the way she looked at me, the way her breathing changed when she stood close, the way her eyes found mine more often than she'd like to admit.

I didn't dare finish my sentence because I wasn't quite sure what she'd do to me—and I didn't want to find out. We lay in tense silence on the lounge chairs beside each other, the ominous sound of the ocean around us, and didn't say a word.

Valentina was looking up at the sky, and it was just my luck that the moon was bright enough, I could make out her profile. The tip of her button nose, prominent jawline, round cheeks. Her hair, tangled up in a high, messy bun. Like she could feel my eyes on her, she asked into the darkness, "You can't just leave me alone?"

There was no need to consider. Or to pretend to consider. "No."

I don't know why either, I wanted to add.

She sighed, and for the second time tonight, it felt like she was giving up. What exactly, I wasn't sure.

"Are you looking at me?" she wondered, still *not* looking at me.

There was no point in denying this either. "Yes."

Another huff. "Do yourself a favor and look at the damn sky, Caden."

My expectations weren't high when I followed her orders (before I had the chance to say something else I'd regret). A partially cloudy sky, some stars to twinkle back at me, that I could perhaps still find the Big Dipper constellation, if I tried really hard. But I did not expect something that looked straight out of a high-budget documentary.

It was a cloudless night. Thousands—*millions* of stars against a black backdrop waving back at me when I looked up. Only that the sky wasn't really dark, instead illuminated by whatever was out there, never to be discovered. It felt life-altering, in a way, to see the vastness of the universe with your naked eyes.

I didn't remember the last time I'd left the city. The last time I'd actively looked at the sky—with the intention of stargazing—was with Alison. And she'd died seven years ago.

"There's so many of them," I muttered, only to keep my mind from going there. "Light pollution really is a bitch."

There was a laugh beside me, singular and too low for the satisfaction that was beginning to curl in the pit of my stomach.

I guess what Valentina had given up earlier was her plan of ignoring me, because she asked, "How good are you with your constellations?"

"I'm not."

Another laugh. Another bloom of pride in my chest.

She pointed a finger at the vast sky, and I didn't have the heart to tell her I had no idea what the hell she was pointing at. Until she said, hesitantly, "Those are the dippers."

And the exact memory I'd been trying to suppress punched me in the gut. Hard.

"Those are the dippers." Alison's head rested on Caden's shoulder, and he felt it was kind of ironic, since his sister's life rested on them, too. Sleepily, the girl pointed at the sky above them. "The small one's down there. The big one's up there. Do you see the thing that could kind of form a kite, as well? That's the Big Dipper."

But Caden wasn't looking up. He had trouble even keeping his eyes from closing; he'd opened the store at six in the morning and managed to squeeze two and a half shifts in today. When he'd told his mom he still wanted to go and see Alison after he got home, she declared him a lunatic.

She still drove him there—all that money that would have been wasted on his license and a second car was going toward Alison instead, and he wouldn't want it any other way. Then, a few more of those opening shifts (a few hundred more of them) and she might even get to come home again.

"Yes," Caden drawled. "The dippers. Beautiful." His head rested on top of Alison's. It wasn't his decision. Really. Unfortunately, he could feel her shifting, then her head flew off his shoulder, and she pointed an accusatory finger.

"Caden!" The laugh bubbled out of her, carefree and happy. Somehow, Alison was still the happiest ten-year-old in the world. "You're not even looking!"

He shook his head vehemently but couldn't suppress a smile. "No, no. I was." His head finally fell back, and he pointed at a random set of stars. "See, there they are," he said and tried to sound as convinced about it as she'd wanted him to. Which meant he didn't sound convincing at all—only to hear his sister laugh again.

"You're a liar." A giggle followed the words, then intensified when Caden gasped dramatically.

"Alison Callahan!" he said. "How dare you accuse me of something so cruel."

In return, she gave him a look. Her brows drew up, and her smile deepened, and for a brief moment, Caden was reminded of how much he would do for his sister—how much he'd already done and how much more he would, if it meant he didn't have to lose her. If it meant he could make her laugh like this forever.

"Alright, alright." His hands drew up in surrender. "Show me the dippers."

And so, on a partially cloudy night, as they sat on a park bench outside the Children's Cancer Center,

Caden Callahan looked up at the night sky with his little sister, one last time.

I blinked rapidly enough that, for a moment, it was so dark, I thought the sky had just been . . . turned off. Taking a deep breath—and then a couple more—I buried that memory back where it came from and turned my head, hearing Valentina's voice.

"You see them?" she asked, and I nodded despite the fact that she was still looking up, not at me. For the first time, her aversion to eye contact was appreciated. At least until I got my shit together.

"Mhm," I hummed.

From the way my body had been reacting to her, I thought my heart might skip a beat or my breath would catch when she finally turned toward me again. But a sense of calm swept through me instead, gently and barely noticeable.

"You're looking at me again," she noted, less taken aback by it. Almost like she'd been expecting it.

"I am."

I couldn't make my eyes follow hers when she looked back up, so I watched her point at another constellation, and the view was just as good.

"That's Orion over there. Leo here."

And to stop her from forcing me to find them, too, I asked, a little impressed, "When did you learn all this?"

Valentina huffed, and her gaze connected with mine again, assessing the sincerity of my question. Another five seconds of her eyes on me, and I couldn't be held accountable for what I might say after.

I want you, maybe. *I need you on a level I didn't know was possible.*

"Whenever I got a free minute," she began and tucked a loose strand behind her ear. Then shook her head and started over. "When I was younger, and I managed to get a free minute, I used to climb onto our roof and just . . . sit there. I looked up, and there was this whole world around us I couldn't explain. An entire world that seemed so quiet and calm and beautiful. I guess it felt like somewhere to escape to? Eventually, I found a used stargazing guide in the bookshop, and the guy behind the counter gave it to me for free. I would've paid him, if I could have. Really! I felt *so* bad—"

Why were free minutes so rare? What kept you so busy as a child? Why couldn't you pay him?

Escape from what?

It felt like crossing a whole bunch of boundaries to get answers to my questions, so I settled on, "So now you're a professional on constellations?"

She laughed again, this time at me. And I thought I might play dumb for the rest of my life if it amused her. I couldn't help it.

"I'm not about to go through two excruciating years of a graduate program for nothing," she snickered. A yawn rattled through her before she extended her hand to me and said, "Geo and Space Physics. Nice to meet you," like she was introducing herself.

Her handshake didn't feel very strong, and her eyes continued falling shut every few seconds. I wasn't sure if she'd remember how *nice* it was to meet me tomorrow. For now, I'd take advantage of it, though.

"Computer Engineering. Pleasure to meet you, Geo and Space Physics."

Valentina giggled, wearily drew back her hand and placed it under her head. Her eyes were closed, but she was still facing me. "Graduate degree?" she asked.

"Yes, ma'am."

Her lips twitched again. She yawned again. "At HBU?"

"Yeah."

"So even after this whole mess, I won't be rid of you? You'll follow me all the way back to school?" She barely managed to get the words out before her breaths evened out. Her eyes stayed closed, and she snuggled deeper into the blanket.

Valentina was asleep, and perhaps that's why I shamelessly said, "And I'm not sorry about it."

CHAPTER 9

VALENTINA

"I didn't know Valentina drools in her sleep."

"I did."

It took me a second to interpret my surroundings: the noise (seagulls fighting, waves rolling against the beach, someone saying I drool), but more so the fact that I was looking at a blue sky, not a white ceiling, and my three best friends were hovering over me like I'd just awoken from a yearlong coma. The concern in their features was missing, though, and they wore matching, wide grins on their lips. You could see the gap between Iris's teeth, which was never a good sign.

I stretched my limbs in every possible direction, my arm almost took out Alfie, I think, before I mumbled, gruffly, "What the fuck?"

Pieces of the puzzle came together slowly. My bucket list. Sleeping outside. A beautiful night sky—

"Good morning, sleepyheads." And Alfie's conspiratorial smile, paired with the plural form he'd just used, finally brought the rest of my memories back.

Yes, the bucket list. But also Caden finding *the bucket list. Sleeping outside, sure. But Caden insisting on sleeping outside with me. A perfect night sky, but Caden looking at me, instead. Caden studying Computer Engineering. Caden talking me to sleep. Caden, Caden, Caden.*

Hadn't this list been about me? Wasn't the point to focus on myself?

And now they'd found us sleeping next to each other. On separate chairs, of course, but still. My eyes darted back to Iris, but judging by the fact that she was still giving me one of those toothy grins, she didn't seem to suspect a thing, which kind of made it worse.

Maybe I *should* still tell her? I'd be a few days late, but at least I wouldn't have to lie to my best friend anymore; as close as Iris and I were, omitting the fact that I'd slept with anyone—and never mind the fact that he was *here*—definitely counted as lying. Plus, nothing had happened between Caden and me since he'd become a part of this. Which meant, technically, she couldn't even be all that mad.

"The last time Caden slept this late," Mike began, interrupting my spiraling thoughts when I noticed him by his friend's side, "he tore a hamstring. That was three years ago." And I couldn't tell whether Mike—his captain—was pleased about the development.

An unidentifiable sound came from somewhere below him, some shifting in the lounge chair beside me—and then a pillow flew right at Mike's head. It messed up his blond hair and left the semblance of a red imprint on his cheek. "Asshole!" he muttered with a smile on his face.

"I'm not the asshole who sees his friend sleeping in for once and decides to . . . wake him up?" I didn't like to admit it, but Caden did have a valid point. And it wasn't just his deep, rough morning voice that convinced me. I promise.

Mike laughed. "Dude, I thought you were dead! It's ten, and you were as still as a stone out there. Literally motionless."

Caden groaned, and I turned my head toward him . . . at the exact second he turned his. Of course I would.

Our gazes crossed—*of course they would*—and for a moment, it seemed like he was trying to assess something. Whether I'd turned back into a bitch, probably. Last night, I was too tired to be mean, and he might've interpreted it as a hatchet burial. We'd slept by the beach together—that should've counted for something, right?

Yes, of course. We'd *stargazed*. I'd told him about my childhood roof nights, basically the reason I'd gone into physics—apart from the fact that I'd googled *college major that will make my family proud* when I was fourteen years old, and physics made the list. Below all the stuff where you either saw blood or had to be very disagreeable. Neither was for me, and physics, apparently, had been.

I'd graduated with honors just two months ago, after all.

Unfortunately, when I'd gotten home with that exact honors degree, the first thing I'd been told was to clean out my room so my sister could move into it. Then whether I was busy (and because I wouldn't be), if I could check what's wrong with the dryer. *It's not working, and you're a physicist now, aren't you? Fix it.*

I'd wanted to say, *The two are not related. I'm not a mechanic.* Instead, I'd checked the dryer, realized it was beyond fixing—it had already been old when I'd still been very young—and bought a new one.

The only acknowledgment of my graduation I'd gotten was from my sister. ("Congrats, by the way. Saw on your Instagram story.")

So maybe the Google search ten years ago had been wrong because that physics degree had not made my family proud. And despite the fact that I'd wanted to give less of a shit about their opinion—I'd made an entire list for this summer because of it—I still thought maybe the master's finally would.

Anyway, telling him about roof nights should've counted for something. I kind of wanted it to. And yet one look at Iris's unsuspecting face, and I knew it could not.

My eyes flicked back to Caden before I gently shook my head. As if to say, *Nope, I still hate you.* He did not seem surprised.

"Well, now that you're awake . . ." Annika hesitated. Her eyes flicked first to Alfie, then Iris, then back to Alfie. As if she wasn't quite sure—

Good thing for her, they both were. In a display of unprecedented coordination between them, Iris reached for my arms, Alfie for my legs, and I was no longer in my glorified lawn chair. Which I suddenly missed very, very much.

Any screaming and kicking was to no avail—and yet when I was carried across the lawn and thrown into the pool, where my manic screams were drowned out, I felt I should've tried harder. But to escape the inevitable was impossible. All I'd managed was to pinch my nose before I felt the cold water engulf me.

I gasped as soon as I breached the water's surface. Anni, Alfie, and Iris stood around the pool, laughing and grasping for air similarly to how I was. Iris was actually sprawled across a lounge chair, holding her stomach, rolling left and right with laughter. "I've never heard you make a sound like that before!" she wheezed out between one laugh and the next.

"I can't believe that just happened." My oversized shirt clung to my body, and I'd be tempted to take it off if I'd been wearing something underneath. If it had been just the four of us, I'd probably take it off either way. But now there were guys to consider.

One of them Annika's boyfriend. The other one . . . well, had actually seen everything there was to see already.

Anyway, it stayed on. Keeping every part of my body underwater made the wet-shirt situation a little . . . not better, per se. But less bad, maybe?

Which meant that my head was the only visible part of me sticking out of the water, and it must've looked ridiculous, because my friends broke out into another fit of giggling and snorting and wheezing.

So distracted, they didn't even see it coming.

One second, Iris was shaking with laughter on the chair, the next she flew into the water beside me. Alfie's eyes widened at the counterattack, right before he started chanting "I'm innocent!" like that might save him. It did not.

Anni did the only reasonable thing: She started running. Around the pool and as far away from Caden as she possibly could have—understandable, if you considered he'd just hurled her coconspirators into the water. Unfortunately, that drove her right into Mike's arms. One look at his face, and we all knew he was not on Anni's side this time.

Annika raised a warning finger, and it was the last thing she did before her boyfriend threw her into the pool. When she came up and screamed "I'm single!" I laughed, and Iris actually *screamed* in amusement. Alfie accidentally gargled water.

Caden and Mike looked at each other from across the pool, like they were congratulating each other on a job well done. There was a silent conversation taking place, I was sure of that much before the boys gave each other a single nod and cannonballed into the pool, kind of like synchronized divers—just really bad ones. We laughed and complained and playfully hit each other (either for laughing or for throwing the other one in) until one big group dissolved into multiple small ones.

At one end of the pool, Anni was playfully scolding Mike. Mike was semiplayfully begging her not to break up with him. Alfie and Iris were dunking each other's heads underwater like the long-lost siblings they were.

I watched them all with a smile on my face, despite their ultimate betrayal ten minutes ago. My chest stayed underwater as I slowly paddled into one corner of the pool. My eyes closed for barely a second, and I didn't need to open them again to know what—*who* was blocking the sun.

"So . . . was that revenge, or do you just love throwing people around?" I asked, my lips curving upward despite myself.

"This was certainly revenge," Caden agreed lazily, his voice lower than I'd expected. Intimate, somehow, despite my friends scattered around us. "But in certain situations, I don't mind throwing . . . *people* around either."

With people, he meant me. And with situations, he meant the one we'd been in four months ago. Because he *had* thrown me around, and I still remembered the way I gasped when I'd landed on his bed and the way his lips curled in satisfaction at the sound.

My stomach dropped, everything within me felt warm and fuzzy, and there was nothing I could do about it. My cheeks were probably taking on a nice, red sheen even when I forced myself not to look at him.

"I remember," I said and tried my hardest to make it seem casual. Like I wasn't remembering *right now.*

Caden hummed. "I'm sure you do."

There was a scratchiness to his voice this morning, probably because we'd both just woken up and despite the cold water—that felt pleasantly warm by now—our bodies hadn't quite caught on yet. It did not make keeping my eyes closed easier. In fact, I'd argue his morning voice was the reason I'd failed.

Caden stood right in front of me, blocking the sun and keeping me from having to blink against it. A lucky coincidence, I supposed. A few freckles spread across his nose, a product of eight-hour-sun days, because I would've remembered if he'd had them the last time we'd met.

They gave him an innocent, boyish look that stood in contrast to everything he'd just said to me and everything he'd done that night. Unfortunately, I was a big fan. And I became an even bigger fan when my eyes dipped lower, just for a second.

Broad shoulders, defined chest—drops of water ran down his torso and back into the pool. I didn't let myself linger, but I remembered his body like the last time I'd seen it—and touched and licked and explored it—was yesterday, not almost half a year ago.

Caden cleared his throat, and my gaze jumped back up. It didn't meet his.

"Should I get you a dry shirt?" he asked, head turned to look at God-knows-what. Anything but me would do.

The reason for that startled a new sense of awareness in me.

Immediately, I dipped my body back underwater. Where it hadn't been for the entirety of our conversation, I feared. Drenched, see-through shirt leaving everything underneath on full display.

I only managed to mutter a "Yes, please." And Caden fled the pool like it had been his personal hell.

Fuck.

CHAPTER 10

CADEN

Valentina Rhodes was going to be the death of me.

CHAPTER 11

VALENTINA

After the pool fiasco, it seemed Caden had needed more distance between us. Like he couldn't look at me without thinking about the outline of my breasts against the wet fabric of my soaked shirt, nipples poking against it. Like he still remembered the way I'd climbed out of the pool after he'd gotten back with a dark shirt, one arm pushing against my chest to spare him the sight a second time.

When we'd split into groups, he'd always make sure to stick with Mike and Anni. When I was the first one to go to sleep, he'd be the last. When I stayed up a little longer, he'd excuse himself in sync with the last person leaving, only to not be left alone with me.

I should've been happy—*relieved*—about it. After all, it was the reason why I'd acted the way I had: so that he'd leave me alone. But it was as refreshing as it was driving me crazy.

The fact that he and Mike had stayed home tonight and weren't with us at Blitz felt . . . strange. It also felt like it was entirely my fault.

What my friends saw it as, though, was the first opportunity to openly talk about him. Which was fair enough. I loved gossiping as much as the next girl in her twenties, but the fact that he was their topic meant I had no excuse not to tell them about what had happened between us. If I didn't do it now, there'd be no way back.

I'd had one opportunity last week and missed my chance, and that couldn't happen again.

"If you love him so much, and you're convinced he loves us, too, why isn't he here then?" Alfie raised an eyebrow and impatiently waited for Iris's counterpoint. Iris, who, *of course*, had been the one convinced that he loved us and had been even more adamant on the point that she loved him.

Because this situation hadn't already been bad enough.

Iris shrugged. "Maybe they needed a boys' night in," she reasoned. "Maybe Mike needed a break from Anni—"

"Hey!" Anni narrowed her eyes, hand brushing through her blonde hair once. "Don't blame me for that. I'm sure they're having a much worse time at home, probably in front of the TV, watching one of their old games." Her head shook in disbelief. "If anything, I feel sorry for Caden that we left him behind. Mike gets a little . . . intense when he's in captain mode. God, I hate that term. *Captain mode* . . ." She trailed off.

Meanwhile, I could've easily put a stop to their guessing games:

Oh, no, guys, it's easy. Caden's trying to stay away from me because I don't want a repeat of what was the best one-night stand of my life, and after I accidentally flashed him in the pool last week, he can't seem to think about anything but *a repeat. Me neither, by the way. I can't look at the man without thinking about the way he'd fucked me. Fun! Right? Right? Why is nobody laughing?*

That's probably how it would've gone. How it *would* go—because I *did* need to tell them, and there was no better opportunity than now.

"Valentina?" Iris asked, nudging my shoulder with raised brows. "What do you think?"

I had a feeling I knew but asked anyway: "About?"

My best friend's eyes rolled, and I couldn't blame her. "Santa Claus!" She snickered. "What kind of question is that? You're sharing a room with Caden—what do you think of him?"

"You've been suspiciously quiet," Alfie added, then seemed to realize, "If you hate him, we can still buy that mattress. I swear the spare room is not *that* bad!"

"It's quite bad," Anni argued. "But not worse than you having to sleep with a guy you don't even like."

That made it sound so bad, I thought I needed to clarify: "I'm not sleeping with him!" Which then sounded a little too hysterical, a little too much like compensation. I was sweating, I think.

The low light above us suddenly felt blindingly bright, like someone was shining a spotlight at me, ready to investigate what exactly had happened between me and Caden four months ago. Iris was wearing a detective hat, smoking a cigar, holding a lamp to my face and angrily glowering until I broke. In my head, that's what the situation had turned into.

I tried to snap out of it, shook my head. "I don't hate him," I said. "He's . . . nice." And while they were all waiting for more than a *he's nice*, I knew this was it.

Alfie took a sip from his drink, Iris checked her phone, and I knew this was the moment. I'd simply open my mouth and casually mention it. I think my eyes closed, and it wasn't a conscious choice. "We've actually . . . met before. So I'm not . . . surprised. That he's nice, I mean."

Silence. Probably because they needed to digest the fact—needed a minute to understand that I'd basically lied to them. I winced when I opened my eyes again.

But no one was looking back at me.

They were focused on Iris's phone, which she'd placed in the middle of the table. And now that I'd opened my eyes, we were all looking at the same Instagram story. Of Jason. The same guy who'd said he didn't want a relationship, then got into one, weeks later. The same guy she'd been seeing again after they'd broken up. And the same guy who'd been the reason I hadn't told her about Caden in the first place.

"They're back together." Iris basically whispered the words, still focused on her phone. A mirror picture of them took up the entire screen. You couldn't see Jason's face, but I trusted Iris to identify him by fingernails alone.

This was not the time for *I told you so*, though. Anni and Alfie both agreed; all we had to do was take a single glance at one another.

"That bastard," Alfie shouted, then snatched Iris's phone off the table and let it disappear in Anni's bag, beside him in the booth.

"We could slash his tires. Throw eggs."

Iris's lips twitched, but she couldn't muster the same enthusiasm yet. Her head fell against my shoulder, and the way my hand disappeared in her hair seemed like second nature. I didn't even have to think about it.

"What do I do now?" she wondered from my shoulder, and a single, humorless laugh accompanied the desperation in her voice. That need to do something when it wasn't her place to do anything at all.

"Block him, then never think about that fuckface again. I promise you'll be better off," I offered.

"I feel like I gave a few good suggestions." Anni was clearly talking about the tire-slashing and egg-throwing combination that I wasn't opposed to either.

"We'll get in a car right now if you want to, Iris," Alfie assured. "Just say the word."

And I kind of thought—*hoped*—she would. Another version of Iris would be on her way to the car right now.

This one, though, just sank farther into her seat, until she slipped from my shoulder to my lap and sighed loudly. Her eyes were shut tightly because she would shed at least one tear otherwise—and she hated doing that for men.

Iris only let herself cry when a girl broke her heart ("At least they're pretty").

An hour later, when we'd adequately debriefed (and still weren't halfway done), Iris remembered my almost-confession. Asked what I'd meant and reminded the rest of the fact that I'd met Caden before, too.

"Just at a party. We talked for a bit," I'd said, because boy problems always reminded Iris of her first of those, which inevitably made her think of the NFR more, as well. So this was hardly the time to tell her I'd like to break it.

Not now, when she needed a good friend so badly. A friend she could trust and rely on. A friend who wouldn't lie to her and who hadn't slept with Caden Callahan.

CHAPTER 12

VALENTINA

Being that good, trustworthy, reliable friend required me to stay away from Caden. And staying away from him was kind of hard when I crawled into my bed every night, and it was directly above his. Harder when, after a week of ignoring me, his head poked over the safety rail of my bunk. At 6:30 in the morning.

I wasn't sure if I was still dreaming when his first words were "We're going running, sleepyhead."

I mumbled an incoherent reply. I don't think I *actually* tried saying anything with substance.

Morning light peeked through the curtains, drenched parts of the room in a soft orange—his face, for example. The sun played in his short, platinum-blond hair; softened his features; and made the smile in the corner of his lips seem . . . ethereal. I blinked at what others might call a heavenly sight, sleep still slurring my thoughts.

"What?" Caden said ironically, and his head tilted in amusement. "I read your list. You wanted to go for a run, which is something I do almost every other day. It seemed selfish not to take you eventually," he explained. I was too tired to argue that it just seemed odd, after he'd ignored me for a week. Odder because I was supposed to ignore him as well. Now more than ever.

I wasn't known to sleep late, but that didn't mean my mornings had to start at six. When someone tried to wake me before eight, it usually didn't end well.

Now, though, I yawned again, then actually meant to sit up. To go running? With Caden?

Only that I was still so tired, I forgot that the ceiling was barely fifteen inches above me, and I would've hit my head. Hard. Borderline-concussion hard. If it weren't for the hand that rushed out, curled around me, and kept me from a potential hospital visit.

Caden's hand lingered on top of my head, and I groaned when I let myself fall back into the pillow. "See?" I said gruffly. "Nothing good comes of me being awake at this hour." *Or us, talking to each other.* When I turned my head, it might've been the first time we'd had eye contact since last week, but I was sincere when I added, "Thank you."

Caden swallowed thickly, then took a deep breath, during which he probably weighed his options. *Be nice to Valentina, who's gone out of her way not to be.* Or *give her the cold shoulder like you have been.*

"Get your ass up, Valentina. We're leaving in ten."

*

I cannot believe I'm doing this. I cannot believe I'm wearing leggings and a sports bra. I cannot believe Caden is carrying my water bottle. I cannot believe I'm running. With him.

But I was. *Uphill.* And at a pace that was probably four minutes a mile slower than his usual time. Partially noticeable by the fact that Caden had barely broken a sweat in the two miles so far. Meanwhile, I didn't remember the last time my pulse had been this high.

We'd almost reached the top of whatever hill he had me running up. At this point, I felt so slow, a fast-paced walk would've probably been faster. I briefly considered stopping but saw Caden slowing down—which meant that he'd made it, which meant that I was about to make it. Probably. Hopefully. If I didn't collapse before.

I did not.

I made it to the top, even if barely, and immediately slumped over. My hands landed on my knees, my eyes closed, and I waited for my breathing to become less ragged. In the corner of my eye, I noticed my bottle and took it without even looking at Caden. And I chugged all sixteen fluid ounces of water.

I think it took me five minutes to fully come back to my senses. My breathing slowed, the metallic taste in my mouth disappeared, and I looked around for the first time.

Caden sighed. "Aren't you glad that I forced you up now?"

Unfortunately, I had to admit that I was lying when I shook my head and said, "No."

Because it was, in fact, breathtaking. In one direction, the sun reflected in the water of the ocean this early in the morning, making it glitter a blinding white. And the fog, still settling over the land behind us in the other direction, cloaked it in an eerily beautiful gray. Everything about the view, in every direction, was beautiful. It seemed like he was returning the favor for our stargazing.

There was a bench overlooking the sea, and the grass it stood on was so green that it seemed painted. The pain of getting here was almost forgotten, and the only reminder was my breathing, still not quite back to normal.

"No?" Caden confirmed. The smile on his lips said he knew I was lying.

I shook my head, finally turned toward him. "No. Especially because it was without a warning. *Especially* because you forced me out of bed after ignoring me for a week."

His eyes narrowed in amusement. The corner of his lip curled deeper, and he tilted his head when he took a single step toward me.

One step too close, my rational thoughts screamed. *Go on, take another one*, an entirely different part of me begged.

"Isn't that what you wanted?" he asked, entirely unconvinced.

"It *is*." It was what I wanted. It was. It was. It was. Maybe if I repeated the words enough times in my head, I'd believe them.

He cocked a brow. "Then what's the issue, Valentina?"

"There is no issue, *Caden*," I mocked back. Hoping it would change the direction I could tell this was heading in. Kind of wishing it would lead us further toward it.

"Good." He nodded, his eyes flitting away from me. A second later, he was back. Attention on me, stepping closer once more. "All I'm doing is trying to respect your boundaries. I might've been ignoring you, but that's only because every time I looked at you, none of my thoughts were holy."

My breath grew heavy again, but it had nothing to do with my cardio and everything to do with what was happening in the pit of my stomach. Heat that unfurled and memories that shot through my head with lightning speed. They weren't holy either.

Right then, on a cliff miles away from my friends—so early, none of them were even aware I was gone—I wanted to kiss him. I played with the possibility, ran the scenario through my mind over and over again. And tried to push every voice in my head (one of them belonged to me, the other to Iris, repeating every reason that I shouldn't do this a million times) away.

But perhaps getting this out—this incessant, continuous need for him—would help. Would let me get over whatever it was that made my eyes follow him whenever he crossed a room and had landed me here in the first place. Maybe if I'd just do it once, I could stop thinking about doing it every time I saw him.

I could stop feeling bad about every time my thoughts were leading me down this exact path, if I just did it now and got it over with. We always wanted what we couldn't have. So having him, technically speaking, should make me stop wanting him.

"Caden—"

"I know, I know." He took a step back, and I panicked. I didn't know what I was doing until I felt myself follow his lead. His brows furrowed. "I know we shouldn't do this. I don't know *why*, but I know that. Don't worry—"

"You're right," I said, then took another step forward. He blinked down at me, motionless. I thought he might be holding his breath until he tilted his head.

"I'm right," he repeated, as if to affirm it to himself. "And yet you're still here." With "here," he didn't mean this cliff, although he might as well have. He meant *here*, in his orbit. Chest almost touching his, hands inches from interlacing with each other.

I swallowed thickly as I nodded. "Yeah." At this point my voice was barely above a whisper. "We shouldn't do this. But maybe we have to. You know?" I traced a single finger up his chest, and he froze under the touch.

"Do I? Know?"

"Well." I shrugged, hoping to get my nerves under control.

I'd kissed enough guys that I shouldn't have felt nervous about this. I'd kissed this particular guy before, and I hadn't been nervous then either. I guess I'd just never kissed a guy while knowing it kind of meant I was betraying my best friend.

I hesitated. Licked my lips and discreetly wiped my sweaty palms on my clothes. My logic was flawed, but it *did* make sense. And now, standing this close to him, it felt like there was no way back.

So I stopped thinking and just went for it. Whatever would come out of my mouth first. No second-guessing. No overthinking.

"I don't know about you, but I can't look at you without remembering how you taste."

And I can't believe I just said that.

"Valentina," Caden warned, my neck craned upward to keep my eyes on his, "don't say that if you don't mean it. I can't—"

"I do." I interrupted him. "I do mean it. I think we should just get it over with. Get it out of our system. If you feel the same—"

I swallowed the rest of my words when his lips landed on mine. And his hands were in my hair, then on my waist, then cupping my ass—like he wasn't quite sure where to place them first, only that he didn't want to miss any part of me. In case I'd regain my ability to think logically and stop this, maybe? But I'd lost that ability. Right around the time he'd groaned against my lips.

It must've looked ridiculous. Two people in unflattering workout clothes, standing on top of a lonely cliff, eating each other. Basically, anyway.

My hands ran through his short hair, and he whispered something against my lips that sounded dangerously close to a plea. I couldn't make it out, but his next words were clearer.

"I really wish," he began. By now, he'd walked me backward against the bench. I leaned against it, and his body pressed mine further into the wood. It should've been uncomfortable, but there wasn't a single part of me that cared about anything but the way he tasted, felt, sounded. "I wish you would've changed your mind somewhere else. Closer to civilization, preferably. Where I wouldn't have to consider the possibility of taking you right here, right now. It's unbecoming."

Despite every urge his words brought up, I managed to get some distance between us. My lips were no longer on his, and his hands fell from my hair back to my waist. A sound of disapproval left him at the distance.

"What's unbecoming?" I asked, breath labored, eyes wide, hands still locked behind his neck.

"My desperation. How much I want you."

"You don't usually consider fucking your conquests on a bench overlooking the ocean?" If I'd cared about his opinion of me, I wouldn't have said it so . . . candidly. But I didn't want Caden to like me. In fact, I still needed him to dislike me after this—if I wanted to successfully stay away from him.

He huffed, the sound somewhere between a laugh and a groan, and kissed me again, despite the distance I'd brought between us. "Apparently I'd never wanted them enough, no. Would you say I've conquered you, then?"

His kisses moved from my lips to my neck, and I vehemently shook my head. “No,” I moaned. I was surprised by the sound myself. Caden hummed against my skin; I could feel the smile on his face. “It takes a lot more to conquer me than a good kiss, Callahan.”

But I wasn’t all that sure about it anymore.

CHAPTER 13

CADEN

Getting it out of our system. What a stupid, stupid idea, Valentina. Kissing her again was like shooting her straight *into* it. She'd been on my mind before, and my body certainly had had a reaction to her, yes, but now she was back. I remembered exactly what she smelled and tasted like, and like an addict gone cold turkey, I craved it. *Her.*

We had walked back to Alfie's completely silent. No eye contact. In fact, I'm pretty sure she was purposely looking anywhere else.

Right before we rounded the last turn of the road and the summerhouse would jump into view again, she stopped. Like she hadn't realized how much time had passed and was surprised to recognize the bush she was now hiding behind. From the house, no one could see us.

That's probably why she turned on her heels and kissed me again. She stretched onto her tiptoes, crossed her arms behind my neck, and my heart dropped into my stomach even before her lips had been on mine.

Why the fuck did she make me so nervous?

This wasn't my first kiss, and it certainly wouldn't be my last—and yet a single taste of Valentina's lips against mine, and I had to stifle a groan. The taste of cherry lip balm and toothpaste mixed on my tongue, and her satisfied sigh might send me into a coma if I wasn't careful.

"Caden?" she mumbled against my lips, and I nodded, eagerly, desperately. Thinking anything she was willing to give me, I'd take. "This changes nothing. You know that, right?"

"I figured as much," I admitted.

If I had any fucking self-respect, I'd stop kissing her neck. I'd stop my teeth from scraping along her skin, and I wouldn't be standing on the side of the road with a raging hard-on, still willing to give her whatever she'd asked for, even if I knew she'd go back to ignoring me in ten minutes.

She untangled herself from me, and I managed not to cling to her like an annoying bug might. Only so I could look at her. Figuring out Valentina Rhodes might become my favorite hobby, with how frequently I did it. For the number of times it happened, though, I was still unbelievably bad at it. For the life of me, I couldn't imagine what she might be thinking. How good a kisser I was, preferably. How she'd missed this and wanted more—hopefully. Probably just that I was a fucking idiot. I tried to snap out of it and started walking back to the house.

Show some independence, Caden.

"So?" I asked. The house materialized around the corner, and I could feel Valentina's guard rising beside me. Walls that seemed almost as high as mine usually were. "Got me out of your system now?"

She rolled her eyes but didn't answer. Which probably meant this little experiment of hers had been unsuccessful. Had probably made the whole thing between us worse. Less bearable. More thought consuming.

I nodded knowingly, like her silence was answer enough. "Yeah," I agreed thoughtfully, stepping onto the gravel leading to the house. "Me neither."

*

Valentina showered, and I thought about myself in there with her. She jumped into the pool—with nothing but that stringy bikini on, *obviously*—and I imagined none of her friends were jumping in with her, so we could finish what we'd started earlier. In the water. On the deck. The lounge chairs we'd slept on last week. Anywhere she'd have me, really.

When her friends split up grocery duty that afternoon, I honest to God imagined hearing my name after hers, hoping to get more time with her—not wanting to wait until tonight.

"That cool with you, Caden?" Iris asked, sitting on the island in the kitchen. On the couch, I blinked out of my Valentina-induced trance to find five pairs of eyes staring at me expectantly. Save for Valentina's, who shook her head, not very subtly, from behind Iris in the kitchen.

"What?"

"You and Valentina. Groceries for the bonfire tonight. Is that fine?"

Oh. So I hadn't imagined it.

"Yeah. Of course." I almost smiled when Valentina, out of sight from the rest of her friends, let her head fall back with a silent groan. I was tempted to blow her a kiss when her eyes slid back to mine in a glare but decided against it. For her sake.

"Sweet. You can take the Bronco."

The way Iris said it seemed casual enough, but by the way Valentina's head shot in her direction, it wasn't.

"What?" she asked, incredulous. "We can take the—what?"

"The Bronco. I'm not letting you chug along with that thing you call a car. And we're taking Mike's actual, properly working vehicle into town." Then she threw her keys at Valentina. She gracefully caught them. "If you hurt her, I'll be very upset."

CHAPTER 14

VALENTINA

I was too afraid of totaling the Bronco, so I didn't drive. Despite the fact that I am a good driver, crashing Iris's favorite car was probably worse than breaking the NFR. And she had enough reason to be mad at me already.

"She doesn't let anyone drive it," I explained to Caden on the way to the store. Apart from firewood, we had to get marshmallows, crackers, chocolate, hot dogs, buns, and whatever Anni needed to make her infamous campfire bread—literally translating to "stick bread" from German.

I hadn't spoken a word to him since we'd gotten back from our run. Out of fear I might say something that would lead us right back to where we'd ended up once today already. But intentionally not speaking to someone was harder than I'd thought, and I'd given up the second we'd gotten in the car. Clearly, I was making up for lost time by sharing every thought that came to mind. For some reason.

"I don't know why she's just letting us drive it, like she hasn't fought tooth and nail to keep those keys out of Anni's and Alfie's hands—well, no, Alfie's I understand. He's an abysmal driver . . ." I trailed off, shaking my head. "It doesn't make sense—"

Caden's eyes flicked to me, then back to the road. Another five minutes until he'd pull up to the store. "Has anyone ever told you how confusing you are, Rhodes?"

My eyes narrowed at him, and he continued. "You don't speak to me the entire time we're home, then you can't seem to shut up the second we're on grocery duty. Did you accidentally flick a switch when we got in the car?"

"Would you look at that," I scoffed, surprised I wasn't taking his words more personally. Anyone else telling me I talked too much would probably shut me up for the rest of my natural life. I'm not kidding. But with Caden, it seemed easy to brush past the insult, simply by throwing one back at him. "Almost as weird as you ignoring me for an entire week, then standing by my bed at six thirty in the morning, demanding attention."

Caden snickered. "*Our* bed," he reminded, then changed back to my earlier topic of rambling. "And your friend gave us her beloved car because she loves you, and she trusts me, apparently. That's the only reason. Is that satisfying enough?"

No. I hated that Iris trusted him. That he'd infiltrated my friend group within a week. A day, and they'd all loved him. Six later, and I'd found myself in a position of breaking their trust. *He'd* put me in a position of breaking that trust. Iris loved me—*needed* me—and I was still thinking about his lips on mine eight hours later.

Getting it out of our system my ass. It still felt like he was all over me.

It seemed logical to take my anger out on him, even if, realistically, it was myself I was mad at. Furious, really. But yelling at Caden let me blow off some steam and drive him further away. A win-win.

"No," I said sternly. A little too loud. "It's not your bed. It's *my* bed that you nestled into without permission. Those are my friends that trust you now, my group that you infiltrated. And none of it is *satisfying*. It's actually quite annoying."

Unfortunately, while my voice was getting louder, my tone harsher, I'd forgotten that our arguing had served as some kind of weird foreplay in the past. When he slammed on the brakes and pulled over to the side of the road, it seemed this one was leading in the same direction.

"That's your problem?" he asked, turning off the engine and finally looking at me. Wait, no. *Unfortunately* looking at me. "Your problem is that your friends like me?"

He wouldn't understand, and maybe that's why I said, "Yes!" Because his apparent likability was why I'd been carrying a boulder of guilt around since he'd gotten here—getting bigger and heavier every time I looked at him and realized I wanted him a little more than the last time our gazes had crossed. Like they did now.

There was a crease between his brows, and I wasn't quite sure if it was anger or confusion that put it there. Maybe the combination of both. He leaned closer, eyes narrowed like he was trying to read me. He probably failed.

"You're proving my point," he said. "You're the most confusing woman I've ever met."

"Congrats. It can only get better from here on out, then." My eyes flicked across his face, and they didn't linger on his lips. For *too* long, at least. I tried to conjure up an image of Iris, of our first bonfire night and how hurt she'd been by *Mr. Doesn't Want a Relationship* a few days ago—tried my very hardest to remember all the reasons that made Caden Callahan an awful choice for company.

He shook his head. "That's the thing," he growled, as if he liked admitting it almost as little as he enjoyed feeling like this, in the first place. "I don't think it can get better. I don't know what you did to me, Valentina. But you're definitely not out of my system."

And he was definitely not out of mine.

I almost caved. Almost banned Iris from my mind again, locked my already guilty conscience into a backroom and climbed over the console, onto his lap. He looked at me—lids heavy, pupils wide, gaze continuously flickering to my lips—like he wanted me to. My hand already hovered by my seat belt.

A single car rushed past us, and it was kind of like the snap of a finger drawing a patient out of hypnosis. I regained some of my ability to think rationally. Grew aware of the fact that our faces almost met in the middle of the car, with how close we'd inched toward each other. Remembered that I could actually speak.

"That's not my fault," I whispered. He was so close, he probably felt the words on his skin.

Caden huffed, and I could feel that, too. "You're saying I'm out of yours, then?" he asked inconspicuously—like his hand hadn't cupped my cheek for a moment, and like he wasn't tracing a finger along my jawline now.

I tried not to shudder under his touch and failed. "You're saying that kiss did it for you?" His hand dipped lower, continued trailing down my neck, touch featherlight. "You don't need anything else I can give you? You don't crave it the way I crave you?"

I wanted to shake my head, but all I managed was to turn it to one side, granting him more access, silently begging for his touch. He knew what it meant—my silence, the goose bumps on my skin, my parted lips.

"Talk to me," he whispered in a low voice, and my eyes closed. Like I'd fallen right back under his spell.

"No—" I wanted to stay strong in my stance. *No, I don't need you. No, I don't want you.* But suddenly, it was his lips on my skin, and the way he placed gentle kisses down my neck, against my collarbone, felt familiar. Good and familiar. Too good and way too familiar.

There was a brief moment of surrender. Right as his kisses moved back to my face and he'd planted one in the corner of my lips, I thought, *I should do this. For myself.* I made the bucket list for myself. Why couldn't I have this, too?

I'd reasoned enough to reciprocate his gentle kiss, to turn my head, to move my lips against his and sigh into his mouth.

"Alright, then," Caden rasped, then pulled away.

The engine roared back to life below us while I was still wrapping my head around his absence from my skin. I was still figuring out why I missed it when he said, knowing smirk on his face, "If that's so."

And we were back to silence.

CHAPTER 15

CADEN

I deserved a medal for my show of restraint. Then another one for winning *Dumbest Guy on the East Coast.* I'd *had* her. Right on the edge, a single push—biting her bottom lip, my hand on her thigh, trailing my fingers across her soft skin again—and I would've fucked Valentina in that car.

But I'd shown restraint, which earned me that second medal. Clearly, because I was still thinking about it now. Surrounded by three of her friends, one of mine, and Valentina herself. Sitting around a bonfire on the beach behind Alfie's house, I was straining against my boxers because I couldn't stop thinking about *What Could've Been.*

Pathetic. But when wasn't I, when it came to that girl?

"Are you feeling alright?" Alfie asked against the sound of the waves, which meant he was basically yelling at Valentina. "That's still your first glass of wine. We're on our second bottle." Each, by the way.

Valentina laughed. The sound probably didn't travel all the way to Alfie on the other side of the fire, but I heard it loud and clear. I was sitting right next to her, after all, and I wasn't quite sure how that had happened; Annika had scooted over when I'd joined last, I think.

"That's not how it works," she said with a snicker, then took a sip as if to emphasize that she was, in fact, not sick. How relieving. "If I was feeling bad, I wouldn't drink at all."

He shrugged, and Iris—whose head had been resting on his shoulder and who'd been suspiciously quiet for at least fifteen minutes now—complained with a very loud groan. She muttered something to Alfie, then presumably repeated it out loud. "Bed," she groaned. Dragged it out, like a zombie who'd acquired a taste for naps, not human flesh. "Beeeeeed."

"I think . . ." Alfie began with a laugh. He got up and dragged Iris off the sand with him. "I should put this one to bed. And I think I'm so drunk, once I'm up there, I will not find my way back down."

They gave their good-nights—Alfie a little more coherently than Iris, but honestly not by much—and staggered back up to the house.

Its lights shone in the distance, an orange hue against the dark backdrop of the night. The sky was as beautiful as it had been the last time I joined Valentina outside. I'd looked up five times so far.

When Annika and Mike got up five minutes later, I wasn't surprised. They'd checked out of the group setting an hour ago, giggling and whispering and kissing like they were teenagers and the only ones here.

Mike being my captain meant that so much as thinking about having alcohol was a federal offense, so I fiddled with my water bottle, dragging it across the sand. Usually, this would be where I'd excuse myself as well. For a week now, I'd done all I could not to be alone with Valentina simply because I didn't trust myself around her. She'd set clear boundaries, and the last thing I'd wanted was to accidentally break those.

This morning, though, she'd broken them herself. She'd kissed me. She'd shown me that she'd wanted more. Right there, on that cliff. Then again, in the car. I couldn't figure her out, but I'd be damned if I robbed myself of another opportunity to try. So I stayed put. For ten minutes, the only sounds were the waves breaching against the beach and the fire crackling in front of us, slowly dying out.

Valentina cleared her throat. "Can you spot the dippers now?" she asked quietly from beside me. Like conversing with me was bad but the uncomfortable silence somehow worse.

I looked up again. "Yeah." And then, maybe because her conversation starter felt like an olive branch of some kind, I surprised myself when I said, "My sister showed them to me once."

Valentina huffed beside me. Out of the corner of my eye, I could see her looking at the sky as well, arms wrapped around her drawn-up legs. "I've tried to show mine. So far, she's told me to fuck off seven times and threatened to tell Mom about the time I snuck out twice. Not that she'd care."

I didn't know she had a sister. Then again, I hadn't known much besides her name a week ago. "How old is she?"

"Eighteen next week." She sighed. "That formative time where they blame you for everything that's ever happened to them—or hasn't happened to them. Been there yet?"

The question felt like a blow to the gut. She couldn't have known how sore a subject this was, couldn't possibly begin to understand the gravity of her words, so I didn't blame her.

I took a deep breath. "She'd be around the same age," I pondered. "I guess I'd know how you feel if she hadn't died seven years ago."

Beside me, Valentina froze. The finger that had been drawing stars into the sand stilled.

"Fuck," she began. I knew what would come next. "Caden, I'm so sorry—"

A single shake of my head cut her off, that's how aware of my reaction she was. "Don't be. You didn't kill her, did you?" I tried to laugh, and usually I managed to bury my grief below a layer of sarcasm. This time, though, it fell flat. Maybe because the way Valentina looked at me was scarily disarming, like she could've seen straight through it, anyway.

"Seriously. I'm sorry. I didn't know." Her brows drew together in concern, and her eyes seemed to get bigger, somehow. Were those the puppy eyes Iris had been talking about? "I would've never—"

"Valentina." Our eyes met, and her mouth shut. "It's fine, really. You didn't know." But guilt was still written all over her face—in her frown, the knitted brows, those damn eyes looking up at me. I kept talking, simply with the hope *something* I'd say would ease her guilty conscience.

"She's still with me." I tapped the spot above my heart, and the beginning of a smile—although sad and pitiful—lifted the corners of her lips. "Every time I look up at the sky. Or kick a ball—and I do that a lot."

This time, I managed to deliver the humor in my tone better. She huffed, and something in the air shifted. Like she was just as glad to leave the ugly topic behind. Eager to move further away from the death portion of the conversation, she asked, "Did she play?"

I shook my head. "No, but she loved watching me play. Her first word was *Caden*, her second *ball*. I don't know if I'd still be playing if it wasn't for her."

But Ali had wanted me to go pro so badly, not pursuing it had felt like a betrayal in and of itself. So I'd applied for a soccer scholarship at HBU when I could've probably covered most of the tuition with all the money I'd earned and saved, working multiple jobs to be able to afford her cancer treatment.

Winning the NCAA championship had been more important to me than passing my courses, and we hadn't even won. There was a reason I'd signed up for a graduate degree—and it wasn't because my bachelor's in Computer Engineering wouldn't leave me with enough options. The opposite, really. Most of the people I'd studied with had above-average-paying entry-level jobs lined up for September. I'd been through a few rounds of interviews myself, just to see.

I was going back to HBU to play soccer, though. The way Alison would have wanted. I'd known that from the very beginning.

Valentina nodded in understanding. "She'd be proud of you, then," she thought out loud, and the words did something to me. "I mean, her big brother: almost captain of the current NCAA champion. That's something, right?"

"Sounds like you've done your research on me, Rhodes." The smile on her face grew, and it felt safe to say we were out of guilt territory. *Good.*

She snickered, attention back on the dying flames in front of us. Their light danced across her face, tinting her features in a soft orange. Making her look more beautiful than she already was.

"Mike told me," she said in defense. Her hand began drawing in the sand again, and she buried her toes in it, too. "He's been talking an awful lot about you, actually." And it sounded like she'd just noticed.

"I did not put him up to it, if that's what you're getting at."

She laughed, and what a sound that was. Still too foreign for my liking. "I'm not sure if I can believe that. It seems like he's caught a bad case of wingmanitis."

I raised an eyebrow, and our eyes met. "Be honest," I tutted. "Do I seem like the type of guy who needs his friends to put in a good word for him?"

Her lips twitched, but I wasn't rewarded with another laugh. "Maybe," she said, for the sake of it. We both knew it wasn't true.

I tilted my head. "When you kissed me this morning, was it because of what Mike said about me?" Never mind that I had no clue *what* he had said. Or why.

Valentina stayed very quiet and very still. But her gaze was still locked with mine. "And when you let me touch you earlier," I reminded her, "was *that* because of what he said?"

Her breath hitched, and it should've been answer enough. But she doubled down, and I wasn't surprised at all. "Maybe hearing about how great of a midfielder you are all week just really put me in the mood."

I snorted a laugh and shouldn't have expected Mike to talk about anything other than soccer. The guy had two brain cells. One for the sport, the other for Annika Schmidt.

"I *am* a great midfielder, but I have a feeling that's not what did it for you."

"No?" Her words were barely a whisper at this point. Breathed against my lips, that's how close we were. I wasn't sure which one of us had closed the distance between us so drastically. Probably me.

And it felt like second nature to follow when she slowly leaned back, onto her arms in the sand. Tomorrow, I don't think I would recall how we'd gotten to this point. Some deep conversation turned flirty banter turned me on top of her. It sounded like the stuff dreams were made of.

"No." I echoed her words. "I think it's simply because you like this, and you like what I could do to you." I placed a single, tender kiss on her neck, and she shuddered underneath the touch. I briefly wondered if she was this sensitive with every guy—then quickly banished any thoughts of Valentina with other men from my mind. Forever, preferably. "But for some reason," I went on, placed another kiss against her skin, "you're not letting it happen. Why is that, sweetheart?"

One of my hands disappeared in her hair, and I could tell, right then, I had her again. Her eyes closed, and her head fell back with a soundless sigh. "Because," she said, then stopped. My face moved back in front of hers, only inches separating us.

"Because?" I asked against her lips, voice low.

"Because I'm not supposed to. You're—" She cut herself off, tried again. "My friends can't know. And I'm not great at lying to them."

It was quite possibly the last thing I'd expected to hear from her. Many more reasonable explanations had crossed my mind since her first rejection: wanting more than casual sex and knowing I couldn't give that to her, for example. I thought maybe she was seeing someone back home or had just met a guy who'd demanded she stay loyal despite his continuous fucking around.

I didn't think . . .

I moved back to look at her, the confusion probably written all over my face. "Your friends said they don't want you to hook up with me?"

Valentina shook her head. "No. No, that's not—" She cut herself off with a groan, and whatever tension there'd been between us was dwindling by the second.

Right now, though, I was far more interested in the explanation I felt coming. She continued, "They don't know about us. And they can't know about us. I don't want them to—"

"You're embarrassed by me?" I'd never had anyone—

"No!" she half shrieked. "God, no. Fuck, Caden. It's got little to do with you and a lot to do with me. Alright?"

That brought a smirk to my lips. The corners of my lips lifted in amusement and some relief. "Aw, Valentina," I cooed, "are you saying it's not me, it's you? How original."

"Technically, yes."

Saying I wasn't dying to dig deeper would be a lie. But it didn't seem like I'd get much more out of her than the vaguest of vague answers. *It's not you, it's me.* Like I hadn't figured as much already.

By now, the fire had gone out; the coals were only glimmering lowly in the sand, one by one dying out. My body physically repelled the thought of moving off Valentina. Of letting more than a few inches get between us and of not feeling her heat below me anymore. But it seemed like the reasonable thing to do.

It was cold, suddenly. The fire out, Valentina gone. She must've noticed at the same time. "I think I'm going to sleep."

Getting up, she tried her best to dust off the sand stuck to her bare legs and the fabric of her black sundress. She failed, of course, but what had almost happened between us—*again*—seemed too recent to offer my help in the matter. Any physical contact would probably lead us right back into the sand.

So all I did was wish her good night before watching her make her way back to the house. It seemed like she needed that time alone, and I gave her ten minutes before I followed into our room.

CHAPTER 16

VALENTINA

I was pacing. Up and down, from the window overlooking the front yard to the dresser opposite it. But trying to walk this off—this pulsing need for Caden right below my skin, pushing closer to the surface every time he touched me or whispered my name or I looked at him for a little too long, really—was harder than I'd imagined.

It was too easy to remember where all the flirting and half kisses could lead. Where it *had* led, four months ago. With his lips all over me, his body between mine, and three orgasms. With sweet nothings whispered against my skin and a warm chest to fall asleep against.

He hadn't seemed like the type of guy to want his girls to stay the night, so I'd left before dawn had even broken.

Behind me, the door creaked open, and it didn't take a genius to know who'd walked into the room. I must've still looked like a deer in headlights by the time Caden closed it behind himself again.

For a long moment, he just stood there, not daring to take a single step closer. He let his gaze fall down and back up my body—too slowly to be considered casual. Too intently to be considered anything but appraising.

"You're still up," he noted, voice low. Presumably not to wake the rest of the house. I appreciated that.

"I left, like, two minutes ago. Of course I'm still up." The bite in my tone wasn't justified. He hadn't done anything wrong—*I* was the one who kept breaking my own rules over and over again. The one who kept jumping between loyalty and selfishness.

With a sigh, Caden leaned against the door behind him, crossing his arms lazily. "Listen," he said, "if you don't want this, it's not happening. That's how simple it is. You don't need a reason to say no."

Didn't I, though? I thought every decision needed some kind of justification.

"You don't need to justify not wanting me, alright?"

I couldn't help but laugh. He didn't know better, but the assumption that I didn't *want* him was so . . . far from the truth, I couldn't hold back my amusement. I waved the look he gave me off. "I'm sorry." I snickered. "It's just—" I hesitated, then thought *fuck it.*

This was Caden, and I'd been brutally honest—borderline mean—to him since he'd gotten here. I still didn't want him to like me, so why tell him anything but the truth?

"Not wanting you is not the issue here, trust me." He perked up—straightened and narrowed his eyes at me, like he was trying to figure me out.

I wasn't quite sure when I'd decided to cross the room, but I stood in front of him five seconds later. "I do want you. So much, I'm considering breaking my morals every time you look at me like that." Lips slightly parted, blue eyes hooded, pupils wide.

He tugged a strand of hair behind my ear, and it took everything in me not to lean into the tender touch.

With a subtle grin, he asked, "Sleeping with me would break your morals? That's how awful I am?"

That's how awful I'd be for doing it.

"In a sense," I said regardless.

The smile on his lips stayed, and he tilted his head, just slightly. "We shouldn't, then," he whispered. His hand still lingered on my cheek, his thumb absentmindedly drawing circles against my skin. Touch, as always, light as a feather.

"No," I agreed. "We shouldn't."

He turned us, brought my back against the wooden door, and let his hand linger where he'd placed it to move me: my waist. "Because of your friends," he said. "Right?"

"Sure." I nodded. "Yes."

"Now here's a thought, though." And I was desperate to hear it, because I knew in which direction it was leading. Because I knew he was going to give me reasons to justify how close he was and that I could have him closer if they were good enough. "Doing something because you want it—"

"Doing *you* because I want it?" I clarified, half a laugh on my lips.

He grinned. "Yes. Doing me because you want it. Kind of like with that list of yours. You're not telling anyone because you want to do that for yourself as well, right?"

"I'm doing that because I don't think anyone would want to do it with me. But sure." Honest truth, again. But I couldn't focus on the admission when his touch danced along my side, up to my chest, then over my waist all the way down to my hips.

"Volunteering as tribute for item number seven." *Sex on the beach.* However presumptuous it sounded, I wasn't at all surprised by the fact that he remembered every list item in order.

"Oh, I'm sure you are."

He grinned—still or again, I wasn't quite sure. His hand lingered below the hem of my dress now, like he didn't want to go further without hearing me say the words. I took a deep breath.

For myself.

Like the bucket list, I would do this for myself as well. Because I was a grown woman who occasionally enjoyed casual sex, even if she had to keep it a secret. Because I didn't have to tell my friends everything, even if they did. Because after this summer, Caden would go his way, and we'd go ours, and while he was part of this group now, he wouldn't be by the time we'd left Oakport. Right?

"Just sex," I confirmed one last time. And it seemed like he really had waited for me to say the words. His hand dove under my dress, and his touch left a trail of goose bumps behind. It lingered on my waist again, only that there was no more fabric separating us. His fingers slid along the waistband of my panties. I pressed the words out before it was too late: "To get it out of our system. For real this time."

He nodded, drew my leg up against his side. I sucked in a breath. "Whatever you want it to be, that's what it'll be." And I was so relieved—so ready to feel and taste him again, I didn't doubt he was about to kiss me until he stopped only an inch short of my lips. His forehead fell to mine, and the smile he gave me was cruel. "Under one condition."

I almost groaned. I wanted him—I wanted him so badly, delaying what had become the inevitable any longer seemed torturous. Since I'd set foot in this room a week ago, I'd thought about little else but having him again. And now, when I was this close—when I'd managed to shove Iris and my guilty conscience out of my mind—

"There are conditions to sleeping with you?" I pretty much panted that laugh. "And I thought I had you all figured out, Callahan."

He huffed, then turned us again, walking me toward our bed. A bunk bed was the opposite of sexy, but we'd have to make do with what we had.

"Well," he said, placing one hand on top of my hair and gently guiding me onto his bunk, careful not to hit my head, "you have your conditions, and I have mine."

Not telling my friends must've been my condition, then. Fair enough.

"Let's hear it."

He hovered above me again, similarly to how he had at the beach. Only now, there was a soft mattress below me and fluffy pillows and covers around. Twenty minutes ago, sleeping with him had been a wild fantasy. Now it seemed inevitable. I'd probably agree to any condition he had—that's how desperate I was.

"That bucket list of yours. I want in."

It wasn't outrageous or scandalous or even particularly crazy. But my features fell regardless, out of sheer confusion. "What?"

"You said no one wants to do it with you. But I'd love to play pool again. Watch the sunrise. *Moonwalk fully.*" He winked, and his words drew another laugh out of me. At the sound, he closed his eyes.

"Are you being serious?" He was still above me, and I couldn't quite believe it. "Your condition to sleeping with me is . . . spending more time together after the fact?"

"Hm," he hummed, considered my words. "Seems that way, yes. What do you say?"

I snickered. "Yes, sure—" Which was when his head dipped into the crook of my neck again. "Just—why?"

I should be focused on the way he was kissing me. The way my back arched off the mattress every time his teeth scraped my skin. But I was still struggling to wrap my mind around his proposal.

"Why?" I think he said. I couldn't be sure because the words were mumbled into my neck, and it seemed he wasn't coming up to have this conversation with me.

"I've been a—*fuck*." His hand was back below my dress, only that this time, its hem came up with it. He drew it all the way up to my waist, fabric bunched up over my underwear. Once, very quickly, his finger slid over my core.

"You've been a what?" His mouth was by my ear until it wasn't. Until he suddenly kissed his way down my neck, my chest, grazed my nipples under the dress, and looked up at me with dark eyes. His finger was still hovering by my panties.

"A bitch," I finally got out. "I've been a bitch to you, and you still want me?"

"I don't think there's anything you could do to make me *not* want you."

"Want me like this, yeah. But—" I shook my head, squirmed when his thumb casually flitted over my clit. Again and again. Still, he was looking at me like we were having this conversation across the breakfast table, no parts of us touching. Like I couldn't feel how it affected him pressing against me.

"But?"

I tried to mirror his nonchalance. "You'll always want to fuck me, sure. But that doesn't mean you'd want to hang out with me. Watch the sunrise, play pool."

Shut up, Valentina. My inner voice kept shouting the words at me. This seemed like a wildly inappropriate moment for this conversation. What if I accidentally succeeded, made him see the flaws of his plan, and he stopped? Stopped touching and kissing and looking at me that way. The thought was almost painful.

Caden shrugged. Like it was nothing, he slid my panties down my thighs. Taking his sweet time, fingers grazing my skin and becoming even slower when he'd almost had them at my calves.

I was not surprised to hear him say, "They're soaked, sweetheart," before he looked back up at me to finally clear up my confusion. "I enjoy your company."

"I've been rude and unaccommodating. Honestly, outright mean—"

He huffed in amusement as he threw my panties somewhere across the room. "Alright. I enjoy your company, even when you're rude and unaccommodating and outright mean."

But that didn't make any sense. "Now," he muttered, and his focus must've drifted off in sync with his gaze, raking up my bare legs, taking me in, basically naked on his bed, "are there any other concerns we need to address right here, right now? Or can we move on to—"

Oh, right. Yes. Move on to finally stilling that pulsing need that had dropped all the way to my core. I reached for the hem of his shirt before he could finish his sentence, and he helped me pull it over his head without a second thought. I meant to reach for his shorts next, but he caught my hands in his. Kissed my knuckles once and shook his head. "So impatient. What I meant to say," he rasped, slowly pushing my arms up and pinning my wrists against the pillow, "can we move on to your first orgasm?"

Every semirational thought still occupying my mind washed away. Made space for Caden and the way he kissed down my body. Chest, torso, hips. He nodded at my hands. "Keep them over your head."

And I didn't want to find out what might happen if I didn't. "Good girl," he hummed against me, and I pulsed in reciprocation. In want, and need, and a million other things on the same spectrum.

"See"—he teased one finger along my core, watched me writhe with anticipation, and still refused to fill me—"how nice you are to me when it's just us, in a dimly lit room in the middle of the night? You're making up for every mean thing you've said to me right now, baby. Just keep being as good as you are."

I didn't have enough time to grasp what his words were doing to me—why my cheeks were burning with pride, not embarrassment—because he was everywhere, suddenly. The tip of his tongue on my clit, his finger inside of me, both moving in sync with the other. Slowly first—like he was savoring the taste and feel of me, remembering what it had been like last time—before picking up his pace.

And it took everything in me not to wake the whole house. Eyes closed, lips parted despite my best efforts, I managed not to let more than soft, muted sounds escape them, and even then, they were panted into the pillow. Suppressed enough, hopefully.

It felt like an eternity of bliss and two minutes all at once. I couldn't say which was reality, in the end, but I had not been prepared to be this quick. To feel release on the horizon when it seemed he'd barely started. But perhaps the entire week leading up to this—the few times

I'd already thought about this exact moment—had had its benefit.

Caden had found my sweet spot, and he knew it, too.

"That's it, hm?" he muttered, and I couldn't do anything other than nod, because opening my mouth meant more than just a simple *Fuck, yes* would escape. Moans, and groans, and please, please, please, repeated over and over again until—

I came.

It couldn't have been more than five minutes, like he'd remembered exactly which buttons to press. Like he'd challenged himself to see how fast he could get me there. Turned out, *very.*

Emerging from between my thighs, he trailed a string of kisses up my legs, stomach, chest—not just leaving goose bumps behind but making me shudder underneath his touch as I came down from my high. When his face popped into my vision, he wore a satisfied smile.

"I'm impressed, Rhodes," he said, voice gravelly. "Keeping that quiet, it couldn't have been easy. For a moment there, you really had me worried this wasn't doing it for you—"

I shook my head, breath still heavy. "Oh, no. It did it. It definitely did it." I took another deep breath, eyes on the upper bunk above us. He sat between my legs. "Sorry. Just with everyone around . . ." I shrugged, like it was explanation enough. "Is it less . . . exciting for you? When I'm not . . ." I hesitated. "Expressing myself?"

How selfish of me, I thought. But the one thing I'd been thinking more than *Wow, Oh my God*, and *He's really good at this* was *Shut up, Valentina, your friends are spread all over this house, and they cannot hear you like this. Not with him, anyway.*

Caden blinked at me, brows furrowing. "Sorry?" he repeated. "You're sorry?" Like he couldn't quite believe the word had come out of my mouth. His hand had moved to my leg, trailing up and down my skin. By now, I'd gotten used to his touch, and instead of sending aftershocks through my body, it just felt soothing. "Seeing you—*feeling* you struggling to hold back might've been the hottest thing I've ever seen," he said unapologetically.

My cheeks flushed pink again, and maybe it encouraged him to keep going. "You have to stop worrying whether I am or am not enjoying myself. You can assume I am. Always just assume I'm having the time of my life when I'm with you."

Like this, I added. *When I'm with you, like this—naked, in bed, giving you orgasms and waiting for mine.* Which reminded me of the fact that he was still straining against his shorts.

When I reached for his bulge, felt it twitch against my hand, and watched his eyes fall shut from the unexpected touch, I hummed in approval. There was a wet spot, right by his tip, that was hard to ignore.

"I am worried, though," I sighed, fiddling with the waistband of his shorts. My fingers dipped behind it, then trailed back out and up his chest. Quite quickly, he'd been turned into the one trembling underneath my touch.

"What about, baby?"

It was hard to believe how quickly I'd had him. One touch, and Caden Callahan, six-foot-something, muscles of steel, almost captain of the HBU soccer team, was willing to do whatever it took. One touch, and he was looking at me like I might be the answer to all his problems.

"You." My hand slid over his bulge again, and he sucked in a sharp breath. "*This.*"

I sat up. Again, his eyes fell shut when I began fiddling with the waistband of his shorts. Only this time, I followed through. Snapped it against his skin once, then pulled them over his bulge. It twitched against his boxer briefs, and the spot of precum was glaringly obvious against the gray fabric. He leaned back with a low sound when I pulled those down, too.

"Need any help with that?" I wondered. My eyes batted open and immediately connected with his.

"Fuck" was all he said, and I took that as answer enough, even before he added, "*Please.*"

The night we'd met, Caden had made me come twice with his mouth and once with his cock, so this was uncharted territory for us: pushing him back against the mattress, my tongue trailing down his body, and my lips gently wrapping around him.

The way his hands found themselves in my hair was new, too.

"Valentina," he whispered, right as I started moving—had closed my lips tightly around him, tongue sweeping over his wet tip once, twice, and a third time, for good measure. He seemed to like it so much, my name sounded like a plea. His grip on my hair tightened but never forced my movement.

When I needed a break, my tongue would swipe up his length, torturously slow before my hand would take over. He'd press his head deeper into the pillow, like that made keeping quiet easier.

I knew what he meant now, though. Watching him trying—and struggling—to hold back was one of the hottest things I'd ever seen, too.

"I'm—" My mouth was back around him, taking inch by inch, until his tip tickled the back of my throat. When his eyes met mine again, watery and wide, his face contorted. "I'm about to—" he began, then started a completely different sentence, like his brain was muddled and coherent sentences were not on the table. "If you want me in any other way tonight, you should really—"

But I didn't. I wanted Caden just like this: twitching against my throat, struggling to speak, and coming in the exact moment we made eye contact again.

And that's exactly how I had him.

CHAPTER 17

CADEN

Last night kind of felt like a spiritual awakening. Only that I hadn't found my way back to God or the Universe but to Valentina Rhodes.

Watching her come apart had been better than what my memory had served me. Watching her take me in her mouth, inch by torturous inch, had exceeded every and any fantasy. And kissing her, sweaty and out of breath but seemingly proud of what she'd done to me, might still be my personal highlight.

When she had suggested *only sex*, I thought I'd hit the jackpot. I'd thought a repeat of the other night would be enough to satisfy my insatiable hunger—but that's exactly what it was: insatiable.

I was disappointed when she climbed back up to her bunk, and not because I'd been rooting for another round in the morning. Only because, somewhere in the back of my mind, there was a piece of me that had wanted to fall asleep next to her. Wake up and have her be the first thing I'd see.

That was new. And scary.

When I got up the next morning, she was still sound asleep, covers thrown wildly across her bed, covering barely half of her. I tiptoed into the bath first, then out of the room, and it hurt a little to leave her there, knowing I was about to spend my time with Mike instead.

Don't get me wrong, I love the guy. But priorities were priorities.

Anything for the HBU soccer team, though. Right?

"Ready?" he asked, standing by the bottom of the stairs as I descended.

"No," I deadpanned.

Mike rolled his eyes, but I followed him outside. "Cheer up, Captain!" He bumped my shoulder in amusement. "A few more weeks until you'll need enough motivation to encourage an entire team. Better start harnessing that good vibe early."

If I couldn't even muster up those good vibes after a night with Valentina, I'm not quite sure how I was supposed to do it in two months. I knew I didn't *want* to. Then again, I knew I didn't have much of a choice either.

Alison's wish lingered in the back of my mind, like a cobweb in the corner of a room you couldn't get to and learned to live with. She would want this. She'd be ecstatic, knowing I was set to captain the current NCAA champion. She'd be happy. She'd be proud.

So I sucked it up.

"Just tired," I explained curtly, then clapped my hands together and managed to at least summon a semienthusiastic "Let's do this!"

One of the soccer balls we'd taken for practices exactly like this one was already in the yard. To warm up, we started passing it across the pool. Good enough motivation not to fuck up, in my opinion, and Mike still felt confident enough to continue talking.

There was rarely a time when he didn't talk, though.

"*Tired*," he echoed, and a knowing smile etched into the corners of his mouth. "How much longer were you guys up?"

My next pass was wonky, and the only reason it hadn't landed in the water between us was Mike. I tried not to sound guilty (of what, I wasn't quite sure) when I asked, panicking, "What?"

Had they heard us last night? *Impossible*. Valentina had done so well, and—no matter how hard it was—I'd been unexpectedly quiet, too. An occasional groan could be anything. They wouldn't immediately jump to the conclusion we'd—

"By the fire?" he clarified, and I visibly relaxed. I easily received his next pass, did some kickups, and passed it back to him. "We left before you guys. How much longer did you stay out there?"

"Ah." I shook my head. "Not long. Fifteen minutes, maybe?"

Fifteen minutes, which wasn't a lie, but I didn't mention the hours in our room after that. There was a part of me that wanted to scream from every rooftop on this island, *Valentina Rhodes wants me!*

There was an entirely different part, though, that liked this—her being my little secret. Me being hers.

Having this thing between us nobody else knew . . . there was something so intimate about the thought. That we existed that way only for each other. That no one else knew how well we'd gotten to know each other—that I knew about the small mole on her hip, and the way her bare skin felt under my fingertips, and that she shuddered when she came. That she could make me come, apparently, just by batting those beautiful lashes at me, eyes watery and lips wrapped around my cock. I don't think she would've had to move at all, and I still would've been satisfied by the end of it.

God, she was fucking spectacular.

Mike's pass landed in the pool. I was not surprised that it was my fault.

Loser had to retrieve. Those were the rules, and I groaned when I pulled the HBU jersey over my head.

Mike raised an eyebrow. "Is she going to be a problem, Callahan?"

I straightened, alert to his tone: captain voice. It was like second nature, really. Nothing I could do about it.

Curtly, I said, "No. Of course not." I stripped out of my shorts and didn't let myself hesitate before jumping into the cold pool, if only to get some time underwater in which he couldn't ask any more questions.

Was she going to be a problem?

Not for me. For my focus, though? Maybe. Which meant it was a problem for him, and for the team. When I emerged from the cold and threw the ball back to Mike, he'd already prepared a whole speech.

"Listen, man," he sighed. I heaved myself out of the water, and he nodded toward the beach, to get started on drills and shots on targets and whatever else he'd cooked up to get me back on my A game, apparently. I followed. "I want you to be captain because in your time on the team, there was no one else more determined than you. You almost failed your classes first semester because you were so focused." *That's not something to be proud of*, I wanted to say. But I kept my mouth shut, just this once. "And when you're officially taking over after the summer, I want to have a good feeling about it. Right now, I do not."

Captain Thatcher had always been blunt. It's like two people lived inside of Mike. One was this stoic, disciplined HBU captain; the other, a thirteen-year-old boy. It had been a little disorienting at first, but you just had to separate Mike at practice from Mike in his personal life.

On this trip, I'd had the luxury of dealing with personal Mike. That had just changed.

"She's not going to be a problem, dude."

And I hoped I was right.

Two hours of a vigorous workout regime in the sand would leave anyone looking like this: sweaty, sand clinging *to* the sweat, flushed and breathing heavily. By the time I'd stepped out of the shower, Valentina was awake, leaning against the desk next to the door.

I'd expected a lot, but not that look on her face. A mixture of guilty and unbelievably tired. She held her phone in her hand, and her gaze flicked between me and the device one last time.

At first I thought the look—*the guilt*—had been about last night, but she swallowed hard, then gave me an apologetic smile before she said, "You got a call."

Which was when I noticed that phone in her hand wasn't hers but . . . mine?

"What?" I was still standing in the doorway to the bathroom.

"Listen!" She started justifying herself before she'd even said anything in need of a defense. "I was asleep. A phone rang—same ringtone as mine, by the way. And it rang, and rang, and didn't stop ringing. I thought it was mine, so I picked up!" she cried. "By the time I noticed it wasn't, it was too late."

"But after you noticed, you obviously hung up. Who was it?"

She grimaced. It was answer enough, even before she said, "Congrats, though! Pete from Anova offered you the job."

The beginning of that amused smile on my lips fell back into a straight line. I was still rooted to the same spot. I blinked at Valentina. "What?"

She could clearly feel the change in attitude, shifted uncomfortably from one foot to the other. "Pete . . . I-Forgot-His-Last-Name. From Anova. You got the job!" She tried to sound chipper, and I understood, kind of. If this were a normal situation, it would be enough reason to celebrate. "Should we get out the champagne?"

The door into the hallway was open, just a crack, but I finally crossed the room to close it. To avoid anyone else overhearing what could cost me everything. It slammed shut, and my first instinct was to get as far away from it as possible—just to lessen those chances a little more.

I dragged Valentina with me, hissed in a tone that was sharper than intended, "If you tell a single soul about this—"

"That you got a job at one of the biggest software developers in the country?" she guessed, understandably confused. "Great entry salary, by the way. One hundred and—"

I cut her off. "I'm being serious," I snapped, again much harsher than intended. But regulating my emotions was last on my list of worries right now. Anova took up those first five spots alone. "You tell anyone about this, and I'm arts-and-crafting a banner that says *Valentina Rhodes slept with Caden Callahan* and hanging it in the living room."

Her features fell and her eyes narrowed and she did not look happy. I wouldn't be, if someone had just threatened me. Which was basically what I was doing, right? Unintentionally, sure. But if Mike found out I'd applied—

Valentina slammed my phone into my hand. "I told Pete to send you an email with the details," she said, but the tone in her voice made it sound like a big, fat *fuck you* before she pulled her wrist out of my grasp and disappeared into the bathroom.

Alone, regret immediately flooded every single one of my rational thoughts. The irrational ones, though, were convinced that keeping Mike from finding out about Anova Inc. was more important than Valentina's feelings.

I just never expected to hear from them again. I'd landed the initial interview through Dylan McCarthy Williams, my roommate, way back when we weren't even fully through with finals. That was followed by two more rounds with different people, an assessment center and another interview. I'd assumed they kept calling me in as some kind of favor to McCarthy's uncle, high up. Ultimately, though, that's all it was. I hadn't thought about that job in over a month. And anyway, I didn't really *want* it.

I was doing the whole grad-school thing, captaining the soccer team, the way Alison would've wanted me to. That had been the plan.

Just thinking about derailing that—her wishes for me and what she thought my future would look like—felt so wrong, like such an incredibly deep betrayal, I wished I'd never applied in the first place.

Pete's email came thirty minutes later.

Dear Mr. Callahan,

On behalf of Anova Inc., I am pleased to offer you the exempt position of Entry Level Software Engineer, located at our offices in Boston, MA, starting October 1.

A salary of $160,000. Health insurance. Retirement plan. Fifteen vacation days.

I skimmed through the offer and benefits attached, like I might actually be considering this. Just to let myself imagine, for a second, before the guilt crept in again.

Then I sent an email back, thanking them profusely, before declining.

For the rest of the day, I was in no mood to celebrate. When everyone suggested going out for dinner and drinks to their local bar, I outright wanted to refuse. If I didn't go, though, I wouldn't be able to see if Valentina let her little phone conversation from this morning slip. Just to be petty. Just to piss me off.

So I went. Sat on the terrace of some place called Blitz and watched the sun set over the ocean, pretending to care about what they were talking about. I thought I'd been listening with one ear, but when Mike kicked my shin under the table, I realized I must've just tuned out completely.

"Huh?" I asked, blinking at him. Thankfully, the rest of the group was busy with another topic altogether and hadn't noticed my lack of attention.

"What's up with you today?" he hissed across the table—voice, for once, low enough not to be noticed. "Is this about this morning? I didn't mean to be harsh, man. But I know you can be better than you have been. I've *seen* you be better. I just want you to get that spark back by the time you're at HBU again."

He was talking about soccer, of course. When was he not? It seemed easiest just to agree, so I nodded, somewhat solemnly.

"I know. I get it. I don't know what's been up my ass lately," I lied. I knew exactly what it was.

That ever-growing awareness that I wasn't doing this because *I* wanted to do it. That I was trying to make someone proud who'd been dead for seven whole years. That I'd applied to jobs and considered other possibilities but couldn't go through with any of them in the end. That, in a year, I'd be twenty-four, and I'd still be at HBU, and nothing will have changed.

The fear that I was missing out on an entire life because I needed to live this one for me *and* my sister.

Mike's foot gave mine a sympathetic nudge below the table. "Don't worry, man. You'll get back into it."

I smiled. Or tried to, at least. Then tried not to drift off again, if only not to cause any more suspicion. My attention latched back onto the rest of the group, just as Iris guffawed across the table—maybe the entire bar, with how loud she was—and Valentina was getting up.

Wait, why was she getting up?

"What's going on?" I asked, faking a laugh to fit in. My gaze trailed after Valentina, eyes fixed on the way her cherry-red hair swayed with each step and trying not to focus on how her ass did, too. Then trying to outright ignore the reminder of how she'd felt underneath me yesterday—how she'd *tasted.*

Fuck. I cleared my throat.

"You see that guy?" Alfie asked, a conspiratorial smile on his lips. His words were hushed, like he might not want anyone else to hear them, but he pointed toward the bar like he couldn't care less who might see.

Through the wide-open French doors, we had the perfect view of a guy. *The* guy, probably. Must've been somewhere in his mid-twenties, blond, floppy hair. Tan skin, no shirt. And Valentina was approaching him.

"Yes," I said, but I had a feeling I wouldn't like where this was going.

"Obsessed with Valentina!" Alfie blurted, like he loved saying it. "They hook up all the time. Honestly, I'm surprised it's been a week and she hasn't seen him yet."

"Usually," Iris agreed, "he's the first number she texts whenever we're here. We had to keep her from doing so the second she got here—that's just desperate."

"It's, like, this summer romance straight out of a movie. Every time we're here, even when it's *not* summer," Alfie swooned. "I swear. I don't know how she can just go back home and not take the guy with her. I'd have kidnapped him by now. That's *not* an exaggeration."

My eyes flicked back to him. By the time Valentina was by his side—and she tapped his shoulder shyly, and I watched him turn, and his eyes widen, and embrace her in a whirlwind hug that lifted her feet off the ground—the fake smile I'd put on was gone. Replaced by a tight frown. Tight enough, it might already have been a grimace.

The feeling settling in the pit of my stomach was unfamiliar, but it intensified when he set her down and I could see her lips crack into a wide, carefree laugh.

“Maybe you’ll finally have your room to yourself tonight. She usually stays over at Finnick’s place.”

Embarrassingly enough, I wasn’t even sure who’d said that. By the time it could have registered, I was already halfway to the bar.

CHAPTER 18

VALENTINA

I hadn't seen Finnick in months.

Still, leaning against the counter, listening to what he'd been up to since the spring—his niece would start primary school soon, surf camp was busier than usual, he'd finally invested in that new board he'd been eyeing—I couldn't care less.

I'd never wanted to get back to my best friends, and farther away from him, more. Which was confusing, because I *liked* Finnick. His smile, his soft, blond hair, the way he talked about his niece and how much he loved the beach and the water—and anything related to the ocean, really. But I seemed to like him less with Caden around, and the latter's grimace wasn't helping.

When he got up, I outright panicked.

My eyes kept flicking back to the man approaching, which was terribly rude. Finnick was still talking about this year's wave quality, after all. His head shook, and the movement drew my eyes back, matching the laugh on Finnick's lips. "I was a little surprised not to hear from you sooner. Thought you might've forgotten about me."

He was joking, but a boulder of guilt still lodged itself in the pit of my stomach. There'd been a few of those recently. Finnick was nice. He was good. And two weeks with Caden had made me forget about him completely.

"We've been so busy." I laughed—or tried my best to, at least, because when Caden shamelessly stopped beside me, it almost knocked the wind out of me. A few feet away. Leaning across the bar to order.

He tilted his head at me, his lips twitched upward as he motioned the bartender over. "You want another drink, Val?" he asked, using a nickname he'd never used. Giving me a sweet smile he'd never given me before.

This morning, he'd gotten all up in my face about a stupid—although very, very generous—job offer, and now he thought himself in a position to offer me a drink? To smile at me like *that*?

With a wide, fake grin, I turned back to Finnick. I held up a finger, then excused myself with a quick, "Would you give me a second?"

To ensure we couldn't be overheard, I walked to Caden's other side. "What the fuck is wrong with you?" I hissed, then gave Finnick another fake smile to signal *So sorry! Everything's fine!*

"I have no idea what you're talking about." Caden's eyes flicked to mine, something shimmering in their usual blue.

Amusement? Annoyance? My guess would be a combination of both.

He ignored the bartender, who'd finally gotten to our end of the counter. "Don't let me keep you from Finnick, Rhodes. He looks quite lost all by himself."

"What do you want?" I narrowed my eyes, his earlier threat not forgotten. I didn't know him well enough to guess how serious he'd been, so I just had to assume *very.* He hadn't left much room for misinterpretation. In my opinion, his threat had been very clear.

His hands raised in mock defense. "Getting a drink."

"You're not drinking," I noted, right as he turned to the raven-haired bartender, tattoos covering her tan skin, to tell her, "Could I have another water?"

Without taking my eyes off him, I added, "Make that two. Please."

Now it was definitely amusement that twinkled in his gaze. It slid back to me, then flicked to Finnick, still patiently waiting a few feet away, pretending to be busy on his phone. Caden hummed, considering his next words—just clearly not long enough. "So this is the guy you had in mind when you put 'sex on the beach (not the drink)' on your bucket list?"

Well, yes.

Finnick Maxwell was the kind of on-again, off-again vacation fling found in any girl's dream. Kind, funny, not bad in bed—but not nearly as good as Caden, I begrudgingly had to admit now. He was ordinary enough not to miss too much when you were away, but things picked up right where they left off when you got back to him.

We got along well, and I usually looked forward to seeing him. Since Caden had made a surprise appearance in my room, I hadn't even thought about reaching out to Finnick, though. When Anni had pointed him out fifteen minutes ago, I had to keep from shrieking in surprise at his existence, and I felt awful about it.

I was at least partly convinced that was Caden's fault. Somehow.

"What?" I snickered at his question. "Not a fan?"

The corner of his lips twisted upward, and his brows followed, like I should know the answer. "Don't get me wrong. Handsome man," he admitted. "But I'm not going to be a fan of you with any guy." He shrugged. "Any guy that isn't me."

Our glasses of water magically appeared between us, and he accepted them with a grateful nod and a ten-dollar bill slid across the bar, while I tried not to let his words go straight to parts of me I didn't want him in anymore.

Yesterday, I'd gotten him out of my system, and that was that. That had been the plan. Strictly physical. Just sex. "A few hours ago, you threatened me," I reminded him. "And now you're jealous?"

Caden sighed, like he might actually regret his actions. "My threat should be irrelevant, because you're not telling anyone about Anova. Right?"

"My sister works at Anova! What about them?"

Our heads shot in Finnick's direction. He'd given up pretending not to listen, and we must've abandoned our whisper-shouting because, otherwise, he wouldn't have heard. Caden probably glared at him—I couldn't see his face—and I gently shook my head in Finnick's direction, silently letting him know this was not a conversation he wanted to be a part of.

The blond's hands shot up in amused defense. "Sorry. I'll go mind my business all the way over there." Pointing at the wooden, creaky staircase that led down to the beach.

"No need!" I managed to squeeze in just before he turned around. Eyes flicking back to Caden, I said "We're done here, anyway" before I joined Finnick by the water.

CHAPTER 19

CADEN

I watched them leave together. Took a sip of my water like it was a shot and leaned back against the bar with a sigh. One look was enough to figure the rest of the group hadn't noticed our little back-and-forth just now—were probably convinced the reason I'd rushed to the bar like it had been on fire was because I'd just been *really* thirsty.

"So." I could place the voice from behind me as the bartender's. When I turned, the amused look on her face surprised me, though.

Her black hair trimmed just above the shoulders, arms covered in a bunch of small tattoos. She wore dark eye makeup, her long lashes probably fake. She was pretty, all in all. Maybe a few years older than me. Twenty-seven, at most.

I could go home with her, I thought. Leave this entire mess—this hot-and-cold game with Valentina—behind and get lost in a woman who actually wanted me. But

I dismissed the thought almost as quickly as it had come—nothing about that seemed exciting, for some reason.

"So," I echoed, my glass raised at her in another thanks. Her eyes, just like mine had, were trailing after Valentina and Finnick. When they jumped back to me, it seemed like she was holding back a laugh.

"You already hooked up? Or about to?"

I groaned, and she finally let her laugh slip. Without another word, like my reaction had been answer enough, she tended to another customer down the line.

We stayed at Blitz for another hour. An hour of pretending not to be far more interested in Valentina and Finnick—sitting in the sand, by the water, talking and laughing and flirting, probably—than whatever conversation was going on around me. We'd had a perfect view of them from our table up here, so it was hardly my fault if I made use of it.

At least I wasn't thinking about that declined job offer anymore. And, I thought, at least Valentina had left with us and not him. I wasn't sure what I would've done otherwise—I wasn't sure I wanted to know.

But being alone in a room with her also meant we were back to arguing with each other. Bickering like little kids.

"There's no way." She shook her head, firm in her stance. She'd changed out of her denim skirt and tank top into something a little warmer—*sweatpants* and a tank top. Instead of flip-flops, she was wearing sneakers. Because she was about to go for a walk. It was almost midnight, and it was a full moon.

Why did half of her bucket list have to be outside, in the middle of the night?

"Valentina," I said with a snicker, like she should know better. *She should.*

Instead of listening, she opened the door out of our room. I followed her into the hallway, and she managed to ignore me all the way down the stairs, through the hallway, until we were outside. Which was where I reminded her, "We had a deal."

We'd hook up, then I'd help her with that list. At least for me, it had been a win-win, when I'd been in no position to make demands in the first place.

"Caden!" she snapped—continued walking, though. Probably hoping to get away from me. "I'm pretty sure our deal is off the table. Don't you think?"

Her tone wasn't ideal, but at least she was saying more than, *I'd rather get kidnapped than have you there.*

To which I'd said, *I don't, though.*

"Aw," I cooed, caught up with her, and adopted her pace. She was walking almost as fast as she'd been running the other day. "Why do you say that? A deal's a deal, I thought."

"Because you threatened me!" she cried, outraged. In the middle of the road, she screeched to a halt. Turned to look at me. "Because you didn't say a word to me all day." Something in her expression softened, almost like she felt bad for saying, "Because you saw me with another guy."

I huffed, honestly a little offended. "If you think I feel threatened every time my girl talks to another man, I'm hurt. Go have your fun with Finnick—I'm not worried."

Only that the feeling in my gut when I'd seen them together was new. I hadn't felt threatened, that much was still true. But I couldn't deny I hadn't been worried either. At least Valentina liked the guy. She was still acting like she despised me, and I'd never had to deal with that before.

"*Your* girl?" The amusement in her tone drew me out of my thoughts, only realizing my mistake right then, when she'd already picked up on it. "What makes you think I'm yours, Callahan?"

Nothing. Nothing at all but wishful thinking.

Which I couldn't say, obviously.

I shrugged. "The way you came around my fingers last night. That you probably wouldn't be opposed to doing it again."

Her head shot in my direction, cheeks flushed. She glared at me regardless. "You *threatened* me," she repeated, much quieter—not sounding all that angry anymore.

Maybe that was the only anchor point for her, even if I hadn't meant it. Even if it had happened out of sheer panic and I hadn't planned on threatening her. The plan had just been to make one thing very clear: She couldn't tell a soul about Anova. And I'd accidentally overplayed my role.

But she couldn't know that, and if she just told herself how awful I was, over and over again, maybe she wouldn't want to repeat last night. By the look on her face, how she swallowed hard and her eyes traced my lips, she wasn't succeeding.

"And she doesn't even try to deny it." I hummed to myself, continued walking. Relief settled in my chest when she followed. "How *was* your date, by the way?"

She groaned but answered. A win was a win. "Good."

"Think you'll tick any more things off your list soon?" I made sure that mask of indifference on my face stayed put. *Please say no, please say no, please say no*, a voice in my head chanted in stark contrast to it.

"The plan is to tick all of them off by the end of summer," she reminded, voice drenched in lazy irony. She was relaxing beside me, and perhaps, with patience, I could still get her to enjoy this. The last thing I'd want was to ruin her summer plans, and that list was a big part of them. She *should* be enjoying this—just not by herself, in the middle of nowhere.

"With Finnick?"

Valentina snickered. Almost laughed, I think. "With anyone who doesn't threaten to tell on me like we're five years old."

And it kind of just burst out of me. Out of guilt, maybe. Or simply because I didn't want her to have that reason to stay away from me anymore.

"My sister is the reason I still play soccer." And this much Valentina already knew—at least somewhat. "By the fire, I said I wouldn't know if I'd still be playing if it wasn't for her. That was a lie." In my periphery, I could see her gaze lifting, studying my profile in the bright, cool moonlight. I looked ahead. "I *know* I wouldn't be. I don't really want to anymore. But it just feels wrong—giving it up. You know?"

She hummed in understanding, and I was kind of glad it was her only response. If I'd told Dylan or Blake or—God forbid—Mike, I'd have heard a thousand opinions by now and a hundred useless solutions to my nonexistent problem. Valentina just listened, like she wanted to hear what I had to say, instead of just responding.

"I felt bad enough just *applying* to Anova. Then they called me back for a second round of interviews, and I felt like I'd spat on my sister's grave. By the fourth round, I felt so . . . guilty, I didn't even know where to put it all. So when Mike asked if I wanted to take over his position—captaining the HBU soccer team—of course I said yes. What else could I have done? Decline and officially flush Alison's dream down the toilet? I couldn't."

I took a deep breath, head shaking. "I just couldn't. I hadn't heard from Anova since accepting that captain thing, and everything seemed to go back to normal. I got into the grad program, Mike was on my ass over soccer. Now I'm here, supposed to be getting back on my A game. Everything was *good*. Like she would've wanted. And then—"

"You got the job offer," she figured, her first words since my outburst. I nodded.

"If Mike found out I'm applying for jobs . . . *Jesus*, he'd probably kick me out—never mind keeping me on as captain. He'd take it away from her, and I can't have that. That guy freaks out when you miss practice to take an exam. I don't think he'd be happy, knowing soccer isn't my first and only plan. If he knew I was considering other options, that would be it."

"Hence the threatening."

"Hence the threatening," I agreed and finally managed to look at her. The glance we shared made both of us stop, without a single word exchanged. Valentina considered me—my tense posture, bottom lip between my teeth, brows drawn together tightly—and she fell against my chest.

She wrapped her arms around my torso, head buried in my shirt, squeezing tightly. I couldn't remember the last time I'd hugged someone—Mom, maybe?—but my arms found themselves around her shoulders regardless.

Her embrace was warm, welcoming. Despite the inches she was missing on my height, it felt safe. The vanilla scent of her shampoo crept up my nose, her breaths even against my chest, and I sighed. Exhaled and relaxed in sync with it.

"What are you gonna do?" she asked, voice muffled. "About Anova?" To look at me, she brought some distance between us, but her touch lingered, like she didn't really want to let go.

"Oh." I waved her off, then brought my hand from her shoulder to her hip. "Nothing. I declined."

Her eyes widened. Then her brows furrowed, disbelief written all over her face. "What?"

"I replied to Pete's email after he sent the offer over. 'Thank you. But no thank you.'"

"You didn't even call them back!" Valentina cried. "You said no to a six-figure salary in an email!" Her confusion turned into full-on denial. "You can't have."

The smile on my lips wasn't voluntary, but I couldn't help it. Honestly, after my confession—the first time I'd talked to anyone about this—I'd expected not to smile for at least twenty-four hours. But here I was, suppressing a damn giggle.

"Two sentences, that's it. I can show you—" I was already grabbing my phone out of the pocket of my shorts, but Valentina pushed my hand back in.

As if to recap, she said "Two lines," then nodded. "Honestly, Caden, I kind of envy you. You don't give a shit about what anyone else thinks, do you?"

Take Alison out of the equation, and she might be right. It didn't sound like an insult, and I wouldn't have taken it as such either way.

"Not more than about myself, no."

Valentina huffed, started walking back the way we came. I followed. "I don't remember the last time I did anything for myself," she blurted.

I tried to think of a time in the past two weeks in which she had. Said no to plans, suggested something else for dinner, or simply disagreed with any of her friends. Nothing came to mind. Even when they'd asked her if she was fine sharing a room with me, she'd lied and said yes.

"Hence the list," I figured, same as she had earlier.

"Hence the list."

We let the silence between us linger for a while. Steps matching against the road, listening to the constant, high-pitched hum of the cicadas, the sound like a constant stream of electricity. From above, the full moon illuminated our surroundings surprisingly well.

Michael Jackson would be proud of us, fully moonwalking so well.

"You have been quite disagreeable with me, though," I mentioned after a while, amusement in my tone.

"Because I don't want you to like me." She shrugged. "Because my life would be a whole lot easier if you didn't, actually."

"Would it?" I held her by the arm, right before we'd round the last turn of the road and see the summerhouse again. It was the same spot we'd stopped at on the way back from our run. The same spot where she'd kissed me, then told me it would change nothing.

Despite our constant bickering, I felt like something had.

"Yes," she said unapologetically. "Because you'd just leave me alone, and I wouldn't have to hold on to every bit of self-restraint to keep away from you."

We were close again, and something dropped to the pit of my stomach at her words—at her proximity and the look in her eyes that told me she was fighting now, too.

My mouth dipped toward her ear. "I'm sorry to disappoint," I whispered, voice strained. "But I don't think there's anything you can do that would make me leave you alone. I can't. It's impossible, Val."

Her breath hitched. "Why?"

I shook my head, and my lips grazed her skin. Honest mistake, but neither of us seemed to mind. I certainly didn't. "I don't know." I shrugged. "What I do know, though," I began and brought my face in front of hers again. "You can't live the one life you have always pleasing the people around you. Say no sometimes, Valentina. Then say yes other times. But only because you want to. Not your friends, not your—"

"Okay," she hurried. "Yes."

And kissed me.

CHAPTER 20

VALENTINA

Caden Callahan was a walking reminder of my betrayal, living proof of how bad of a friend I was. Looking at him made my heart plummet to the pit of my stomach, that's how guilty I felt. For breaking the NFR, yes. But even more so for lying to my friends, betraying Iris when she'd just been betrayed by some loser who didn't deserve her anyway (again).

Maybe that's what I was, as well. A loser who didn't deserve her.

Maybe that was why, the second I was alone with Caden, despite my guilty conscience, his lips would be on mine again. Sometimes for a peck, sometimes for five minutes that left us sexually frustrated and panting against each other. Depending on how much time we'd had.

You can't live the one life you have always pleasing the people around you. Say no sometimes, Valentina. Then say yes other times.

I'd thought about his words a lot in the past week. Although they'd been a little hypocritical, twenty minutes after he'd told me every major life decision he'd made recently had been for his sister, not himself. Anyone with a sibling could understand, though. It's why, despite the fact that I'd never get my family to love and appreciate me the way I wanted them to, I'd just dialed my own sister's number regardless.

One thing she loved more than ignoring me was attention. So while she didn't usually pick up my calls (asking about school, wondering what she'd had for breakfast or lunch or dinner, wishing her luck on an exam she'd mentioned months prior), on her birthday, she did. Crossing the kitchen to go outside—and trying my best to ignore Caden cutting up fruit on the island—the line beeped for a total of three times before it crackled and I heard her voice. "Thank you," she said by way of greeting.

"No words have come out of my mouth yet," I reminded her quickly, before adding, sincerely, "Happy birthday, Lisa."

"Thank you," she repeated, and I could hear some giggling in the background, music coming from another room.

"Where are you celebrating?" Because it sure as shit wouldn't be at home. "Has Mom said anything?"

Lisa snorted, like I should've known better than to ask in the first place. "She said, 'You look nice today.'" And her voice rose an octave when she imitated Mom. "Which, I guess, is an improvement over last year, when she asked if I could drive her to work, then wanted to ground me when I said I was busy."

I cringed at the memory. "Sorry." For reminding her, maybe. Or the fact that I'd left her for college in the first place. For never managing to fix Mom's . . . problem and letting my little sister deal with it on her own. Honestly, there were a lot of things worth apologizing for in our past.

She huffed, and I knew the sound was paired with an eye roll. I'd gotten so many of them in my lifetime, I knew all the tells. "I'm at Stacy's. Having some people over," she added, circling back to my earlier question and further away from the uncomfortable topic of Mom.

It's how our conversations always felt: flat. Awkward. Trying to navigate through topics that wouldn't make us remember how fucked up our entire upbringing had been. Turned out, there weren't many left.

"That's nice." I nodded, although she couldn't see. "Tell her I said hi." I knew she wouldn't, even when she hummed in agreement. Pressing my phone between shoulder and ear, I slid the door to the yard open. "Have you heard from any colleges yet?"

Closing it behind me, I couldn't help but sneak a single glance at the guy in the kitchen, dumping his fruit into the blender. I closed the door quickly.

This time, she outright groaned into the phone. "Nope, Valentina. I'm not having this conversation with you. It's my birthday! Just for one day, can't you just drop the act of—" She cut herself off with another loud sigh. She must've gone back into the room because the music was louder and I could hear some chatter. "Whatever. I have to go. Thanks for calling."

Lisa hung up before I could've said so much as *Enjoy your day.* I mirrored her groan when I fell onto the lounge chair outside, trying to keep my spiraling thoughts from falling down the rabbit hole of *She hates you.*

That's what happened when you tried to desperately get someone to love you: the exact opposite. Another reminder of why I'd vowed to stop trying. And another reminder of why things with Caden had been so easy. I wasn't fighting for his constant approval, and I couldn't remember the last time that had been the case.

Outside, Alfie and Anni were alternating between playing mermaids and ungracefully jumping into the water—whoever managed to get a louder complaint from Iris, tanning on an inflatable air mattress in the pool, won.

Despite the commotion around her, Iris lifted her head to send me a look. "You alright?" She adjusted her cap to actually see me, and her eyes narrowed.

My head fell back onto the chair. "Lisa," I explained curtly. "Mom forgot about her birthday."

"She didn't ask her to chauffeur her around again, did she?!" The outrage in her voice tipped the corners of my lips up despite the situation. "Wait, let me get some water, then we'll dissect—"

Iris wobbled on her inflatable, tried to paddle to the edge of the pool before I could even tell her, "I'll get it for you. Don't worry!"

At the moment, I'd jump at any opportunity to be good to her—to make up for the fact that I was playing the role of worst best friend there ever was a little too well. I'd gladly listen every time she complained about Jason, then throw in some insults myself. I'd probably kill the guy if I had to. If only to make her happy.

She'd been handling the whole thing better than last time—probably because Oakport meant distraction, and how much could you really drown in despair and sorrows when you had your friends around every waking hour? I was still worried, though. One wrong thing—say, finding out your best friend had been lying to you for weeks or that said best friend hooked up with a guy she wasn't supposed to hook up with—and she might slip into that state of despair, regardless.

I couldn't risk it.

Getting her a bottle of water seemed like the least I could do to compensate. I was halfway to the door before she could've complained.

So it was my guilty conscience that propelled me into the kitchen. Not Caden, who was alone in there. Not the fact that it'd been a few hours since I'd last felt his lips on mine or that after that disaster of a phone call, what I needed most was distraction.

Definitely not.

He stood by the blender, one hand on top of it, the other scrolling through his phone. Banana peels, a half-empty strawberry package, and a tub of protein powder were scattered on the island in front of him. He'd been so immersed in his phone, he couldn't have heard me come in over the noise, and still, like he was attuned to my presence, he looked up. Looked around. Then looked back at me, the corners of his lips twisting upward.

My eyes rolled, but only to distract from that feeling plummeting to the pit of my stomach. That's all it took—him, looking at me like that. I stalked in his direction. The fridge was behind him, after all.

"Need something?" he asked, hand falling from the blender as he turned with me. By the time I'd crossed the living room, he was leaning against the island behind him.

"Water," I said. I made no move to get any, though. "For Iris."

Just saying her name in his presence felt wrong at this point, but . . . *You can't live the one life you have always pleasing the people around you.* So I said yes to Caden.

In my mind, I'd been saying yes to him for a while. For myself.

He nodded, then let his gaze slide down my body. Excruciatingly slowly. Like it was the first time I was wearing that red-and-white-checkered bikini when it was not. And like it was the first time he'd seen me in it—when he'd seen me with much less on.

He reached for my hip, pulled me closer, and it didn't even seem like a conscious decision. "I don't know if I'll ever get used to this," he muttered. I was surprised I understood anything he said at all, over the sound of fruit still mixing beside us.

My head tilted. "What?"

Caden's blue eyes jumped back to mine, pupils wide. "You. In this." His hand traced up my back, along my shoulders, then dipped all the way down to my waist again. "It's my favorite." He smiled.

"Why am I not surprised your favorite outfit of mine is the one that covers the least?" I laughed and tried to ignore the goose bumps his touch left behind. Partly due to the AC blasting in here, I'm sure. The same went for how hard my nipples were. It was cold, that's all.

Caden shook his head, inched his face a little closer to mine. "Noooo," he whined. "My favorite *bikini*," he corrected. "My favorite outfit is that dress of yours. The black one, with the white, low neckline." He huffed, placed a single kiss against my collarbones. "Makes your boobs look great." He grinned.

I snickered and laughed and snorted—all in one, somehow—and then I kissed him.

It's where this exchange would've led, anyway. I was just accelerating the process, because I didn't know how much time we'd have by ourselves, and it would be a shame to waste it.

He hummed against my mouth, content and pleased. A little surprised—but not really. Without even looking, he turned the blender off, and it was silent. From outside, you could hear water splashing and amused screeches.

But it was still quiet enough to notice his breaths turning heavy and the way he groaned when his palm spread over my bare ass. He fiddled with the strings of my bikini, frustrated by the fact that he couldn't untie and take it off.

"I want you," he groaned into my mouth, and the sound traveled straight between my legs. "All the way, Val. Taste you, feel you, hear you."

"Impossible." And it frustrated me just as much. I'd hoped, now that we'd been touching whenever we could, I'd be more satisfied. Wouldn't want him as badly as I did back when I couldn't touch him at all. But it had made it worse. Tasting his lips on mine, his teeth playfully digging into my lower lip, his hands all over me, and all those filthy sounds and words whispered against my skin. It drove me crazy. "With everyone around. We can't—"

"I know." His lips traveled down my neck, and I threw my head back in response. My lips parted, and every sound that wanted to make it past them, I held back. "This will have to do, I know. But a man can dream."

So could a woman.

And I was. Of a reality in which Caden and I were the only ones living here. Where I could wear nothing but oversized shirts, and he could walk around with that God-forsaken towel hanging low on his waist. Where a single, fleeting touch would leave us naked, sprawled across various surfaces—couch, kitchen island, sun chairs. A reality in which we could have each other anywhere, all the time, and wouldn't have to worry about the sounds we might make when we came in sync because no one was around to hear them.

The thought alone was enough to consider having him right here, right now. I *could*. If I'd had the guts, I'd get on my knees, take him out of those swim shorts, and wrap my lips around him right here, behind the kitchen island.

Thankfully, my consideration was cut short. Somewhere behind us, I heard the door to the yard slide open. We had about two seconds before—

"Valentina?"

We shot apart. Caden started frantically cleaning the kitchen, and I turned on my heels to get to the fridge. By the time Iris could see us, I was neck deep in it—not to find the cooled water but to regulate my body back to a normal temperature. To get that blush off my cheeks.

"Water!" I announced, then closed the fridge forcefully with a bottle in hand. I threw it at Iris and was lucky she caught it before it broke her nose. "Sorry," I winced.

Her brows furrowed, eyes scanning the chilled bottle in her hand before returning to me. Once, they flicked to Caden, pouring his smoothie into a glass.

Could we be any more obvious?

Before she could make an observation, Anni and Alfie joined us inside, dripping across the floor. "Ready?" The blonde sent a questioning glance across the three of us, who were tiptoeing around (what I thought was) the obvious.

Caden jumped at the opportunity. "For what?" he asked around a mouthful of smoothie. I was impressed it wasn't dripping down his chin.

And it seemed—lucky me—Iris dismissed her suspicion. It only made me feel worse, though. "We wanted to head into Isleton," she said and took a sip of water. "Get ice cream, stroll along the boardwalk for a bit." Her eyes found mine, and her brows rose questioningly. "Talk about that phone call," she added, only to me.

Alfie, oblivious, announced, "Go shopping, maybe."

I thought of Caden's hypocritical words. *Say no sometimes, Valentina. Then say yes other times.*

Maybe this was a harmless enough thing to say no to—just to try it out? See what it felt like? If they didn't like it, I could still just let myself be convinced.

I glanced around the room. "Why don't you go ahead? I think I'm gonna pass this time."

Anni's head flew in my direction. Iris, already looking at me, furrowed her brows. Alfie seemed outright shellshocked, blinking at me with wide, blue eyes. Then all three of them shot toward me at once.

"Are you okay?" Anni asked.

"Do you feel sick?" Alfie wondered at the same time.

The back of Iris's hand pressed against my forehead while she concluded, "It's the heat, isn't it? You've got heatstroke? You need to sit, Valentina."

As if the task needed three people, they walked me over to the couch, pushed me into the pillows, and looked at me with wide, concerned eyes. Caden walked around the couch, amusement across his features. When Iris gestured for me to lie back, I couldn't help a laugh.

"Guys," I muttered but did as I was told regardless. Iris's hand was on my forehead again. "I'm fine. Really," I added when they just looked at me like I'd lied under oath.

"So what? You just . . . don't want to go?" Anni asked, still doubtful.

My eyes flicked to Caden behind the group, and he inclined his head in an encouraging nod. On his lips, he wore a smile I hadn't seen on him before. Proud, maybe? Excited, most definitely.

I was well on my way to mirror the sentiment, but that was obliterated when Iris said, "Oh."

My heart plummeted to the pit of my stomach, because my brain couldn't differentiate between sensing disappointment and being held at gunpoint.

I couldn't quite figure out what the look on her face meant. They were mad, probably. Thinking I wasn't appreciating my time with them, wondering if they'd done anything wrong—

"Alright then!" Iris clapped her hands together. "Fair enough. Anyone going with us, we're leaving in fifteen minutes. Chop-chop!" To me, she whisper-shouted, "But don't think I forgot about Lisa."

Like the nonbiological siblings they were, Alfie and Anni raced each other to their rooms. Iris blew me a kiss, then ran after them. And not one of them seemed upset about my decision.

And maybe dreams did come true, because half an hour later, Caden and I had the house to ourselves.

CHAPTER 21

CADEN

"Remind me again what we'd been doing when we were so brutally interrupted?"

Valentina looked up from the lounge chair where she'd gotten comfortable, making use of the last rays of the day. The sun was about to disappear behind the house. She had another twenty minutes, tops.

Her lips tipped upward, and the book in her hands landed on the small table next to her without much consideration. "Just so we're clear: When summer's over and I barely managed to read *one* book, I'm going to blame you," she said, sitting up, leaning back onto her elbows.

Two braids parted her cherry-red hair in the middle, the sun had left her skin flushed, sweat collecting in her hairline and brows. Her bikini, a little crooked, showed off her tan lines.

I held my hand out to her. "I can live with that. Cool down?" I asked and nodded toward the pool beside us. It must've still been eighty-six degrees, at least. In the sun, it felt more like ninety or more. So I wasn't surprised when it didn't take her long to say, "Lead the way."

I took my phone out of my pocket and jumped in headfirst, only so I could watch her take the ladder. I had no problem admitting to my selfishness—and seeing Valentina climb into the pool, hips swaying with each step, was high up on my personal hierarchy of needs. She didn't hesitate, but those five seconds it took her to get in were still beautiful. With a relieved sigh, she pushed off the wall, then let herself float toward me on her back. Her brown eyes opened, sunlight playing in their color, and I was blinking down at her with a smile that had become more common around her.

"Hi," she said, and her nose crinkled with a silent laugh.

My heart swelled, then squeezed tightly in my chest. *What the fuck was she doing to me?* Unheard of, for my heart to react before my dick did. Somewhere, very far back in a corner of my mind, alarm sirens went off. Signaling that if I wasn't careful with her, I might actually start to like her. Care for her. Give her the power to destroy me, if she so chose to.

Somehow, Valentina Rhodes didn't seem like the type of girl that should have that kind of power over me. Her hot-and-cold attitude hardly said, *Your heart is safe with me.* Quite the opposite, actually.

Unfortunately, something much louder and much more present in my head loved to see her smile. Loved *making* her smile. Loved touching and kissing her. And made sure those sirens were not taken seriously at all. They were forgotten as soon as she wrapped her legs around my waist.

My dick did react this time. To her face, so close to mine. My hands, which had instinctively found themselves on her ass. And to the fact that this time, no one could stop me from untying her bikini.

"Earlier," I started confessing, "all I'd wanted was to be alone with you. So that I could do this." My fingers played with the ribbon tying the bottom half of her bikini together. A single tug, and it fell open. One side first, then the other. When I slid them away from under her, my finger swiped along her core.

Her eyes widened, and she looked genuinely surprised when she said, "Me too." Arms locked behind my neck, hips pressing against my hard cock. She must've noticed because she ground against me in anticipation, and her eyes fluttered shut, just for a moment. When they connected with mine again, hazy and dark, my restraint—barely there to begin with—snapped.

I'd do anything to make her come apart for me. Right here, right now. I walked us to the edge of the pool, bikini forgotten on the other side. When her back hit the wall, she moaned. Quietly, but enough to make me lose my mind, regardless. One hand traced up from her ass, over her hips, all the way between her legs. Lingering, caressing her thigh as I watched and felt her getting impatient in my arms.

"*Caden*," she complained, and the sound was dangerously close to another moan. Dangerously close to driving me completely and utterly out of my mind. Especially after we'd had to be so quiet here.

"I'm so proud of you," I whispered against her neck, leaving one kiss, then another, and trailing all the way up until my face hovered in front of hers. "Look at you, looking out for yourself. Saying no to your friends earlier, now grinding against me. I'm so proud of you," I repeated, more of a groan than anything else.

She writhed in my arms, searching for more friction, trying to find any part of me underwater to give her what she wanted. When I pressed a kiss to her forehead, my thumb finally finding her clit and two fingers driving into her, she fell apart against me.

Valentina's head crashed to my shoulders, burying itself in the crook of my neck. She tried to kiss me, sucked and nibbled my skin whenever her lips didn't part in moans that became progressively louder. Never *loud*, but louder than I'd heard them in a while. Loud enough to draw encouraging noises out of my mouth, too.

I was honest to God going to explode in my shorts just getting her off. Just feeling her clench around my fingers, grinding her hips against mine. Hearing her pant before whispering my name into my skin, like a forbidden prayer.

Over and over and over again.

On the chair behind us, my phone rang. The shrill sound echoed through the backyard, but it seemed Valentina didn't have half a mind to notice, and I didn't care at all. About anything but the girl in my arms, about to come for me.

Her hips started moving against my fingers, pushing me deeper, increasing my thumb's friction against her. Her head fell back, and my lips found themselves on her neck again. Trailed down to her chest and pushed the triangle of fabric covering her breasts to one side. "That's it," I groaned into her skin, seriously struggling to keep myself in check when my mouth puckered around her nipple. "Be a good girl and take what you need from me."

And Valentina rode herself to orgasm on my fingers.

"Fuck," she panted, head back on my shoulder, chest rising and falling rapidly against me. "Caden—*fuck*."

"I'm going to need a minute," I confessed. I swallowed thickly, my nose buried in her hair, that still smelled like vanilla and salt and *her*.

I sighed, but it was more of an exhausted, frustrated groan. My fingers slipped out of her, and she breathed a satisfied sound against my shoulder.

When she accidentally moved her hips against me, I feared I might actually just come. For the sake of every other person still wanting to use this pool, I held back. Ground my teeth together and prayed for my cock to stop twitching against her core, pressed against me again, now that my hand was gone.

Valentina, of course, grinned triumphantly.

"Don't tell me you're close," she gasped, scandalized. "Caden Callahan, the same guy who kept me busy for *hours*. No way—" Her taunts turned into a surprised squeal when I lifted her out of the water, onto the edge of the pool. I needed to get out of here before I threw my reason and common sense to hell.

My hands slid from her waist down her thighs, drops of water shimmering on her skin in the light of the setting sun. "It's different now," I tried to explain.

Her head tilted. I could get used to seeing her like this, looking down on me with the faintest blush on her cheeks. Her chest was still heaving. She still wasn't wearing anything and had just put her bikini top back in place.

"Is it?" she asked, watched as I climbed the ladder out of the pool right beside us. Without thinking about it, she got up once I was out. "Why?"

Good fucking question.

I considered it as I walked her backward onto the lounge chair. Watched her cautiously sit, interlace our hands, and pull me down to her, until I hovered over her again.

She'd always been pretty—her lips had been just as kissable, her hair just as pullable, her eyes just as big and beautiful. The dips and curves of her body had always intrigued me, but something *was* different.

Something that made me want to study her, know her fully inside and out—what made her laugh, what made her cry, what made her a begging mess underneath me. I didn't just want to enjoy her; I wanted to figure her out.

And that was fucking terrifying, wasn't it?

"Hm?" Valentina pushed. Not just her question but her hips against mine, arching her back, ready for round two, it seemed. Her lids were heavy, the way she blinked up at me slowly. "What makes this different, Caden?"

Delicious, the way she said my name.

"Nothing," I said, then reconsidered. "Everything." I shook my head. "I don't know." And fortunately, my phone started ringing again, keeping any follow-up questions at bay. It was the third time since we'd gotten into the pool.

My breath shuddered in my throat when I looked from the device back to her. "I'm just going to take this, get myself under control, and we can finish what we started. To make it worth your while." Right now, I didn't think I'd last three minutes inside her.

Valentina grinned knowingly and nodded. "I guess anticipation is our thing, huh?"

I guess it was.

Leaving her behind—naked and ready—was almost painful. But I grabbed my phone from the next chair and hurried inside, hoping some distance might clear my mind. Right now, she was playing on a loop:

Valentina. Valentina. Valentina. Valentina.

The caller ID on my phone surprised me. "Dylan?" I said into the device, sliding the door to the yard behind me shut.

"The one and only," my former roommate replied dryly and cut right to the chase. "Why the fuck did my uncle just tell me you declined the Anova offer?"

The distracted smile on my lips fell. Valentina was no longer on my mind, and I didn't welcome her replacement.

Dylan had been the one to get me that interview at Anova Inc. a few months ago. He'd actually been *excited* to get me the interview. *"You're gonna rot away at HBU if you keep this up,"* he'd said. *"Who needs a master's degree these days, anyway? All you're doing is overqualifying yourself."*

He was probably right. I just didn't really care if he was.

"Listen—" I tried to justify myself, not because I had to, but because he'd done me a solid, and I owed him that much.

He cut me off: "No, man. *You* listen. My uncle and I are not . . . great. I told you, if you want the interview, you need to be sure—"

"And when you said that, I told you to forget about it—"

"That's not the point," he snapped, voice low. "The point is you took the interview. Then the next one, and the one after that. You aced their fucking assessment center bullshit, and I thought, *Wow. Caden is really doing this—getting out of Hall Beck University. He's not going to rot away doing a useless grad program.*" Easy thing for him to say, with millions at his disposal and billions at his girlfriend's. He liked to think himself a common man, but he really wasn't. "And now you're—what? Turning down a six-figure salary to captain a soccer team that's already won the championship? Two years of work experience are worth so much more than a master's. This is dumb, man. Really, really dumb."

"Are you done?" I asked roughly, trying to ignore the voice in my head that was calling him reasonable.

"Yes."

"And you know this isn't going to change anything, right?" *It couldn't.* No matter how much I might want it to.

He sighed on the other end of the line, and it lowered my guard—at least a little bit. "I assumed as much." There was a strange noise in the background, a screech, then a very distant, very excited, "Oh my God! Dolphins!"

My brows furrowed. "Where the fuck are you?"

I could hear the smile on his face when he said, "On a boat. Somewhere in Portugal." It was quiet for a moment, nothing but blurred voices and inaudible pieces of conversation coming out of my speaker, until the line snapped, and he was back. "Athalia says hi. Listen, I just wanted to check in, give you a piece of my mind. That's what friends are for, right?"

I snickered, half amused, half annoyed—mostly by the fact that I wasn't as pissed off as I should have been about his ambush. "Consider me in possession of a piece of your mind."

"Great. I've gotta go. Dolphins, apparently. Can you believe it? Yes, I'm coming, princess!" he said and hung up before I could even reply.

My head still shook in disbelief when I made it back outside, ready to kick that conversation out of my thoughts to make space for Valentina and her body, her moans, her soft skin, and her gentle pleas.

On the chair, she'd curled up under a towel with the book she'd discarded earlier. But instead of finding her reading, her eyes were closed and her breaths even.

I didn't mean to smile, really. This meant I wouldn't have her the way I'd desperately wanted her, after all. But I still couldn't find a shred of disappointment in me. All I could think of was how cute she looked when she slept. How peaceful and content. *Just sex* my ass.

Gently, carefully, I carried her upstairs. Scared to wake her, I tucked her into my own bed, then just stood there, like a creep, watching her sleep. My eyes were drawn away from her only when the phone in my pocket vibrated with an email notification.

Dear Mr. Callahan,

As we understand, you have declined our latest offer of employment at Anova Inc. in Boston, MA. Find our follow-up offer attached to this email. Please take your time and hopefully reconsider. We would love to have you on board.

Best Wishes,
Pete Klein

CHAPTER 22

VALENTINA

Everything we did on Oakport was somewhat of a tradition. From the bottomless margaritas and Chester's karaoke performance down to the boardwalk strolls and grocery trips. Iris would always get into the shopping cart, Alfie would always wheel her around, and Anni and I would always walk twenty feet behind, so as to not be associated with either of them.

Another meaningless—but ultimately very near and dear to my heart—tradition was pool at Blitz. Alfie's dad had basically forced him to learn how to play when he was barely heavier than the cue stick itself. Iris's parents had met playing, so they insisted Iris wouldn't have been adopted by them if it weren't for pool, which meant she had this sentimental attachment to it. And according to Anni, it was just a thing over in Germany—she also, to the others' great horror, still insisted it was called billiards, not pool. Which it was not.

All of this meant that my friends were pro pool players, and I'd never touched a cue in my life. When they had suggested we play a round our first time here, I said I'd sit it out. Who wanted to play something they were really good at with someone who had no idea what they were doing?

They'd asked the guys sitting a table over—because without me, there weren't an even number of players, and they couldn't team up—and Finnick Maxwell had happily obliged. That night had ended with us making out against his car, and we'd been inseparable vacation flings since.

By now, I *have* held a cue, but I've still never played a round. Which was the reason for the eighth item on my summer bucket list:

play pool

I gnawed on my bottom lip as I inspected the game, red lipstick probably all over my teeth. The fifteen balls formed a triangle in the center of the table, and it shouldn't be so goddamn hard to figure out how to make the white one hit the rest of them. But I could barely balance the cue. Didn't know how to hold it or which fingers the tip should rest on. Or between? Under?

I was playing with Anni—ultimately, she was still worse than Alfie and Iris. From our booth beside the tables, the latter shouted, "Someone give poor, helpless Valentina a hand, please!" Amusement lingered in her tone, and I lovingly shoved my middle finger in her direction. Her cackle rang through the lively bar.

This was a bad idea.

"I can't help you. It's against my best interest," Anni muttered, an amused smile on her lips at my sixth attempt of leaning forward, finally doing it—and aborting the mission.

My gaze helplessly flicked to Mike, leaning against the table. Emotional support for Anni, I assumed—only that I was pretty sure she'd be fine without any kind of support. I think she was starting to realize that, too.

Mike's hands shot up in playful surrender. "Sorry. Wrong team."

My eyes rolled, but my snicker got stuck in my throat when he added, shouting toward our booth, "Caden! Would you get your ass over here?"

Since he'd carried me up to our room and tucked me into *his* bed, contact between us had been limited. There were still fleeting touches, stolen kisses, and, yes, heavy make-out sessions before bed that would leave the both of us so sexually frustrated, we'd swear to never do it again. Only to do it again exactly twenty-four hours later. But I didn't trust myself around him with others there as well, and he must've felt the same way. We'd sit at opposite ends of dinner tables, I'd wait to get a drink until he was out of the kitchen, and when he was in the pool, I definitely stayed out of it. Today, I'd sat in the corner of the booth to make sure our knees wouldn't touch beneath the table and to make sure he couldn't stretch his long legs to reach my side of it.

A safe distance between us was mandatory, and if he—

"What's up?" His voice sent a *zing* of awareness through me, and I stood up a little straighter, leaned onto the cue, and tried not to look completely helpless.

"Valentina is struggling," Mike stated plainly. Honestly, there was no point in denying it, so I just trained all my attention on that triangle of balls on the green table. To focus on anything but Caden's amused glance, which I could still see out of the corner of my eye.

"Is she?"

The color I'd worked so hard on banishing from my face returned. Embarrassing. This was simply, and easily, the most embarrassing thing I'd ever experienced. That's what it felt like, at least.

Who thought putting play pool *on that stupid list had been a good idea?*

"You know what?" I pressed through pursed lips. "I'm giving up."

"We haven't even started!" Anni cried a laugh from the other end of the table. "C'mon, just hit it. Caden's gonna show you. Easy."

"He really doesn't have—"

"It's fine, Caden will do it," he said in third person, moving to stand by my side. The smirk on his lips had become audible in his tone, so I knew it was there even before I looked at him. Still, the low-light, backward-cap combination was deadly. Something plummeted to the pit of my stomach when our gazes met.

I glared at him regardless. Tried to let him know that us, this close, in front of my friends, was not a great idea—without using words.

Relax, he mouthed, then came up behind me. My eyes immediately flicked across the rest of our group; I couldn't help it. Alfie and Iris were busy stacking cards in the booth, and she had that hateful look in her eyes that let me know they were talking shit about Jason. So at least she was busy.

Anni was standing against a wooden beam, with Mike leaning over her, talking and giggling and probably heavily flirting. They'd most likely given up on anything spectacular happening with this game.

The only spectacular thing happening over here was Caden, bending me over the pool table, one hand on mine, the other supporting the weight of the cue. And that was probably much more spectacular for me than for any bystander watching.

"What are you doing?" I hissed lowly, turning my head just enough to see him. The smile on his lips was so wide, it was borderline goofy.

"Showing you how to play pool." He placed the cue between my thumb and pointer finger, then let his touch linger against my hand. His mouth was right by my ear, and I wondered if he had to resist the urge to kiss my neck, as strongly as I was resisting my urge to lean farther into him.

In hindsight, wearing a short denim skirt when you'd planned on playing pool—an activity in which you famously had to bend over tables—had been a bad idea. At least with him right behind me, no one could look up my skirt.

His arm aligned with mine, veins and muscles rippling through it. I'd never quite noticed how nice his hands were, but it was undeniable now, when I was looking right at them, on top of my own. I shifted underneath his weight, and I wasn't quite sure what it was supposed to achieve either. Bring some distance between us, maybe? Distract me from my ass aligning perfectly with his crotch, most definitely.

It did the exact opposite.

He exhaled forcefully, and his hand around the cue tightened. The cue stick wobbled in our shared grip (most likely because, despite my hands on it, Caden was doing all the heavy lifting). "*Don't*," he stressed.

"Don't wha—?" I tried to turn my head in his direction, and he pressed himself tighter against me.

"Move," he snapped, but the bite in his tone was missing entirely. "Don't move, Val. Please." He cleared his throat, and a low groan played in the sound. Still, no one was paying any attention to us. Which was fortunate because I didn't think I could play this situation cool.

Him, hard, pressing against my backside. In the middle of a crowded bar. Ten feet from my friends, who were convinced this was the first time we'd been this close.

"Caden." I hissed his name, but that didn't help the fact that this entire situation was a little too much, and he was a little too close, and I was very, very turned on. Inappropriate, to say the least. "They're gonna know."

It felt like he'd been hanging over me for an hour, honestly. How couldn't they be a little suspicious—at least *curious*? But still, one glance around showed that no one was paying us any mind. Anni and Mike were still kissing. Alfie and Iris were still talking shit.

Caden tried his best to align the cue in our hands again. He pulled it back, and the polished wood grazed my skin. "If you stop blushing, they won't suspect a thing, sweetheart." Then like it was nothing, he—*we?*—hit the cue ball just right, and the previously neatly aligned balls shot in all possible directions. Two solids went in.

At the loud *clang*, everyone's heads shot in our direction again. Caden stood up, then took a step back. Stick in hand, he lazily leaned on it, a content smile on his lips.

"Damn." Anni's eyes narrowed as she assessed the game. "Can Caden help *me*, too?"

"Hey!" Mike complained, and she blew him a consolation kiss in return.

Though, if Caden would help Anni the way he'd helped me—bulge pressing against my ass, whispering sweet nicknames into my ear, and trying his very best to keep himself from searching for more friction against me—I understood why Mike wouldn't be a fan of the idea.

My eyes slid back to Caden, fixing the cap on his head when our eyes connected. Tension still filled the air between us, even with the space that separated us now.

It's like I could still feel his skin on mine, and it was hard to keep my eyes from trailing all the way down his toned arms to his hands. Strong and firm and precise. Not just when he was playing pool but when his fingers would find the perfect spot between my legs or his thumb rolled across my clit just right.

"Bathroom!" I yelped before I could fall down that particular rabbit hole. "I'll be right back."

When Anni said, "Two balls went in. You have another turn." I shook my head, already on my way. "Caden can take it," I half shouted as I disappeared into the secluded hallway leading to the bathrooms.

It was exactly what I'd feared it would be like, the reason why I'd done my very best to stay away from Caden Callahan—first completely, then at least when anyone else was around. It's like self-control flew out the window the second he touched me or looked at me or said my name in *that* way. Even worse when he used one of the nicknames he'd made a common practice.

Val. Sweetheart. Baby.

All of them were doing things to me. So awful and dangerous, it shouldn't be possible that they felt so good at the same time.

I wanted to run my face under ice-cold water, but my makeup prevented that. Instead, I stood in the dimly lit bathroom, fanning my face in front of the mirror with one hand and running cold water over the other. Something—*anything*—to cool me down. To wash Caden off me. To regain control.

I took a deep breath. Reapplied my red lipstick, color matching my hair. Looked at myself in the mirror until I stared back at a less flustered version of myself. Cool, calm, and collected. Or at least something like it.

Another hour, maybe, until we'd be back behind our shared door, where no one could see us, devouring each other. *I've got this.*

One more deep breath, and I pushed the door into the hallway open—and ran straight into a chest. Caden's chest.

"Fuck!" I wasn't quite sure what was more prominent: my surprise or my frustration. I'd just gotten myself under control again, and there he was, ready to ruin all that progress. "*What* are you doing here?"

"Officially?" he said as he leaned against the wall behind him. The hallway was so narrow, though, that we'd barely be able to pass each other, so he was still too close. "I'm getting another round of drinks."

"And unofficially?"

He raised his brows, like it should be obvious. Maybe it was. To underline his point, his gaze flicked down my body, then slowly lifted back to my eyes, lingering at the hem of my skirt. Instinctively, I inched it lower.

That's what he was here for, then? Blowing off some steam, working out the frustration he'd channeled during the time his cock had been resting against my ass?

"You okay?" he asked instead.

And somehow, knowing he'd come here to check on me—not to kiss me or touch me or make use of one of the empty bathroom stalls behind us—made it worse. The bare minimum tugged at my heartstrings, made my insides clench and told me I was *so* fucked.

"I'm fine." My head shook. "Please don't start being nice to me as well."

"When have I not?" His tone was mocking, kind of in the same way his touch was, when he hooked his finger under my chin and tilted it upward, until our eyes connected. "Hm, Val?"

Val. Sweetheart. Baby.

I'm sure there'd been times in which he hadn't been nice to me. If every part of my brain wasn't consumed by him—his touch, his scent, his *presence*—I would've come up with plenty of examples. Now, like this, with the way he tugged a strand of hair behind my ear, my mind was blank. As far as I was concerned, Caden had always been as angelic as he seemed now.

Maybe he really had been.

"I don't know," I confessed, voice barely above a whisper. And then, because I couldn't take this—the tension, and *maybes*, and the obvious way he was looking at my lips—I kissed him. In some dingy hallway leading to the bathroom of a bar, my friends around the corner, I kissed Caden. Again and again and again.

When he tried to pull away, I followed. When I tried to pull away, he followed. Like we were stuck in some cat-and-mouse game neither of us wanted to win.

He let his head fall back against the wall, sighing at the way my lips trailed along his neck, biting and teasing until his breath turned heavy and his eyes dark. I shouldn't enjoy him this much. I shouldn't enjoy him at all.

"We—" I breathed, my face in front of his again, only inches apart.

"I know." He shook his head, like he was hoping it would snap him out of whatever trance we'd transported each other into. "We shouldn't, I know. It's just so hard—"

His eyes ran down my frame again. This time, I didn't adjust my skirt. "When you came out of our bathroom wearing this"—his fingers, still sprawled across my waist, played with the waistband of the denim skirt—"I wished we could've just stayed home. I wished I could've just—" He leaned toward me, lowered his voice, and his lips were tickling my ear when he whispered, voice rough, "I wished I could've just bent you over the windowsill."

To underline his point, his hand dipped to the back of my thigh, grazing my bare skin, inching the denim upward—just slightly, to prove he could. I shivered.

Quite honestly, he could do pretty much anything, and I'd be completely defenseless. Even now, touching me in a very open, very public hallway, I couldn't tell him to stop because I didn't want him to.

My last attempt at being reasonable was half-assed and weak. "Should we get back?" At this point, I was whispering. My voice was strained, and I squinted to read his face in the low light. Above us, a single bulb burned at half its capacity. Every now and then, it flickered.

Still, I could see Caden's lips curving into a smile. "We *should* get back," he agreed, and to my horror, his absence left behind an aching cold. "Before I can't guarantee ever letting you go again."

Which meant we'd disappear into a stall, and he'd fuck me thoroughly and wholly, and it would still be good, even if we were in a public restroom. Because he was Caden Callahan, and anything he did to me left me feeling blissful and on top of the fucking world. For cruel, unknown reasons.

I hurried out of the hallway, half of my mind on him, the other on the fact that I needed to seem less . . . *on edge* when I got back to the group. Behind me, Caden went the other way, toward the bar.

Thank God he was still thinking rationally because I'd completely forgotten about the lie he'd told our friends. I was starting to get careless, which, arguably, was the worst part about this. He distracted me so much, consumed me so fully, that I almost forgot my friends could never find out.

I slid into the booth as I ruffled through my own hair—hoping it would explain why it looked three minutes post–heavy make-out. It seemed Anni had abandoned our game of pool because she and Mike sat on the other side of the table. "Giving up?" I asked with a grin.

Anni rolled her eyes. "I don't stand a chance with Caden on your side."

From beside her, Mike gasped. "Babe, I told you I'd team up with you," he said, faking outrage and crossing his arms.

"My bad." Anni snickered in amusement. "*We* don't stand a chance with Caden on your side." She pressed a kiss to his cheek, and Mike tried not to smile. Unsuccessfully. "Plus," she continued, "these guys were heckling us for the table. It seems they're a lot more serious about their billiards." They were yelling and cheering and booing and flipping each other off—simultaneously.

I wasn't mad at the abandoned game. It seemed like the safe option, considering the last time I had the cue in hand, I felt Caden's hard dick against my ass, and the insinuation genuinely had me considering sex in a bathroom stall. That would be one hell of a broken law for my bucket list: public indecency.

"Oh well, let them have their fun." *Better than me having mine, for anyone involved.*

My eyes drifted off the four guys to the lively bar. Conversations were loud, the music louder, and it was late enough to see some action on the dance floor. From early teens—definitely too young to legally drink—to retirees, Blitz catered to every audience. Well-informed tourists and regular locals roamed the bar, enjoyed a cool drink inside or on the deck or (if they asked really nicely and promised to bring the glasses back) on the beach below, accessible via those creaky, wooden stairs. When Caden parted the diverse crowd, a tray of drinks in hand, my eyes widened.

In horror. And mortification.

He placed it on the table between us, and Iris screamed before I could give him a heads-up. My cheeks were turning the color of a very bad sunburn.

"Caden!" she gasped, her grin too wide to sell the scandalized tone in her voice. Iris pointed at him. His neck.

To be more precise, my lipstick residue in the form of a million kisses on his skin.

I grabbed one of the glasses from the tray, hoping the clear liquid was water, and took a big sip, then—hopefully as inconspicuously as I'd hoped—wiped the back of my arm over my lips.

Fuck. How could I not have noticed that?

Clueless, Caden's brows furrowed. "What?" he asked, the picture of innocence and confusion. I almost felt bad for him.

Mike's eyes flicked back and forth between us, and I tried to ignore it. Iris, still giggling, pulled out her phone and swiped to the camera. Triumphantly, she showed Caden his own reflection. "*Getting drinks* my ass! Who did you just hook up with?!" she asked, looking around the bar frantically. Thankfully, that meant she wasn't suspecting me, at least.

Again, that made it worse, somehow.

"Oh," he said with a lightness and amusement in his voice I couldn't have faked. He scratched his neck, presumably to smear the crystal-clear shape of my lips. Then he tutted, "I don't kiss and tell, Iris."

I just hoped he'd stick to that.

CHAPTER 23

CADEN

There'd been other close calls with Valentina since that night at Blitz.

Mostly because she was such a great distraction, and I needed a lot of that at the moment. Whenever my thoughts threatened to linger on that unanswered Anova offer in my inbox, I sought her out.

In the kitchen, when we thought no one else was in the house—and we'd only realized we'd been wrong because Mike stomped downstairs like he weighed five hundred pounds. When she'd been on top of me in my bunk, and Alfie thought it would be fun to ding-dong ditch our room—Valentina had flown off my lap so fast, she hit her head on the desk opposite our bed. Another time, when we'd all been playing cards outside, and Valentina had been out first, so bored she'd fallen asleep against my shoulder, drool down her chin and everything. Back in our room, I'd kissed her into oblivion and mercilessly teased her for the stain on my hoodie. We'd forgotten to close the door behind us.

All in all, we'd gotten less careful and more needy. Which was a dangerous combination—she knew that just as well as I did, and it was probably why she was in the bunk over mine and not just next to me.

"You've been quiet," she noted from above me. "Everything alright?" There was something in her tone I didn't quite recognize. Concern? Interest? Kindness? In the four weeks we'd been here, the only side she'd shown me was the one that pretended *not* to like me.

Lying on my back, my head shook, although she couldn't see. "This is just by far not my best experience with you on top," I tried to joke.

She laughed, and I could tell by the way her voice hitched halfway through the sound, she was rolling her eyes. Then she playfully hit her mattress, and it would've probably been my shoulder or arm or thigh if I'd been next to her.

"Not just now." She snickered. "Today. And yesterday. Seems like you've got something on your mind."

Yeah, a yearly salary of two hundred thousand American dollars.

"And since when do you worry about the quality of my day?" I didn't mean to sound as snappy as I did. It was supposed to be another joke that would keep us from actually talking about my feelings, but my tone was all off.

To my surprise, she answered sincerely. "I'm not sure," she said. "Since that night you tickled my back, maybe?"

For a solid thirty minutes, and I'd have done it sixty more if she hadn't gone completely rigid from one second to the other, then bolted to the bunk above mine. It had taken her an hour to fall asleep.

I sighed. Her truth made me want to level the playing field. "Anova sent me another offer." The words came out so fast, I wasn't quite sure if she caught it all.

"And, of course," she said with sarcastic disbelief in her tone, "somehow, this is a bad thing."

"Awful," I agreed.

"I don't understand you, Callahan." She shifted above me, and I found myself holding my breath to hear what she'd say next. "You tell me I should live for myself, then you throw opportunities away for something you don't even want—"

"Ali was diagnosed when she was six." I wasn't quite sure where *that* came from, but I went on. "She was the happiest baby I knew, honestly. She never cried, she never complained. She ate whatever Mom put on her plate—vegetables and everything." I blinked rapidly, then decided to just close my eyes. "You'd think once she was told she had leukemia, that would change, but it didn't. She cheered me on from the sidelines just as enthusiastically—probably more enthusiastically, the older she got. Like she didn't care at all about the fact that she might die.

"I started working a lot. Three part-time jobs to save for medical expenses. My parents weren't well-off so we didn't have great health care, and our college funds ran out a year into her treatment. Two years later, there was this new, experimental way to target blood cancer even in critical stages like hers, and I probably slept a total of three hours a night for about six months, trying to make enough money to get us on the eligibility list. I had it, really. I was *nearly* there. Ali died that month."

I paused, let that reality settle. It still hurt the same way it did seven years ago. I still remembered it the same way, too.

Caden thought she would die at home. They had prepared for Alison's transfer from the CCC back into her bedroom next week, and the doctors had said it would be enough time. She'd still have a few weeks at home. A month, even. Two.

She would not.

He'd expected it to be quick and messy and unbelievably horrible—limbs twitching, heavy breathing, screams and tears and his mother passing out beside the hospital bed. He'd never seen anyone die, so he wouldn't know.

But Alison had fallen asleep a few hours ago, her tiny hand in his, holding tightly, still breathing as normally as someone who'd die soon, and there was no sign that said she'd never open her eyes again.

Caden just knew.

The way he'd known her favorite songs and what she'd want for dinner and when to stop tickling her before she got seriously annoyed—and would fight *back.*

It was the first time in days he'd been alone with his sister, and perhaps that played into it as well. That Alison knew as well as he did . . . his parents might not survive being there when she passed. That she'd held on long enough for it to be just the two of them. Because he was her big brother. The one who hadn't shed a single tear in front of her. Who'd read her bedtime stories even when she'd been unconscious and laughed at bad jokes she'd barely managed to get out anymore.

Strong and invincible. For her.

She couldn't know that the same strong, invincible big brother would fall into their mother's arms whenever they were out of earshot, sobbing. Wishing he could change things. Feeling useless and empty and a million other things he couldn't even put into words.

Now, though, noticing her grip around his hand loosening, he felt relieved. That he was there to carry this burden for the rest of his family. That he could be strong for Alison one last time and let her go. Without a fuss, so she wouldn't have to feel bad.

"Mom's getting coffee. Dad's with her," he said, like his sister might need the confirmation. "It's just me. It's okay." His eyes were burning, his nose was running, but he did nothing about it.

He was being strong for her. One last time. Like he'd promised himself. "You can let go. If you want."

And for the very first time, Alison listened to her brother.

Whoever said time healed all wounds must not have had their sibling die.

"She was the light of my life, Valentina. I would've done anything for her. She wanted to be a doctor, you know? Help children that were going through the same thing she was and *make them healthy again*. Those are big dreams, and she never got to live them. Who would I be . . . how selfish would it be if I got the opportunity to live my dream—*her dream for me*—and didn't take it?"

Above me, I could hear a muted sniffle, some shuffling of blankets. Silence for a long while.

Fuck.

This was what oversharing felt like, then? Knowing you'd said way too much, way too fast, to someone who probably didn't care all that much, leaving them speechless and trying to find the right words.

I'm so sorry, Caden. Is there anything I can do to help? What do you need?

My sister back would be a start.

I expected the same standard reply from Valentina, and I would've understood. But she surprised me.

"Don't you think—" she hesitated, and I understood that, too. "Don't you think if she'd had the opportunity, she'd have wanted to live a happy life, above all else? Don't you think if she had to choose between success or happiness for you, she'd choose the latter?"

Always.

"It just seems wrong." I sighed despite her valid point.

She echoed the sound. "I know," she said gently. "It sucks thinking that every choice you'd make for yourself would disappoint someone else."

Silence, and I was glad she decided to fill it a few seconds later. "That's why I don't. That's why I never complained when I had to pack my own lunches, cook dinner, do the dishes, work to keep the lights on. I thought, if I just keep going, my family is going to be so grateful. If I study something really hard—like physics—they *had* to be proud. If I graduated with honors, they *had* to acknowledge it. Sorry, I didn't mean to make this about myself," she added.

But I was quite glad to get the attention off my dead sister, to be honest. "I assume they didn't?"

"My sister said, 'Congrats, by the way.' Mom was probably too high to notice. Sorry," she said again. "That's awkward. I didn't mean to overshare. I love my mom, she's just—sorry."

I snickered. "I just trauma-dumped my sister's death on you. I don't think you can beat my oversharing. Don't worry."

"I just mean—" she continued, hesitating again. "A wise man once told me, 'You can't live the one life you have always pleasing the people around you.'"

To my surprise, I could feel the corners of my lips twitching, threatening to lift. "A wise man?" I teased.

"A semiwise man. A sometimes wise, sometimes very dumb man," she corrected.

A sometimes wise, sometimes very dumb man, who, perhaps, needed to start listening to his own advice.

CHAPTER 24

VALENTINA

I couldn't sleep. I didn't know if it was Caden's sister or that I had let my mother's substance-abuse problem slip or perhaps the heat, but it was a fact. I twisted and turned, threw the covers off, then pulled them back up. And I felt awful because I wasn't the only one in the room.

I tried to remind myself I wasn't supposed to care about what Caden thought—if he could sleep or not, if the noise I was making kept him up—but there was no point pretending anymore. It was exhausting, frankly, to convince myself I didn't like the guy. Somewhat, at least.

After a thousand shared kisses and four weeks in close proximity, who wouldn't?

Something about this was different, though, and made him special. He was still talking and laughing with me, kissing and touching me, even when I'd shown him my worst side. When I'd been cranky, and sassy, and mean, and I hadn't tried to impress him at all—Caden still seemed . . . impressed. At the very least interested.

"We should get back. Before I can't guarantee ever letting you go again."

I'd said no to him more times than I'd said yes, and he was still here. I'd frowned at him more times than I'd smiled, and he was still here. Caden was still here when I hadn't tried my hardest to get him to stay. When I'd pushed him away, over and over again.

I threw the blanket off me again, groaning into the crook of my arm. "Caden?" I whispered into the darkness around us. The only light was coming through the crack in the curtains beside the bed. "Are you awake?"

For the first time in thirty minutes, the blanket below me rustled, like he'd been waiting to get an opportunity to move. "Of course."

It surprised me a little bit, how quickly it came, how naturally. "Of course?" I wondered. "Is it that obvious?"

He huffed in amusement, and I wish I could've seen how his lips twitched when he was trying his best to keep them at bay. "It usually takes you a while to fall asleep, so I wait until you do. Make sure you're fine—that you won't need anything. I sleep better that way, too."

I froze in my bed. Breathing shallow, eyes on the ceiling. "Caden—" I warned, but there was nothing threatening in my tone. It was a beg, a plea, maybe. That he needed to stop being this nice, and this considerate, and this . . . lovely. Plain and simple.

"Valentina," he smiled in answer. I could hear it in his tone.

Still, I wanted to cling to reason. I hadn't even *tried* to make him like me, so how could he? "That's impossible. You fall asleep almost instantaneously. There's never a sound coming from your bunk."

Caden snickered. "Because I try my best *not* to make a sound. Because I don't want to accidentally wake you—or, well, keep you from falling asleep."

I was about to melt. Not from the heat—which was climbing into my cheeks more furiously than the temperatures in this room could make it—but from his words. I was about to break, crack in two, and leave the part behind that told me I couldn't have him. But I shouldn't do that . . .

I shouldn't. I shouldn't. I shouldn't.

The room was spinning, and I was sweating, and everything was a little too much—for the fact that it was midnight and that I'd been unable to fall asleep, despite how tired I'd been. I short-circuited. I didn't mean to ask, "Come down to the beach with me?"

At least it would be cooler there, I thought. At least there'd be a breeze and the sound of waves gently rolling against the sand that would fill the silence between us. I thought it would be a good idea, and he must've, too, because he agreed. He didn't even hesitate.

Without thinking, I'd grabbed my blanket to sit on, and he'd grabbed his, and it reminded me a little bit of that night I'd tried to run away from him, too. When I'd packed my things and slept on one of the lounge chairs outside—and I'd genuinely thought getting rid of Caden Callahan would be that easy.

But he was a very persistent man. That much was clear. And despite all my efforts, he was still here.

"It was too hot in there," I said when I could finally feel that breeze and hear those waves. When we were lying next to each other on our blankets at the beach, looking up into the night sky. "I could barely breathe."

I honestly wasn't sure if I could blame the heat for that or if it had been entirely Caden's fault. But I liked to imagine it was the former. For my own peace of mind.

He nodded beside me, then turned his head. I could see it out of the corner of my eye. And with the way my stomach dropped when his eyes found me, then intently scanned my profile, I shouldn't have returned his gaze.

But I did, of course. And that feeling in my chest intensified in sync with his smile.

He sighed but never took his eyes off me. He muttered, still smiling, "I'm so fucked." Like he didn't mind at all. I didn't have a spare breath to ask why, but he told me, anyway. "I know I'm not supposed to kiss you. I'm not supposed to want to kiss you. You don't want me, and that's why I shouldn't want you, but—"

I kissed him. I rolled over, pressed him into the blanket below us, straddled his hips, and kissed his confusion away. The confusion *I'd* put there.

"It was never about—" I wanted to explain, but he pressed his mouth to mine again and kept his hands behind my head to keep me put. I tried again. "Never about not wanting you."

Because it never had been. The problem had always been that I wanted him too much for my own good. More than I should, given the No-Fraternization Rule, which I'd tried not to think about whenever I looked at him. Given the fact that he was the reason I was lying to my friends, acting carelessly and selfishly for the first time in my life.

"No?" he asked, teasingly biting my bottom lip.

"No." His hand slid from the back of my head, down my neck, shoulder, back, until, without a second thought, it slipped into my panties. I was only wearing those and an oversized shirt, and apparently, that made access a lot easier. He groaned into my mouth when he squeezed my ass, and I instinctively rolled my hips against him. It drew desperate sounds out of both of us.

"What was it about, then?" he asked, breath heavy, voice guttural and raw against my lips.

"Not being able to have you. Wanting you so much and knowing I can't have you." Knowing that, if it came down to it, I'd choose my friends over a man any day of the week. Even if that man was Caden and I was really starting to like him.

"None of what you say makes sense," he said, but he didn't sound angry. He didn't give me time to explain either. "But it's okay. It doesn't have to. Just tell me what you want now, sweetheart, and I'll give it to you." He turned us, swiftly and without much fuss. When I looked up at him, eyes wide, he only smiled.

My chest was heaving underneath his, breath uneven and messy. "What if it's the moon and the stars?"

"I'll get those, too. I'll find a way."

But I shook my head, tried to ignore the way his words tugged at my heartstrings. Squeezed the whole damn thing tightly in my chest. "Just you," I said, almost pleading. With him and myself. "I just want you."

"So you'll have me. It's that easy."

The way he kissed me was different. Like a promise and a plea. For what, I wasn't sure. The weight of him settled between my legs, my knees angled on either side of his body. It was addictive, the way his tongue danced with mine, the sounds he breathed into my mouth, the way he buckled under my touch.

What used to be a neatly shaved buzzcut had turned into hair just long enough to run my fingers through, and he groaned against my lips again, then trailed his kisses to my neck, sucking and nibbling and coaxing the same sounds out of me.

"You taste so good," he muttered, took a deep breath, head still buried in the crook of my neck. "Smell so sweet. Like vanilla and candy."

My back arched at his efforts against my neck, or his words, or just him, groaning against me. I wondered if he was thinking about how good he'd feel buried deep inside of me, too.

And like he was, he confessed, "I want you. I *need* you."

I chuckled, threw my head back in a laugh and a moan and disbelief. "Can you read my mind, Callahan? Is that why you've been so good?"

He emerged from the depths of my neck to look at me, a playful grin on his lips. The moon illuminated his face just enough to make out his rugged nose, the thick eyebrows. The blue of his eyes was less intense but still there. Deep and dark and perfect to get lost in—hoping to find some spark of its actual color in the moonlight.

"Why?" he asked teasingly, and his fingers trailed down my chest, stomach, hips. Played with the hem of my shirt. I squirmed under his gentle touch, still dampened by the fabric separating us. "Are you thinking about my head between your thighs, too? Or are you just wondering how long it'll be until I'm finally inside of you?"

His hand dipped lower again, below my shirt and to the waistband of my panties. Black and lacy, but it hardly mattered—they were off in seconds. In a skillful motion, he slid them down my legs and nudged the fabric of my shirt up with his head. Simultaneously, I felt his teeth scrape my nipples and the breeze against my core.

"Yes," I moaned. *No sense in anything but the truth*, I thought as my back arched off the blanket below us. "I need to feel you, Caden."

He hummed against my skin, a groan of approval, and it sent shivers down my spine. "You moan my name like that again—"

He kissed his way up my body, until his face hovered above mine again. Until we looked each other in the eyes, and he said, "I'm afraid I'll come right there and then." It was a fact, that's how he'd stated it. No embarrassment, no shame—just the truth of the matter whispered onto my lips.

It was a rush, knowing what I did to him without much effort. "Better hurry then, before the fun's over. *Caden*," I added.

He ground his hips against mine, and we both moaned at the contact. "God, you are so lucky," he began. "That I had the foresight to bring one of these." Out of the waistband of his boxers, he pulled a condom.

Despite taking birth control, that shouldn't have been the last thing on my mind. But I could barely think at all, never mind be asked to stay reasonable.

"My hero," I muttered and kissed his neck, shoulder, chest—anything I could reach while he took his shirt and briefs off, then carelessly threw them in the sand.

I looked up at him, sitting on his knees. A cloud passed in front of the moon, and I could barely make him out, the way he pumped his cock once, twice, then threw his head back before he managed to concentrate on the task at hand again.

I think, honestly, I could've just watched him. I could've just watched a barely there silhouette of Caden jerk off on a lonely beach in the middle of the night, and it would've done it for me—simply because it was him. But he ripped the package open, slid the condom on, and when our eyes connected again, anticipation threatened to tie a knot around my throat. My breath hitched.

"Am I still reading your mind?" he asked, attention on me again. I'd leaned back against my elbows, watching as he crawled over me. All I could do was nod. "Do you still want me? Right here?" A finger teased where I needed him most and he groaned at first contact, the same way I writhed against his touch with a whine. "Fuck—" he cursed. "You're so ready for me, aren't you? Talk to me, baby," he added when I, again, could only nod, lips parted in a soundless moan.

"Please," I managed to squeeze out, and one could hardly classify it as talking, to be honest. I moaned, maybe. I groaned and pleaded, maybe. But I wasn't talking to him. This wasn't a fair conversation because suddenly, I could feel his tip against me. "Please. *Please*," I repeated.

He groaned a laugh against my lips, aligned with his again. "Yeah?" he asked, pushed into me, barely an inch. When my hips arched against him, he pulled back.

Where was he getting this self-control from?

Caden tutted playfully, the smile on his lips dark and devious. "So impatient," he teased, kissed me, and pushed another inch forward—still not enough. At all. My whine said as much. "We've been working toward this for a month, Val. Shouldn't we enjoy it?"

Just that it wasn't enjoyable at all. That the seams of my anticipation were about to burst, that my need to feel him fill me completely was so strong, my fingertips tingled and my head was buzzing.

Another inch. Torturous and slow. This one seemed to affect him as much as it did me, and a deep, guttural sound escaped his throat. "You felt so good that first night a few months ago," he said, voice hushed, strained. "But this—"

I knew exactly why he'd paused because I felt it, too. This was different. This was so much better. That night felt incomparable to what was happening now. To the way he groaned, and moaned, and said my name when he pushed a little deeper once more. "Valentina, you're fucking spectacular."

He hadn't even fucked me yet—he wasn't even fully inside of me, and I thought the way he said my name might still burn me wholeheartedly and completely to the ground. I pulsed around him, and for a second, with the way he moaned right into my ear, I thought I might actually come. I didn't know how, but I held back.

Caden must've been struggling, too, because he was beginning to get impatient—as restless and desperate as I had been all along. He added another inch barely ten seconds after the last. His lids threatened to flutter shut, and his lips formed a soundless *O*.

Underneath him, my entire body was humming his name. It wouldn't surprise me if I were trembling.

"A word of warning," he said, and his voice was so deep, so rough, it traveled right to my core, pulsing. He groaned. "I don't know what you're doing to me, but I'm not going to last a minute fucking you the way I plan to." Again, it seemed like a fact. Like he knew what he was capable of and what capabilities I was, apparently, robbing him of. "I promise, I'll make it up to you. I'll make you come as often as you'd like. I just can't—"

I shook my head. "I'm right there with you," I breathed.

I couldn't get my voice to be above a whisper. But I, too, was on the verge of an orgasm before we'd even really started. I could feel it, buzzing in the background, waiting to be unleashed by the right words, a touch, or six rough snaps of his hips against mine—any of those would do, I think. That's how close I was.

His eyes shot wide in surprise. "You—?"

"I'm close, Caden. And I want us to finish this together."

His patience was hurled into the dark sea at our feet. His restraint snapped. His moan was unapologetic and right by my ear. When he added that last inch, filled me completely and to the brink, I lost all sense—of anything.

Of up and down, right and wrong, left and right. Just bliss, thrumming across the surface of my skin, catapulting me into an alternate reality where all it took was four strokes and a canon of nicknames whispered against my lips, parted in a loud moan, before we came in sync at the fifth.

Where he made me come with his mouth and fingers and filthy words three more times, breaking our record, before we fell asleep right there, on the beach, my head nestled in the crook of his neck.

I woke at dawn. With the sound of waves rolling against the beach, the cackle of seagulls, and the morning fog settling over the land around me. *Us.* Caden slept peacefully beside me. Features relaxed, breaths even, and the accidental hickey I must've left last night already fading.

I tried not to panic at the prospect of it—at the fact that it was proof, *evidence*, that we'd gone all the way. That I had slept with him, and, unfortunately, it had been as life altering as our one-night stand had been. Just by a lot more.

The only thing keeping me from a full-on panic attack—because kissing and even the occasional orgasm were one thing, but sleeping with him, enjoying it, and not even really regretting it were another altogether—was the slowly rising sun on the horizon and the way Caden's chest rose and fell evenly beside me.

I watched as the sun—initially nothing but a red circle—peeked out across the water, painting the sky a light orange and tinting the few clouds above us the same color. It rose, and its red turned to orange to yellow, the sky a gradient of the same tones, and I wondered how mad my friends would be.

I wondered how seriously they really took the No-Fraternization Rule but suspected: very. Iris did, at least. It was her rule, her trauma attached to it, and I'd bulldozed right through it. Had driven full speed at Caden, who'd invited me in with open arms. Meanwhile, I'd invited him in with open legs.

In front of me, one of those relaxing videos was playing in real life—the sunrise, the roaring of the ocean: all that was missing was the musical backdrop. And yet all I could think about was the man still sleeping beside me.

CHAPTER 25

CADEN

My first thought was Valentina, even before I'd opened my eyes.

In a highlight reel that woke my dick before my brain had the chance, last night's events flooded back to me. The way she arched below me, moaned my name, and came as quickly as I did.

What a marvel that woman was. Just fucking spectacular.

I squinted against the sun, groaned as I stretched, and was glad to discover that we must've put our clothes back on before we passed out last night. I was wearing my briefs and the shirt I'd left the room in. Valentina's underwear wasn't flying around the beach either.

Neither was she, though.

The spot beside me on the blanket was empty and probably cold. I thought it was funny, the way my heart gave one little squeeze, like it was trying to find a connection to hers that didn't exist. I thought it was even funnier that I got up, collected my blanket, and stepped up the small boardwalk back to the house without a second thought. Without even fully realizing.

Like maybe there was a connection after all, and it was leading me back to her all on its own.

I got back to the house, and three pairs of eyes blinked at me from around the breakfast table. *Fuck*. It must've been later than I'd realized. Iris, Anni, and Alfie were, mostly, confused, judging by the looks on their faces. I couldn't blame them, as I was standing in the yard with nothing but a thick blanket bunched up under my arm, wearing boxers and a shirt. I stopped short, like a kid caught doing something they weren't supposed to.

"Morning," I managed to say, then hurried through the sliding door back into the house.

They were probably too blindsided to comment, but I could hear their chatter loudly the second I disappeared out of sight. I just didn't care enough to stay and listen, because thirty seconds later, I carefully opened the door to our room, unsure what to expect.

Half of me was convinced Valentina would simply forget last night happened and put so much distance between us—physically and mentally and spiritually and any other way she could find—that I'd start to think it was just some deluded dream I'd play over and over in my head a hundred more times. The other part of me hoped. For what, I didn't know—until our eyes connected.

Valentina sat at the small desk opposite our bunk beds. Her eyes moved away from the notebook in front of her, and her entire face lit up despite the fact that she was probably trying hard to hide it. The corners of her mouth curled, her eyes widened, and she blushed.

And, apparently, it was exactly what I'd been hoping for because I mirrored her every action. Down to the fucking color in her cheeks.

"Hi," she breathed, and I finally closed the door behind me. Dumped the sandy blanket in a corner and promised myself to remember to wash it later. I'd probably forget. Half a second later, I stood behind Valentina's chair and tried to play my fast-beating heart off as casual. I wouldn't know what else to do with it. I'd never had to deal with that.

"Hey," I said. "How'd you sleep?"

"Good." She swallowed thickly, and I could feel my smile growing when she emphasized, "Very good."

My eyes flicked from her face to the notebook she'd been leaning over a minute ago. Her summer bucket list beamed at me brightly, and it really only hit me how much time had passed when I realized most of the items on it were scratched out. Done.

~~sleep outside~~
~~go for a run~~
~~full-moon walk~~
skinny-dipping
~~break a law~~

~~watch the sunrise~~
~~sex on the beach (not the drink)~~
~~play pool~~

I huffed, feeling kind of sentimental about the whole thing. It wasn't even *my* list, so I steered away from the feeling. "What law did you break?" I asked in amusement. "Public indecency?"

Apparently, this was the wrong thing to say. Her lips twitched first, as if she wanted to laugh, then remembered it wasn't funny. For a moment, I honestly thought she was about to lecture me on why breaking laws wasn't a laughing matter before making me promise not to seduce her in public places again (I couldn't do that; I'd be lying).

Instead, she shook her head and ignored my comment. Her eyes flickered across me restlessly until they focused on my neck. "We need to do something about that," she said as she got up, like I hadn't said anything at all. She lifted her hand, let her fingertips graze my neck.

I nearly shivered underneath her touch. My knees almost buckled, and the wind almost got knocked out of my lungs. *Really.*

"Huh?" I unnecessarily tried to turn my head, but it only left us closer. Only left my lips a hair's breadth from hers, if it weren't for the height difference between us. She looked up at me, then trailed her fingers across the same spot on my neck again.

"Apparently, I'm sixteen years old again and leaving hickeys behind. Sorry." She scrunched her nose, and her lips thinned into an apologetic smile.

"Territorial much?" I joked, and she punched my arm—somewhat playfully. "But at this point, you should know I have no problem with that. Mark your territory, if you want to." We both knew she wouldn't purposely do that, not with her friends around. Not when I was still nothing but her little secret.

Stealing a glance at the mirror above the dresser, I quite liked the look of it, though. I think it might just be the fact that it was proof last night really happened. That it had happened, and she hadn't disappeared again.

Another laugh bubbled out of her, and Valentina rolled her eyes. "You're my territory?" she asked, doubtful. "Aren't you free as a bird? Tied to nothing and no one but yourself? You're not anyone's."

I could be yours.

The thought was so brief, I almost paid no mind to it. Then it scared the fuck out of me.

I couldn't really be anyone's—I'd never *been* anyone's. Probably because after Alison, the thought of loving someone and then losing them had been enough of a deterrent, I kept every girl I'd ever talked to at arm's length. I'd built walls to keep my grief in and posted guards at the gates to keep people out.

Only that Valentina had snuck past them easily. My guard hadn't been up, and she'd slipped right through the cracks. Long enough ago that I was considering being *hers*. That the thought came naturally and the implications only followed after long consideration.

Long consideration in which I hadn't said anything, by the way. I blinked back into the present: Valentina standing in front of me, her hand still on my neck, fingers dancing across my skin absentmindedly. What was the last thing she'd said?

You're not anyone's.

"Well . . ." I shrugged, tried to play it cool. Tried not to show how much she affected me, how I had to resist the urge to breathe in her smell, lean into her touch. "Yours, apparently. I mean, you *marked* me." I gasped, scandalized, and with another eye roll, she brushed past me. Her absence—although she was still right there, only disappearing into the bathroom and rummaging through something, by the sound of it—left a cold imprint behind.

"Let's fix that. Sorry," she repeated, voice still muffled out of the adjacent room. Valentina came back with a clear tube of makeup. Concealer, maybe? It'd been a while since Alison had forced me to sit model for one of her very elaborate, very colorful makeup looks. Her live commentary still haunted some distant corner of my mind, but what Valentina was about to smother onto my neck, I couldn't say.

It irked me, forgetting things about my sister. "Concealer?" I guessed.

"Wow." She unscrewed the top, revealing a little wand covered in something at least *close* to my skin tone, and stopped right by my side again. *Good*, something inside of me screamed. "You know your makeup. Is that why your skin looks airbrushed? Have you been deceiving all of us?"

She always squinted when she laughed at her own jokes. I stored that piece of information with the rest of them. Right between the fact that she played with her necklace when she was nervous and that little sound she made right when she was on the edge of an orgasm.

Feeling the cool tip of it against my neck, knowing she was the one gently brushing it across my skin, sent a shiver down my spine and goose bumps up my neck. I exhaled—sighed contentedly, really.

"Thank you," I teased, and for a moment, she froze, like she hadn't noticed her compliment.

Quickly, she closed the concealer, threw it on top of her bunk, and got back to blending it into my skin. I'd expected a sponge but got her fingers instead. "I thank my skin-care routine for this." I pointed at my own face, circling it in emphasis. "Three steps, a pain in the ass every morning and night. But it gets the job done."

She nodded knowingly. Another glance at the round mirror beside us, and like I'd suspected, any trace of a hickey was gone. But she was still touching me. "How do you know, then? Girlfriend?" she asked, and her voice wasn't carrying quite the same confidence it usually did.

Despite the right answer being my dead sister, I couldn't help but smile. *That* was new. "Why? Jealous?"

She huffed, tried to get the concealer from her bed to put it back but didn't get that far. My hand curled around her wrist before I really knew it, and I tugged her back against my body. Her round eyes blinked up at me, long lashes batting against her cheeks. "Have I ever given you a reason to be jealous?"

"You mean apart from your reputation as the fuckiest fuckboy on campus?"

I snickered, and for a second, her eyes flicked to my fingers around her wrist, like she was just as aware of every point of contact between us. "I wouldn't go *that* far. And friendly reminder, you were the one that snuck out of my room a few months ago."

"I don't usually do that," she clarified, like it should've been obvious. Her eyes narrowed in faked offense, but all I could think of was how cute she looked. How kissable, and holdable, and touchable. Which was probably the opposite of the reaction she'd hoped for. But I couldn't help it.

My fingers slid up her arm, behind her back, and she took one more step toward me, letting us stand toe-to-toe. Nose-to-nose. Lips-to-lips. "But you did."

"Like you would've wanted," she guessed, but it was barely a whisper. I could feel her breath on my lips. They were tingling from her close proximity.

She was probably right. I didn't usually fall asleep cuddling, and I didn't usually wake up with a woman in my bed—or me in hers. But waking up lonely when there'd been someone you'd fallen asleep with, even if it had been an accident, had been . . . weird, to say the least. It was at least part of the reason why I'd still been thinking about Valentina four months after the fact. It's probably why, when she'd walked into our room a month ago, my heart had plummeted into the pit of my stomach.

"I think maybe I would've liked it," I said lowly. My voice was rougher than I'd intended it to be, and I cleared my throat. "Definitely, at least, making you come again the next morning would've been fun." She meant to retort something—cheeks red again, eyes narrowing again—but I cut her off. "See what your people-pleasing tendencies have robbed us of?"

At least we'd made up for whatever we'd missed that morning. We'd exceeded everything it could've been, by a lot.

She gnawed on her bottom lip in thought, eyes jumping back to mine. She played with the necklace previously hidden under her shirt. "Alright," was the response she settled on after a long pause. She swallowed thickly. "Okay. Maybe you're right. Maybe I should focus on what I want more than what others might want from me."

"And all it took for you to admit it was realizing you missed out on great sex with Caden Callahan. Incredible," I muttered, amused, pulling her closer again. Letting my hand brush down her back, settling on the lower half.

The kiss I placed on her lips was slow, and sweet, and fleeting. The way she followed my lips when I pulled away was heartbreakingly wholesome. Same as the sound she made somewhere in the back of her throat.

I didn't remember the last time I'd kissed someone that way. I wasn't sure if I ever had. Short and sweet and without the intention of eventually taking things further.

"But then," she said, and perhaps Valentina *was* trying to take things further, because she started nudging me toward our bed. Without even the thought of complaining, I tripped onto the lower bunk and pulled her onto my lap—legs on either side of me. "I feel like it's only fair you start making certain life choices for yourself as well."

Her voice was soft, tone gentle and kind. She was, again, playing with the charm on her necklace. A shimmering, orange crystal. I leaned back onto my elbows, pillow behind me, eyes trained on her.

I was waiting for the usual fight-or-flight reaction when certain life choices of mine were questioned or the topic of my sister came up. For another row of bricks to be put on top of my walls and for the guards at the gates to unsheathe their swords. But nothing.

Valentina still sat on my lap, having abandoned her necklace to let her fingers draw up and down my shirt absentmindedly. Her eyes were ferociously trained on her hands, and even when I grabbed the one now fiddling with the hem of my shirt, she didn't look up.

"You're so beautiful, Val." Which finally did make her look at me. Her eyes jumped to mine, and there was a red sheen to her cheeks again—one that told me she liked my compliments, despite how uncomfortable they made her. One that told me she liked when I called her Val, even though she'd never expressed it.

I wasn't usually great at reading people, and she was still a mystery to me, but in situations like this, it was so easy with her. Like she was written for me. Like I'd known how to interpret every twitch of her brow before I'd even met her.

Her lips quirked, then her eyes rolled, then she hit my chest playfully. "Don't try to change the subject," she scolded half-heartedly. Somehow, my hands had landed on her hips.

"Sorry," I said. "What did you say?" Valentina sat on top of me, nothing but her panties and my boxer briefs separating us, and I was only a man, after all. More helpless than most others when I was in her presence.

She snickered, got closer regardless. Her red hair fell into her face when she leaned toward me, over me, until her face hovered in front of mine. "You deserve to live the life *you* want, Caden. If I'm supposed to focus more on what I want, you should do what you want, too."

"I don't know," I muttered, half a mind on her, the other on captain duties and the Anova offer, still unanswered in my inbox. "What I want, I mean. I don't know what I'm supposed to do." And there was something in the way my voice broke that I didn't recognize. Vulnerability, maybe? Desperation?

All I knew was that I'd just cracked open like an egg. That Valentina had cracked me, and all the things not meant to come to the surface started oozing out.

The fact that deep down, I was still the sixteen-year-old boy grieving his little sister, wanting to make her proud. That I pretended to know what the fuck I was doing but really had no idea. That I was desperate for someone to just tell me what the right thing was.

And maybe she was that. "I think you do." And her smile was pitiful. "I think you just don't want to do it. Even when you know you should."

Accept the offer. Fuck captaining.

It seemed easy enough, only that when I looked at that choice, all I saw was: Be selfish. Destroy Ali's dream. And suddenly it wasn't all that easy anymore.

All my defenses were down, disarmed and disabled one by one—by the woman still sitting on top of me, so close I could count her lashes if I'd wanted to. "I don't know if I *can*," I corrected. "I want to. I *should* accept that offer. I just don't think I can. I don't know." I shook my head again, let it fall back, and closed my eyes in frustration and confusion and, honestly, annoyance. At myself and my feelings for making this so much more difficult than it should be. Rational decisions were easy; it's when the heart got involved that things became complicated.

"You love Alison," she said, letting her fingers run through my short hair. My sister's name out of her mouth felt so right, it actually sent shivers down my spine. "And she loves you. That's why I'm having a hard time imagining her wanting anything but the best for you. Anything other than your happiness probably wasn't an option for her. Just like you wouldn't have cared if she'd ended up being a doctor or a—"

"Dog sitter. When she didn't want to be a doctor, she wanted to pet dogs for a living." I smiled at the reminder.

"Can't blame her," Valentina agreed thoughtfully, and her lips quirked again. She thought for a mere moment, then rolled off me, and I was ready and willing to complain loudly before I realized that she was staying close to my side. Instead of swinging out of bed and leaving because I'd let her in, and that's usually when everyone else would leave—her head landed on my chest. Our fingers interlaced. Her leg sprawled over mine, and she cuddled into my side.

I held my breath, that's how unexpected it was. "Comfortable?" I asked, not quite sure if I wanted to get away from the topic or continue talking about it because it had felt kind of . . . nice. Getting it all out there. Having someone who knows enough about me and my sister to have an opinion on it. Someone who cares enough to voice it.

I'd never really talked to anyone about Alison like that.

"Very," Valentina sighed. She kissed my neck, messily and distractedly. Her voice was muffled. "Let's just stay like this for a while. Tell me something, if you want. Don't, if you don't."

So I was talking, and she was listening, right up until her breath evened out, and the fingers that had been tickling up and down my biceps stilled. "Just," she mumbled into my shirt, "taking a quick nap."

And I was surprised she managed to warn me at all before she fell asleep against me. I was out like a light thirty seconds later.

CHAPTER 26

VALENTINA

I didn't remember falling asleep. I remembered his arm around my head, his fingers in my hair, and the low, calm cadence of his voice. I remembered the smile on my lips. Most importantly, I remembered the way I'd felt—*still* felt.

Safe. Understood. Seen. Without the fear of doing something wrong and scaring him away—because I'd done all the wrong things, and he'd never even taken a step back.

I groaned into the crook of his neck, stretched my arms against the bottom of my bunk over us. Last night must've been too short and this had been desperately needed. It took me another minute to properly open my eyes. I sat up—slowly and carefully so as to not wake the man beside me—and blinked through the room.

Straight at Alfie, motionless in the door.

My eyes widened, my pulse spiked, and my lips parted—ready to word-vomit an explanation and apology and justification simultaneously. But not a single word came out of my mouth. Like I'd gone mute.

Silently, we regarded each other through the small room. He looked as shocked as I felt, eyes continuing to jump back and forth between me and a peacefully sleeping Caden, whose arm I was still tracing my fingers up and down on. I stopped. Alfie finally moved.

"Valentina!" he gasped, closed the door behind him, and leaned against it, eyes still wide, shock and confusion and a million other things still in his expression. So far, I couldn't see disappointment, but the rest of his emotions would probably make space for it soon. Once the fact settled, once he'd gotten all the details, it would come.

Caden disregarded, I jumped out of the bottom bunk—unsure how we'd both fit in the first place. I hit my head, stumbled over my own feet, and finally made it to him with multiple injuries. My hands were on his shoulders, and they were shaking. Just slightly.

"Alfie," I warned or pleaded, I wasn't sure either, "this is not what it looks like, I swear."

It's like he blinked out of a trance, rapidly and more often than he needed to. He whisper-shouted his next words at me. "So you weren't cuddling Caden Callahan in your bed? Hands and legs and whatever other body parts all over each other?"

"Well—"

"And you're not hooking up?"

"Okay." I nodded to myself, my lips thinning into an apologetic expression. "Maybe it is what it looks like."

"Valentina!" he repeated, and now his hands were on my shoulders, too. There was less outrage in his voice and more . . . excitement?

"No." I shook my head. Looked at him for a second and then shook it again. "No. No, no, no. This isn't a good thing, Alfie. I fucked up. Majorly."

But the smile on his lips was irreversible, and I knew its implication, even before he said anything. "How was it? How is he?" His eyes trailed behind me, and he gave an impressed expression when he looked back at me. "Valentina Rhodes, I'm truly impressed. Not a bad catch."

"Alfie!" I groaned. "How good it was is not the point. If—"

"Good, then? How good, would you say? Scale of one to ten?"

"Alfie!" My head fell back, and another groan fled my lips. Once this guy smelled gossip, he suddenly liked being a journalist at his dad's college paper—as if he'd print every scandalous situation in next week's issue of the *Hall Beck Post*. "Eleven, but that's not—"

"Oooooh," he said, then whistled lowly. "Well, damn. Your ratings usually don't go above a six, Valentina."

I shook my head, tried to ignore his tangent. "Alfie, listen to me. You can't tell anyone. If Iris finds out, and she really meant what she said about him being part of the group—"

"She said that?" At least he'd calmed down enough to hear me.

"Yes. On, like, day two."

He shook his head. "She can't have meant it. We didn't even know the guy."

"And if she did?" I shrugged at my own words, let the truth of the matter consume me again.

I'd tried to ignore it since the first time Caden had touched me. When I'd realized I wasn't physically capable of keeping my distance from him and when I'd realized no matter what I did and how much of an asshole I was, he wasn't keeping his either.

Alfie deflated at my realistic hypothesis. "No fraternization," he sighed, like it was more of a burden for him than me. "But don't you think"—his eyes flicked to Caden sleeping behind me once more, then back—"maybe she'd understand. It's been *years*. She knows we'd never leave her. She knows you wouldn't—"

"I don't want to find out." Because I had no idea how Iris would have reacted if she'd been the one to accidentally walk into this. "I tried to tell you guys, and then Jason happened, and the moment passed. Now is not the time to hurt her even more, right? She needs us."

I needed her. After realizing my family would never truly care—who else did I have left except her? Except Iris, and Anni, and Alfie.

At the mention of Jason, Alfie's nose twitched. "Fuck that guy," he muttered, just for the sake of it. I agreed. "He always messes her up worse than anyone else."

"Which is why I don't want to hurt her more by telling her I've been lying." *Since the second we'd woken up on Oakport the first time, really.* "Please don't say anything?"

Not sure how it was possible, but Alfie deflated more. Leaned against the door behind him and sighed loudly, like he might actually have understood where I was coming from. "Morning, Caden," he said absentmindedly. "This really is a mess you've put us in."

I whirled around to find Alfie hadn't lost his mind talking to people who weren't conscious. Caden sat up, slowly blinking at us. Confusion and sleep narrowed his eyes, and they jumped back and forth between us. "What's going on?" he asked, and the roughness of his voice almost let me forget this entire problem.

Made me, at least, want to forget Alfie still in the room with us. Alfie knowing and Alfie being the biggest blabbermouth on campus. I focused back on him.

"I'm being serious, Dunbridge. Don't tell anyone. You can't tell anyone." My finger hovered threateningly in front of his chest, and I poked it once—for good measure.

"You'll have to, eventually."

My head shook, and I wanted to ask why. Explain that this wasn't anything serious, that it wasn't going anywhere, and that in a few weeks, we'd probably never see each other again. Caden would hopefully move to Boston; I'd do my grad program at HBU. Our paths would not cross. But everything about it felt wrong. The thought, then voicing it. Knowing Caden was awake and would hear. He probably couldn't care less, but I kept my mouth shut, anyway.

"Promise?" I asked, glaring at him until he gave me the answer I was waiting for with an eye roll.

"Promise." Once more, his attention flicked to the bed behind me. "Congrats, Caden. You've got yourself a great girl." And with that, he leveled me with another look before leaving the room. I closed the door behind him, then turned around.

Humor played in the blond's expression. His eyes narrowed and his lips quirked. Alone again, at last.

"Have I pushed Finnick Maxwell off your summer-fling throne, then?"

Without even having to put up a fight, I thought. But it felt mean, a little bit. Finnick had always been good to me, so I didn't need to compare him with Caden, then voice that comparison out loud.

Still, I meant it when I said, "Yes." Voice level and even. Like we were having a casual conversation about the weather, not how he—and his performance—held up against others.

He tutted. "Give me some credit, Val. I thought an eleven out of ten would get a little more praise than that."

I could feel the blood rush into my cheeks, embarrassment taking over. My hands flew up, and I buried my face in them with a groan. "I thought you were asleep," I muttered through my fingers. "How much of that did you hear?"

He huffed, slid back against the wall to make room on his bed, and patted the space on the mattress in front of him. "What makes you think I wouldn't wake up when someone jumps over me, cursing like a sailor? Come here," he added, a knowing look on his face. His head tilted, and I could do nothing about my feet starting to move.

Like I'd been hypnotized by his inviting voice and beautiful smile alone. Like I'd been under his spell for God knows how long.

"I hit my head." I justified the cursing as I scooted in beside him, greeted by his warm body and familiar scent under the blanket. "Sorry. I thought I was being discreet."

"As discreet as a seven-thousand-pound elephant in the room," he agreed—or I guess didn't. But he said it so sweetly, kissed my forehead so tenderly, one could assume he had.

"Sorry," I said again, and if he wouldn't have brought it up, I might just forget Alfie had ever been in this room. For the sake of my peace of mind and for the sake of *this*. Being held and kissed and called sweet nicknames. Some selective amnesia was worth that, was it not?

"Do you think he'll tell them?" His voice was soft, his fingers dancing up and down my arm. Goose bumps followed his touch like a trusted companion. And before I could answer, he added a much more important question: "What's the no-fraternization thing he mentioned?"

I froze, my back against his stomach went rigid. He noticed, of course, but his fingers continued caressing my skin. For a brief moment, I considered lying. Telling him the reason I'd wanted to stay away from him hadn't been part of the plan. Letting him in enough to understand the ins and outs of my friends and our dynamic wasn't part of it either.

But not a single bone in my body wanted to carry the burden of lying to Caden, too, and so I told him.

CHAPTER 27

CADEN

I almost didn't ask. I'd almost let it be, forgotten Alfie was ever in the room, and never found out what the No-Fraternization Rule was. It had clearly been what Valentina would've wanted, but I was glad I'd listened to my gut this time, because five weeks in, I'd given up on figuring out why Valentina was so vehemently against the idea of us.

Yeah, she'd said it wasn't me and that her friends just wouldn't approve and that she wasn't embarrassed—but no matter how robust my ego, these thoughts had still been flying around in my head regardless.

"I'm sorry," she said again. For the fiftieth time, probably. "It's stupid, I know. But Iris—"

"Hey, it's not." Her nose had been buried in my chest the entire time she'd told me about the NFR. I snickered. "I mean, it is a little bit. But I get it. You love Iris, and this is her . . . thing. You don't want to disappoint her." I meant it, even if that disappointment was . . . me.

Valentina finally emerged out of the depth of my shirt, a vicious glare in her eyes that only made her look cuter. Honestly, it wasn't all that vicious to begin with. Her lips were twitching upward, and all her efforts were going into keeping them in a straight line. Unsuccessfully.

She finally gave up. "It is her thing. Only that it being her thing made it our thing."

"I can't help that I'm *so* great, you wanted to sleep with me from day one, while Iris wanted to be my friend. I didn't know it would be a conflict of interest; otherwise, I'd have been a little more rude to her."

She sighed, rolling onto her back. "You are unbearable."

"Am I?"

"No." Our eyes connected again. Something plummeted to the pit of my stomach. I tried not to think about it further.

It was a known routine for me at this point. The smile on my lips, as always, was inevitable.

She sighed. "Now what?" Like I could give her the answers to that. If it were up to me, the truth—*our truth*—would already be out in the open. If it were up to me, every minute we'd not spend on top of each other, at least her hand would be in mine. Friends around or not.

Despite knowing better, I suggested it. "Alfie said you're going to have to tell them eventually." The unspoken words that hung between us were, *So you might as well just do it.*

"I can't. She'll hate me." Valentina took a deep breath. "What if she leaves?"

And I think that's what her people-pleasing tendencies boiled down to. That she didn't realize how fucking great she was. That the people around her were around because they *liked* her, not because she did things for them and said yes to anything they wanted. And that they wouldn't just abandon her, because for once in her life, Valentina Rhodes made a decision for herself.

"I don't think she will," I muttered in response. "I think she loves you a little too much."

There was a long pause. Valentina gnawed on her bottom lip, eyes on the top bunk above us. She was considering something, I could tell by the twitch of her nose and the slightly furrowed brows. Finally, she said, very quietly, "I thought Dad did."

I don't think she'd mentioned her father before. Her mother's substance-abuse problem, yes. Her sister's lack of interest in her life, yes. Her dad, though? I'd never heard about him. "What happened?"

Valentina tried to shrug it off, make it less of a big deal than it obviously was. I let her, just for the sake of her own comfort. "Oh, nothing." She snickered. "Are you sure you want to hear this? It's not even that big of a—"

"Yes." I cut her off. "Stop making your issues seem less important than everyone else's, sweetheart. Tell me."

The smile on her lips turned genuine. Sweet and appreciative, and something inside of me bloomed at the sight—with pride, I think, for putting it there. I nudged her. "Please?"

She laughed with an eye roll. "It really isn't that big of a deal," she repeated, but the look I sent shut her up. "Growing up, my dad and I were really close. *Daddy's little princess*," she mocked. "Had a baby overall with the print and everything. He used to pick me up from daycare, then kindergarten, then school. Basically all of my childhood memories were with him. My parents fought a lot, but I always thought they'd be fine. I'd come home to them yelling at each other, and I thought if I'd just do my homework extra fast and better than anyone else, it would make up for that. When I could hear them fighting at night, I thought I'd prepare a nice breakfast in the morning, and everything would be okay again. I thought that would be enough, you know?

"I was ten, I think, when he left." Valentina blinked rapidly. "Turns out he had a whole other family. Just one town over. He's still a dad to those kids now, but we haven't heard from him at all. Despite their constant fighting, Mom hasn't been the same since either. And I can't help but think that if I'd just done more, supported them better, been a little less difficult sometimes, he'd still be there. And Mom would still be clean—"

I couldn't help the interruption. "You were a child, Val. You can't honestly think that."

"I can, and I have." We thought to sit up at the same time. Me ducking to avoid hitting my head, Valentina leaning against the wall behind her, legs drawn up to her chest. "I mean, it makes sense. He wouldn't have left if I'd been enough, right? That's not how that works. Think about it." She clearly had. For the past decade. "Maybe his other daughter was smarter and nicer and listened better than I had."

And so I assumed she'd just started being nicer, listening, and always giving her prettiest smile while doing everything for everyone else but never herself. Thinking that becoming what everyone wanted her to be would keep them around. Forgetting that in the process, she'd lost a pretty big part of herself.

I shook my head, tilted it slightly. "Your dad didn't leave because you weren't enough," I said carefully. By the look on her face, perhaps it was the first time she was hearing it. "Maybe he left because he didn't love your mom anymore. Maybe he left because the fighting was too much. None of that makes it better, but it had nothing to do with a sweet, little ten-year-old girl who did everything in her power to make him stay."

"You don't know—"

"I promise you, I do. I'd bet a lot of things on it. All of my things, actually."

Her head fell back against the wall, hair still messily flying in all directions after our nap. "But," she said, then didn't finish the sentence.

"No buts," I tutted. "Your friends don't like you because you'd try and give them the moon and the stars if they'd ask. They love you because you're you."

Again, she shook her head. Her teeth dug into her bottom lip. "You don't know them well enough to say that."

"This is another one of those things I'm absolutely certain about, Rhodes. It took me a day to figure it out, and I've had weeks at this point to prove myself right over and over again." I shrugged. "I mean, you've been an A-class ass to me, and I still like you. Scowls and insults and all."

And I think she was trying to ignore that little confession as much as I was now. Five seconds of silence later, regretting it heavily. *And I still like you.* But I did, didn't I? More than just a friend, definitely more than anyone else before.

Finally, she caught herself. "Because you're weird, Callahan." She nudged me with her foot, and her eyes rolled. "Maybe you've got a degradation kink."

"Only one way to find out." She blushed in sync with my wink, hiding her face behind her hands. *Giggling.* The sound tugged at something in my chest. And I realized then, I was so unconditionally, irrevocably gone for her.

"Fuck," she groaned into her hands. Then, lower, she asked God knows who, "What are you doing to me?" Valentina's eyes connected with mine, and I had no idea why it was doing the things it was doing to me either. Chest tightening. Fingertips tingling. Goose bumps crawling down my back and arms and neck.

Every single part of my body had some kind of reaction to her. Every. Single. One.

"I should be worried," she said, contemplative. Her head tilted, like she was genuinely confused. When she got on her knees and crawled the short space over to me until she sat on my lap, my heart actually stopped. Skipped a single beat, then doubled its speed. "About Alfie knowing and Iris finding out. I should want to stay as far away from you as humanly possible. But—"

She was not far at all. Her breath fanned against my lips, her eyes were so close, I could see every single shade of brown in them. Like it was instinctive, my hands found her backside, cupped her ass. I couldn't have done anything about it, even if I'd wanted to.

"But?" I asked.

My throat worked, and she blinked at me, trying to find the right words. "But I'm not feeling any of the things I should feel. Instead, this seems like the only *right* place to be."

In my bed. On my lap. Lips basically grazing mine. Here. With me.

My entire body buzzed with relief once my lips found hers—chanted *finally* over and over and over again. Finally, I could taste her on my tongue again. Finally, she arched into my touch again. Finally, her hips rolled against mine, and our groans mixed between our mouths, and I wanted her so much, it was hard to keep my head clear.

All five of my senses had been taken over by her, so getting out a coherent thought was . . . challenging. "Your friends—" But her hand dipped to the waistband of my boxers between us, and she started fiddling with the fabric.

"Val. Baby," I breathed, hoping to get her attention off my lips long enough to finish my sentence. But the words only seemed to encourage her. Her hand grazed across the outline of my hard dick, cupped it, and continued teasing up and down my length.

Torturous, I thought. *Fucking perfect*, I corrected.

I twitched against my boxer briefs, and Valentina moaned against my lips; half a mind on what she was doing with her hands, the other on kissing me so wholly, I forgot my concerns for a weak second.

"I need you," she confessed, brought some distance between us to look at me. Her hand was still busy teasing the shit out of me. "Now. Here. Please," she pleaded again, just like she had last night. Only that last night, we'd been on a deserted beach, out of earshot of the house and the people inside it.

"Your friends," I tried to reason again, but it was getting significantly harder the more turned on I was. Which, we'd established already, was: very.

Valentina shook her head, round eyes blinking innocently at me. Those were her puppy eyes, that look Iris had warned me about. The one that would get her anything she'd wanted, including me, apparently. "I'll be quiet. I promise." And the desperation in her voice was so hot, I almost fell for it.

I raised my brows. "Can you?" I asked, lips twitching. "That would be news to me."

My eyes flitted through the room, trying to find a solution to our problem before I threw her reasons to hell and she'd regret it the second I pulled out of her. The windowsill I'd been wanting to bend her over looked inviting but wouldn't do much to muffle her—or, honestly, *our*—sounds. Same with the small desk or the dresser beside the door to the bathroom.

I blinked one, two, three times, my eyes glued to it. "Fucking Eureka," I muttered, looking at the solution to our problem.

Valentina followed my gaze, twisted and turned on my lap until she was looking at the bathroom, too. I tried not to let her wiggling against my hard cock affect me and failed when I groaned lowly, hands flexing on her waist.

The look in her eyes spoke volumes, and I knew she'd come to the same realization when she'd said, "Shower. Now."

I'd never gotten up faster.

Secured in my arms, her legs wrapped around my waist, I carried Valentina into the bathroom, and we barely managed to close and lock the door behind us before we were at it again. Her body pressed against the door, one hand curling around my neck, the other busy with the waistband of my boxers again.

"We're so stupid," she whispered against my lips, out of breath. "We could've been doing this the entire time, and we never once thought about showering together."

"Wrong," I interjected. "I thought about it a number of times. Every time I was in here by myself, probably." Pumping my cock to the thought of her, trying to relieve some of that sexual frustration we'd been working up for weeks.

The bathroom wasn't big. Sink to the left, toilet beside it, and the walk-in shower stretching across the short wall opposite the door. Blue tiles inside, gold accents all around. Pretty, honestly, but not what I was focused on right now. The girl pinned against the door made me not even dare a glance around.

"Really?" she asked, but she didn't seem surprised. "And you kept the idea all to yourself. How selfish of you, Caden."

My name out of her mouth was like music to my ears. Made the last bit of restraint I was holding on to snap. My hands roamed her body, stripped the oversized shirt over her head, and she stood in front of me with nothing but her panties on. The lacy ones from a few months ago—I'd recognize the way they hugged her curves anywhere. For months, I'd seen it every time I'd closed my eyes.

"Valentina," I breathed, and I didn't mean to. My fingertips grazed along her collarbones, watching her squirm under my touch, blush under my gaze. I was discerning every single one of her reactions, every subtle twitch of her eyes when she wanted to let them fall shut, every time her lips parted in a soundless moan. Touch traveling down her skin, across her breasts, to the dip of her waist and the curve of her hips, until they played with the fabric of her panties.

I was straining against my own underwear, so hard it was almost painful—in the good way. In the way that made me know that whatever happened next would be spectacular. My lips followed the path my fingers had carved. Kissed her collarbones, sucked on her nipple, then trailed down her waist and hips until I kneeled in front of her. Until my teeth hooked under the fabric and I slowly slid them down her body.

From above me, I heard a whimper, and I wasn't even touching her yet. Her panties fell the rest of the way to the floor, and my eyes batted open to look at her. A mess, arched off the door behind her, hand in my short hair, teeth digging into her bottom lip. "You said you'd be able to keep quiet," I reminded her with a knowing smile. "The water's not even running yet."

Valentina tried to glare at me, but the second I placed a gentle kiss against her core, let my tongue roll against her clit just once, she was done for. Her head fell back with a thud against the wood, and the hand not in my hair tried to grasp for purchase, landing on the door handle.

Seeing her this way, sprawled against a wall, completely naked and ready for me, my cock was about to burst through my briefs. And as much as I'd love for her to take me out of them, I couldn't wait. I made quick work of it, shrugged off my underwear and threw it somewhere behind me. With my dick sprung against my stomach, twitching, tip glistening, I got off my knees. I was so turned on, for a second, I worried I couldn't even stand straight.

Five seconds later, after her gaze slowly wandered up my legs, lingered on my cock, and then snapped to my eyes, I turned us, walked her backward until she hit the shower glass. Anticipation hummed in the air between us once the water pattered against the floor. I gave it ten seconds to warm up, then walked us under the stream.

And there was something magical about Valentina Rhodes, naked and wet, soaked hair streaking her face, round eyes expectantly looking up at me with a million unspoken words on her lips. So turned on, her hand had disappeared between her own thighs. So needy, the other had wrapped around my cock.

"Have I told you how beautiful you are?" I asked, kissing along her shoulders, nibbling and sucking her skin long and hard enough to coerce quiet sounds out of her. She was still playing with herself, and I kind of liked seeing her take initiative like that. After all, no matter how good she thought I was—an eleven out of ten, apparently—she could still do it better herself.

I turned her, back against my stomach, lips continuing to trail along her wet skin, shoulders, spine. "Hm? Have I?" I pushed, when all I'd gotten in response was her head thrown back against my chest.

"Maybe," she moaned. "I don't know. Are you—?" She cut herself off, and I wasn't sure if it was a shred of embarrassment or the fact that my fingers started playing with her nipples that cut her off. Maybe a combination of both.

"Am I what?"

She hesitated, threw a glance at me across her shoulder. She must've seen the same desperation, the same kind of visceral need, in my eyes, and it made her go on. "You're clean, right? You get tested regularly?"

And I knew exactly what the question insinuated, the second I remembered that the condoms were not here with us but on the other side of that door. The thought almost made me lose my breath. "Of course."

"Good." She sighed, and there was genuine relief in the sound and the way she aligned us. "I'm on birth control. Can you just fuck me?"

I slipped inside her, and it was the easiest thing I'd ever done. Wet and ready and perfect. Like she'd been molded specifically for me—or maybe I'd been made just for her. Her words cut off with sounds that, hopefully, were drowned out by the sounds of the shower. A moan that mixed with my own unapologetic groan in the air between us.

"Like this?" I asked, and she bent over without my instruction, holding on to the shower wall while I tried my best to support her weight with the arm around her waist. The other was still busy with her breasts.

I tested the waters. I needed to know how much of this I could take—how to draw it out long enough for both of us to have our fun. So maybe I'd last longer than a pubescent teenager this time around.

Slowly at first, I drew in and out of her. Feeling her walls clench around me, feeling myself twitch inside of her. Knowing every single thing she liked just by the way she arched her back a little farther, pulsed around me, or the string of little noises and sweet curses escaping her lips.

This, too, was like music to my ears.

I'd adjusted to the feel of her around me, and she must've adjusted to my size, too—tauntingly defying my rhythm and rocking against me, burying me inside her to the hilt. "Fuck," I ground out between gritted teeth, head thrown back, pace picking up. "I don't think anything feels as good as you, Val. I don't know if anything ever could."

Her response, as always, was a deep moan. Praise did that, I'd realized—when I'd told her how well she was taking my fingers, how proud I was that she was keeping quiet so well, a few days ago. It made her come apart at the seams, unraveled her from the inside out. It was no different now.

Our eye contact was unexpected. The way she glanced back, across her shoulder, and locked her eyes straight with mine had me stutter in my rhythm, made me twitch inside of her and forced me to stop, just until I knew I wasn't about to finish this thing early for us. The look she gave me was teasing.

"Scoring a goal?" she asked, then started moving against me, way before I'd been ready. Somehow, I managed to hold off the inevitable. "Doesn't that feel better than this?"

My head shook. "Not in a million years."

"Winning the championship last year?"

I was finding my footing again, matched her rhythm, then sped up. "Not even close, sweetheart."

The smile on her lips deepened, from teasing to appreciative. Her head fell back, her moan was drowned out by the water still raining down on us, and my full focus was on her. A world outside of this bathroom—the shower—did not exist. Her ass nestled against my crotch, and she was taking me deeper and better than I thought possible. *She* was better than I thought possible. Everything about her.

Her hands twitched against the tiles, trying to hold on to something and finding no purchase. Her breathing *had* been uneven, but now it was picking up. Her voice was hoarse, her moans more uncontrolled. And I just needed to see her.

Quickly, without much but that primal need, I turned her, pinned her against the shower wall, and angled her just right in my arms. For me to hit new spots inside of her, legs wrapped around my waist, and for her to finally find something to hold on to: me.

Watching her face contort, a soundless gasp on her lips, eyes closed, that was it for me. I had a minute, tops. One in which I needed to get her there, too. The showerhead was an option. My fingers weren't, but hers were; she'd used them earlier, so why not—?

There was a knock on the door.

A knock, then another, and an attempt to open the door. Then, probably right out of Valentina's worst nightmare: "Caden? Valentina? Which one of you is in there?" *Iris.*

I froze. Still inside of her, buried to the hilt, unable to move without the possibility of an orgasm that couldn't be timed worse. The moan on her lips died down to a frustrated groan, hopefully drowned out by the shower. I upped the pressure, just to make it a little louder. Just in case.

We exchanged a single glance, her brown eyes wide—in shock by what could've turned into the second discovery today, maybe. Or in desperation to come and knowing it had been delayed. At least I thought it had.

"Me!" Valentina shouted before her head snapped back in my direction. She circled her hips as best as she could while still in my arms, slowly, just once—as if she were testing the waters, too. And as if she couldn't help herself. "I was right there," she breathed, more of a frustrated complaint whispered against my lips. "You said I should do things for myself, right? Not care about anything else?" She was paraphrasing, but I couldn't find it in me to correct her when she moved again, and her head fell to my shoulder with another sigh. "This is what I want. You. Now."

And I was only just a man. Fueled by Valentina Rhodes, naked in my arms, moving on my cock—encouraging me. I shouldn't. We shouldn't.

"Ah." It came from outside, reminding me once more of the reason. That the way I was slowly dragging in and out of her was a bad idea. But how could it be, *really*, if it felt this good? "Have you seen Caden? Did you guys fight?"

I wouldn't necessarily call this fighting. The way her back arched and she leaned back against the shower wall, lips parted, hips moving against mine. Only when I nudged her, with a smile I couldn't have possibly hidden, did she remember to reply.

"No!" But her voice wasn't carrying the conviction it should have—it had been more of a whimper. An encouraging sound, really. So I picked up my pace. "Why?" Valentina added, before her lips parted in a soundless moan again.

There was a thud against the door, and Iris was probably leaning against it now. "I think he slept outside?" Her tone was a mixture of amusement and actual concern, I think. But I couldn't be sure; my entire focus was on Valentina. And the little sounds she usually made right before she'd come. My sign to keep it up.

My lips puckered around her nipple, and I could feel it, too. That sense of sweet relief crawling closer. Only that it wasn't crawling but sprinting. Fast and selfishly.

"Valentina?" Who'd been too busy keeping her voice down to remember to answer her best friend outside. "You okay? Did you slip and fall in there? Do I need to burst through this door?"

"No!" I chuckled against her skin at the gunshot of an answer, straightened back up, and put everything I had into what would undoubtedly be my last few strokes. "I didn't know he—" She swallowed another moan. "He slept outside. I thought he . . . went running. Or something," she added.

"Look at you," I whispered against her lips, a hair's breadth away from mine. "Doing so well. Taking me so well. Do you think you can be this quiet when we come?"

The words she'd soundlessly formed on her lips were exactly what I needed to see. *I'm about to. I'm close.*

Close was an understatement for me. My feet were dangling off the cliff. I was about to fucking fall.

"Tell her to look for—" She understood before I'd even said the name.

"Mike!" There were better things than hearing your girl moan another dude's name, but this was a delicate situation, and I'd excuse it. "I'm sure he—" Valentina squirmed in my grip, rolled her hips against mine, matching my rhythm, shuddering against me. "He'll know. Ask him," she managed to squeeze past her lips before another moan escaped them, whispered into my shoulder. Her teeth dug into the skin to keep those that followed quiet.

From outside, I think I'd heard a "Yeah, maybe," followed by departing steps, but Valentina twitched and pulsed around me, quite literally squeezing me to what might go down as the most spectacular orgasm of my entire life. And there'd been a few.

Around my hips, her legs were shaking. Her head was thrown against the wall I still had her pinned to, and her arms were around my neck, nails dragging across my back as she slowly blinked back into the present.

Into the reality where I'd fucked her in the shower, Iris on the other side of the door, and she'd come just seconds after her friend's departure. Who knew if she'd even made it out of our room yet?

And I think Valentina was realizing the same thing.

CHAPTER 28

VALENTINA

I admit, my logic was flawed. It didn't make all that much sense: sleeping with him to distract me from the fact that I'd slept with him—and that Alfie had found out. But you try to resist Caden Callahan, sex God and the only guy who'd ever managed to make me come through penetrative sex, and then we'd talk.

Apparently, not even another person there had been able to make me not want him. Even if that person had been my best friend, who could never ever find out about us. Even if that person had been talking to me through the door while he'd been balls-deep inside of me.

It had been a little thrilling, doing something I wasn't supposed to. Exciting and new, taking initiative. Thinking about myself. Saying yes to Caden—and everything that came with him.

He'd snuck out of our room after, pretended to come back from his run, and Iris was no longer worried about where he might've been. Mystery solved. Everything went back to normal. That didn't mean I'd forgotten, though.

The thoughts—and images and sounds—still fluttered through my mind six hours later. Of the surprise on his face when I'd continued moving despite our interruption and of the surprise on *mine*. Of those deep, guttural sounds in the back of his throat, edging me close when he seemed nowhere near it.

I'd never be able to shower again without thinking about him. How good he was—and how much better we'd been together.

But I wasn't in the shower, and this was hardly an appropriate situation to replay our sexcapades. In the kitchen, with all our friends around us, trying to cook a simple pasta dish and failing miserably.

Then again, his hand on my ass wasn't appropriate either, and here we were—on the other side of the kitchen island, leaving the rest of them to ruin the food.

"I think Valentina should help. At least she can cook." Iris scowled at Alfie, currently dumping a bunch of spices into what was supposed to turn into Alfredo sauce. "That's too much pepper!" she cried, then snatched it out of his hand.

Now Alfie was scowling, too. Synchronized, their eyes found mine, as if somehow I was responsible for settling their argument. My hands shot up, palms toward them. "Nope. I'm not getting involved."

"Too many cooks spoil the broth," Anni, on pasta duty, commented. Next to her, Mike was cutting up the cooked chicken. He'd been uncharacteristically quiet today.

"What she said," I agreed.

"Okay, then I think Valentina should be the *one* person that *doesn't* spoil the broth. She can cook. So why should we have to eat the mess he's spicing, when—ouch!" Iris rubbed the spot Alfie had hit. Even if he was facing the pan again, continuing to throw salt and parsley into the sauce, I knew he was smiling. Probably keeping from outright laughing.

I leaned onto the island separating me from my friends, and Caden's hand unsuspectingly slipped below the hem of my dress. Beside me, he was casually leaning against the same counter; if it hadn't been my skin he was grazing, I'd never guess what he was up to. The bored expression on his face was almost believable if it weren't for the tent in his shorts.

I snickered. "Exactly. Why should I rob you guys of a learning experience? This will be good for you. Now help Alfie instead of complaining." I laughed.

"Yes, chef." Iris turned back around, purposefully hitting Alfie's shoulder with her own. He nudged her back—and turned their cooking into bickering within five seconds.

"Who knew you could be so bossy," Caden muttered under his breath, head tilting when he finally looked at me. I'd been waiting all evening for our gazes to accidentally cross, but he'd been more careful since the Alfie incident, followed by the shower incident. I was glad for it because I'd thrown caution out the window. If I hadn't, he wouldn't be touching me the way he was now. His fingers wouldn't dance across my bare ass, and I wouldn't be playing with the thought of palming him through his shorts.

Clearing my throat, I stirred away from those images as best as I could. "I have my moments," I agreed and tried not to look suspicious. All their backs were turned toward us, chatter and the bubbling of water and the sound of the fan were filling the air, but we still didn't have to risk it.

He hummed in agreement, hands crossing on the island and leaving my skin cold and empty. His lips were by my ear, breath tickling my neck when he whispered "You sure do" before rounding the counter and helping Mike.

Or trying to. "Nah, man. I'm good," he said, voice so gruff, even Anni beside him was taken aback. By the look on her face—brows furrowed, lips parted—she had no idea what was going on with her boyfriend either. He hadn't said a word, and I hadn't seen him and Caden together in . . . a few days, at least.

"You can't let me at least pretend to be helpful?" Caden tried to joke.

Mike snickered, but there was no humor in the sound at all. Anni's eyes narrowed even before he spoke. "You're good at that, aren't you?" He wasn't even looking at the guy, just continued cutting up the chicken more aggressively than he needed to. I was afraid of what he might do with that knife once he was done with the meat. What he wanted to do, clearly, was use it on Caden.

"Excuse me?"

"At pretending you're helpful," he unnecessarily explained. "The same way you pretend to be *all in* for the team. Or that you want to be captain in the fall. Right?"

"Babe!" Anni finally intervened, but I wasn't looking at her.

Caden tensed, his fingers flexed, and his head tilted in confusion—or anger? I couldn't tell from here; all I could see was his profile. Which didn't look happy regardless. There was a tense silence in the kitchen; Alfie and Iris had stopped bickering, and the only sounds were the fan and the boiling water. But they didn't do much to fill the awkward silence either.

For a second, I thought I was about to see two grown men brawl. Although his back was still turned toward me, by his tone, I figured Mike was ready to punch his friend square in the jaw.

But Caden's hands shot up in surrender, eyes flicking across the rest of us before he said, with a fake lightness in his voice, "If you wanted all the chicken glory, you could've just said that." Then he kept himself busy by starting to lay the table and completely ignored the way Anni dragged her boyfriend past him into the backyard, then slid the door shut.

I grabbed the forks and knives and helped Caden with the table. *Pretending to be helpful.* "What crawled up his ass?"

Caden startled, and his eyes flew in my direction, like he'd been deep in thoughts before I rudely dragged him out of them. I was about to apologize when the scowl on his lips turned into a genuine smile, and he placed the next plate. "Fuck knows," he muttered. "Maybe he thinks I'm not training enough. Maybe he thinks I'm not good enough. Maybe—" He shook his head. "Maybe he's just in a bad mood."

"Right." I shrugged and came up beside him, a little too close. I placed the cutlery next to the plate he'd just put down. "So you're okay?"

Caden gave me a bright smile, perfect teeth and all. "'Course." Then quieter, closer, he whispered, "I don't think there's anything in the world that could ruin today for me. You were so fucking spectacular, Val. I'm still thinking about it."

And I knew exactly what he was referring to. Heat rushed into my cheeks, and I hurried with the cutlery, if only to get some space between us that would keep me from jumping him, right here, right now. From a safer distance, our eyes locked again, and by the smirk on his lips, he'd interpreted my reaction just right.

"I'm still thinking about it, too."

Just ten minutes ago, I'd been replaying the way he'd taken me in that shower. I'd been playing with the possibility of dragging him back up there to take another one.

"Still thinking about what?" Iris's cheery voice snapped me out of fantasy land and made me remember where we were: the very public, very open living room of Alfie's house, with all my friends gathered around.

Iris placed the pan of chicken Alfredo—enough fettuccine inside it to feed an entire village—on the trivet in the center of the table. Alfie was carrying two bottles of white wine and dumped them into the ice bucket we'd prepared beforehand.

"Oh," I quipped, trying to find an answer that wasn't *Thinking about the way he'd fucked me.* "Our run. We went running the other day."

"You run?" Iris's brows furrowed, her voice carried a note of disbelief as we sat down. Then, instead of a note, it turned into a truckload when she added, "I don't think I've ever seen you run." Her eyes flicked to Alfie, whose gaze had been jumping back and forth between Caden and me. "Have you?"

He shook his head too quickly. "Never," he said, and I gave him a warning look. *Don't fuck this up*, it said. *You promised.* "I mean, sometimes," Alfie corrected, fiddling with his fork until it clinked loudly against his plate. He was a mess. I'd never known him to be *this* bad of a liar. "Actually, yes. Now that you mention it. I've seen them run together a few times. At least once."

Now replace *run* with *cuddle*, and it wouldn't even be a lie anymore.

Iris was about to ask another follow-up question, but the door slid open, and Anni and Mike were back. Sitting opposite me, Caden tensed, gaze trained on his friend. Or captain? I could never quite figure out their dynamic, to be honest.

Without a word, Mike sat at the other end of the table, trying his best not to scowl—and failing, obviously. Anni, an apologetic smile on her lips, sat across from him. "Sorry for the wait. Shall we?"

And so we did.

The awkward tension was quickly forgotten once we'd noticed Alfie had done an amazing job with the seasoning. Iris had taken off her imaginary hat, bowed to him, and formally apologized for doubting his skills. In my direction, she whispered, "You still would've done it better." For which Alfie hit her shoulder again because Iris didn't have the ability to do anything quietly.

She was loud and boisterous and unapologetic, and it's what I loved so much about her. She fit like a missing puzzle piece into my inability to say no and turn into whatever the people around me needed. It was inspiring, really, how she was just Iris Zhang, no ifs or buts.

Just honest, funny, laughs-like-she's-dying Iris. And I was lying to her.

Three of us—sitting on the couch or passed out on the living room floor after dinner, wineglasses forgotten as we passed bottle two around like joints—were lying to her, and she had no idea. She was laughing with us like we weren't betraying the fundaments of our friendship and the pact it had been built upon.

I hadn't meant to drown my guilty conscience in wine. That logic was flawed as well because alcohol had the ability to remove the filter between my brain and mouth, and I often turned into a chatty mess once it got to my head.

"Never have I ever . . ." Anni paused in thought. "Ah, got it! Made out with my professor, then still failed his class." Very pointedly, she looked at Alfie, and, well . . . yes, he drank. After viciously glaring at her.

"Come on," he snickered, taking the bottle from his mouth. "We've all been there, right?"

We broke into what must've been the one hundredth fit of cackles and giggling of the night, and even Mike, still uncharacteristically quiet, suppressed a smile.

Iris looked around the room, assessing the people inside only for a second before saying, "Never have I ever had sex in public—wait, no!" she cried. "Now I have to drink." With a pout, she brought the bottle to her mouth, took a sip, then groaned. "I hate this game."

My eyes locked with Caden's, although I'd tried so hard not to look at him all night—scared that my need for him would be written all over my face. In the span of ten seconds, we'd had an entire silent conversation.

Does yesterday count?

Technically, no one saw us.

Someone could've seen us, though.

But they did not.

In the end, Caden won and gestured for a bottle, which Iris passed to him. She didn't seem surprised when he drank, but once I tipped my head back, bottle by my lips, she gasped.

Or screeched. Or outright screamed? With Iris, you could never tell.

"Valentina!" she shrieked. "When? How? What?" Her head flew in Alfie's direction, then Anni's. "What?!" she repeated. "How do we not know anything about this?"

Well, funny you should ask. It only happened yesterday. With a guy currently in this room. A guy you wouldn't want to see me with.

"Pretty recently." I cleared my throat, then decided to take another sip, because today was national flawed-logic day, apparently. "I don't know."

"Unbelievable," Anni commented, shaking her head in fake disappointment. "Are we even friends anymore?" Thank God her amused grin gave her irony away.

"Come on, then," Iris urged. "*Spill.*"

"I don't know—" I hadn't meant to look at Caden again, but this time my friends' gazes followed mine.

"Don't worry about Callahan. He can take some of the dirty details. Can't you?" she asked but didn't wait for a reply. By the smirk on his lips, though, it seemed Caden was just dying to hear about his performance. "He won't judge you. He's part of this now, and I'll cut his balls off if he does."

Laughter around the room again, but all I'd heard was, *He's part of this now.*

Part of our group. One of our friends. Equal to all of us, included in the NFR. My thoughts began spiraling, and I couldn't do anything about it.

Liar, liar, liar. How could you do this? She's going to find out, and she'll leave, and she'll take Alfie and Anni and Mike with her. You'll be by yourself again—because no matter how much effort you put into your friendships, no matter how many parts of yourself you're losing along the way, it'll never be enough. You'll never be enough.

Caden tried to intervene, and I appreciated the effort. "I really don't need to know what my bunkmate's been up to, Iris. Don't put those images in my head."

Iris threw her head back with a cackle, and once again I cursed Caden for his effortless charm and ability to make people laugh. My best friend shook her head, still smiling. "You're too nice. It's the puppy eyes, isn't it? She's used them on you?"

"I'm a victim," he agreed, not looking away from me.

"Aren't we all?" Iris sighed before blowing me a kiss. "Who's next?"

For the past ten rounds, we'd skipped Mike, who was beside me. "Never have I ever," he said now, eyes on Caden. Glaring, vigorously and unrelentingly. The easy smile on Caden's lips fell, like he knew the entire evening was about to change. Like he could sense it, somehow.

He was right.

"Never have I ever," Mike repeated, "wanted to quit soccer to work for Anova."

Out of instinct—because all our questions had been at least a little funny—Iris laughed, then immediately shut up when something in the air shifted. I think we all felt it: something falling off its axis, disturbing our carefully maintained equilibrium.

"What?" Alfie whispered to no one in particular. I think neither Mike nor Caden heard him. For both of them, the situation was clear as day; the looks they exchanged said as much.

"Excuse me?" Caden said regardless. Maybe in an effort to salvage what could be salvaged, he'd opted for politeness and manners? Maybe this was all just some big misunderstanding?

"Or maybe this one: Never have I ever thought about abandoning a team that's counting on me." Mike's voice might actually have been shaking—that's how angry he sounded. "Never have I ever been a selfish bastard. I think you'll have to drink, Callahan. Don't you?"

No room for misunderstandings, then.

Who the fuck had Caden told about Anova? If it hadn't been me who told Mike . . .

Caden's gaze snapped to mine. Gone were the knowing smirks, hidden smiles, and fiery looks he'd been sending me all night, and I had the awful feeling his thoughts had led him down the same path mine had. Only that he couldn't know I'd kept my mouth shut. And if he really hadn't told anyone else—

Right then, he wasn't thinking about Mike, the (very real) accusation, or what it might mean to either of them. His attention was still on me, and he was thinking one thing: *Why would she tell him?*

I knew it like they were my own thoughts.

I could sense disappointment before actually seeing it. Usually, Caden was tough to read. His walls were high, his facade flawless, and there'd been cracks only a number of times. Before every single one of my orgasms, there was this awe and wonder in his eyes that I didn't think he was faking. Whenever he spoke about his sister, his heartache and grief were *real*. I could add this moment to the list of times Caden Callahan's facade cracked.

His brows drew up, his lips parted, his breathing picked up—I could see it from here. He frowned, as if confused, then swallowed thickly, like he'd come to a decision. Then looked at me like he was about to do something he knew he'd regret. But he did it, anyway.

"My turn. Never have I ever lied to my friends," he said slowly, like a threat. "Never have I ever hooked up with Caden Callahan. Never have I ever *fraternized* within this group."

There was a ringing in my ears—growing louder, like it was getting closer somehow. Voices, drowned out around me, definitely talking to me. *What*s and *huh*s. But my vision had tunneled.

All I could see was Caden, opposite me. All I could see was the realization on his face that selling me out hadn't been nearly as satisfying as he'd thought.

A second later—or maybe a minute or ten—Mike dragged him outside, and I couldn't help but hope he still wanted to punch him square in the jaw. I'd give him permission now. I'd encourage it.

I blinked back into reality. Anni and Iris looked at me with wide eyes, mouths agape, probably pinching themselves to figure out if this was a dream—or nightmare. Alfie was fiddling with his hands in his lap, eyes trained on them vigorously.

"Valentina?" Iris asked, carefully, confused, dumbfounded. "What the fuck?"

CHAPTER 29

CADEN

The last thing I should be thinking about was Valentina. I should be worried about the guy I'd considered one of my best friends being ready to knock me out with a single punch. I should be worried about my future on the HBU soccer team. My possible future at Anova. My relationship with Mike. Whatever the fuck I thought I owed Alison.

Not a secret summer fling that shouldn't mean anything—one Valentina would've forgotten about the second we'd left Oakport, guaranteed. She hadn't planned on telling her friends, so the only logical conclusion was that she thought she'd never see me again to begin with.

That I meant about as much as Finnick Fucking Maxwell to her.

So she'd spilled my secret, and I'd spilled hers. I'd warned her. A few weeks ago, I'd basically threatened to tell her friends if she ever so much as thought about opening her mouth about Anova. Now she had, for whatever fucking reason. And so I had, too.

A promise was a promise. A threat was a threat.

And maybe it was better this way. Have her fuck me over before this—whatever *this* between us had been—could become an even bigger mess. Involving feelings and trust and, worst of all, an admission of both. Before I'd dismantled my walls, reached in, and given her my heart whole.

Before I'd given her the power to destroy it with a single, delicate squeeze. Like this had been.

Opening up, trusting, loving, only to end up losing that person the same way I'd lost Ali, completely and irreversibly.

Coming home from the hospital and still finding one of her plushies in the living room. Zapping through TV programs and getting stuck on her favorite show. Still hearing her laugh ring out in the hall, like she'd burst through the door any second. For a single second forgetting she was gone until the reminder hit me like a truck.

I didn't think I could go through that again. I'd rather be alone for the rest of my life. Keep myself locked up behind walls ten times as high as me and make sure not to let anyone slip through the cracks, like Valentina easily had.

"You don't even want to explain yourself?"

I shook the lingering memories off. It was dark, but I could still make out Mike's silhouette, the way he paced up and down, arms crossed, then uncrossed, hands flexing into fists, before uncurling. If one thing was clear, it was that he wasn't quite sure how to feel.

I shrugged, tried to steer my thoughts away from cherry-red hair, brown eyes, rosy cheeks. And failed. "Well. What's she told you?"

Honestly, I didn't think he'd heard me. That rush of anger clouded his judgment, drowned out his surroundings. All he noticed was that I'd said *something*, and it was enough to make him lose his fucking mind again.

I had a glimmer of hope our conversation would turn out to be productive once he'd let it all out. He cursed and shouted and continued pacing, and not for a single second of it did he look at me. At last, he asked, "How long?" His eyes finally locked with mine. "Have you known? How long have you been considering?" he corrected.

And how on earth would more lies help? "A few months. Since graduation, maybe."

"Dude." Some of the anger in his voice evaporated, like the truth was so devastating, he wasn't quite sure what to do with it. "You've got to be fucking with me. Why would you throw away everything you've worked so hard for?" He shook his head. "For some stupid job that'll still be there in two years?"

Because I'd never wanted it. Because I'd never done it for *me*. Because I'm selfish, but when it came to my sister, I'd give her the world—dead or alive.

Just with this . . . I wasn't sure if I could make the decision for anyone but myself.

All thoughts Valentina had put into my head, I begrudgingly realized.

I settled on, "I don't think it makes me happy, man."

And it was the first time I'd admitted it to myself as well. Unfortunately, Mike's reaction wasn't as understanding as I'd hoped. It was barely accepting.

He laughed, only to make a point. The boisterous sound echoed through the yard, bounced off the summerhouse and across the flat surface of the pool, illuminated by its lights below the water.

"Who the fuck are you, and what have you done to Caden Callahan?"

"Funny," I deadpanned.

"It's not," he shot back. "That's the problem, dude. You're captain—you were *supposed* to be captain, because the only thing that actually made you happy was winning. You didn't light up the same way when you aced an exam or went home with a beautiful woman—" He cut his own thoughts off. "This is about Rhodes. It has to be."

"It's got nothing to do with her."

"Stop lying to me. It's fucking insulting. You *like* her."

I snickered, tried to wave the accusation away like it wasn't a big deal. Like it hadn't taken a whole lot of mental strength to convince myself I wasn't. "Bullshit. When have I ever liked anyone?"

"Exactly. So what is it?" he challenged. "She's not going to grad school? You guys want to move to Boston together? She's promised you the world, if only you don't go back to school in the fall?"

"No." Talking about her shouldn't have been a big deal. The way he'd said her name should have been irrelevant. I tried to act like it was, but I gritted my teeth, clenched my hands into fists behind my back, and I didn't know why. Something about his tone, maybe.

"She doesn't like all the female attention you got as an athlete? She's scared you'll leave her for the next best cheerleader?" he continued guessing.

My hands continued flexing. My jaw tensed.

Either oblivious or aware of exactly what his words did to me, he carried on. "She wants to be your priority? Damn, Callahan, I never thought I'd see you this pussy-whipped. See you throw your life away for a good fuck—"

My hand twitched, one last time, before flying against his face. The force of my knuckles connecting with his face rang through my veins. Adrenaline rushed into every single part of my body, vision red, only for a moment.

"It's got nothing to do with her," I spat while he recoiled. "I don't know how much Anni would like you talking about her friend that way, though. Think twice, next time you put her name in your mouth."

He looked back at me, and no matter how great it had felt, I was glad to see he wasn't bleeding and that his nose didn't seem broken. Mike rubbed his jaw, glared at me. "God, you've always been so fucking oblivious." Again, he shook his head. "You're off the fucking team, by the way. I'm calling Coach Hepburn tomorrow, and I'll be damned if someone who didn't even want it takes my spot next month."

And maybe it was better that way.

CHAPTER 30

VALENTINA

I could fucking kill him. If this is going to cost me my friends—if breaking the NFR would make them leave, forget about me, and move on—I'd make him regret it. Then, in seventy years, after I'd died, I'd haunt him all the way into his own afterlife.

He'd never been worth this mess. All the men in the world combined couldn't be worth more than Anni and Alfie and Iris. Not even Caden. Not even the way he'd so effortlessly made me laugh, had been so understanding and sweet and kind. Had stayed when all the odds had been against it.

If he wasn't worth it, though, why was I still thinking about him now? The way disappointment had settled into his features, the way his brows had drawn together, his mouth had twitched into a frown, only for a second, before he'd gone and ruined my life.

"So," Anni said, "let me get this straight. You hooked up with him months ago and never told us." And I knew the tone in her voice was there just to make me feel more guilty. "Then he shows up here, and you *still* don't tell us." Side-eye from Iris. "Then you hook up. A few times—wait! How many times?"

I fiddled with my necklace, gaze skipping through the room to avoid theirs. "A few times sounds about right."

In my periphery, Anni shook her head quickly. Alfie was trying not to draw attention to himself and the fact that he'd been complicit since today. Iris hadn't said a single word. The blonde tutted. "Nuh-uh. Specifics. Number of kisses, sex, and *other* stuff."

I genuinely couldn't put a number on the times his lips had been on mine. Hundreds? Thousands? So I skipped it. "Twice," I said. "To the sex."

The first time had been last night, on the beach. Then again today, in the shower. I could feel myself blush just at the reminder.

"*Twice*?!" I didn't expect Iris's voice, and my head shot in her direction all on its own. Our eyes connected, and my stomach twisted: guilt and more guilt.

She'd been sitting on a chair dragged from the dining table to the couch, the wrong way around so her arms could rest on its back. "You couldn't even—oh, whatever." Iris got up so forcefully, the chair wobbled on the carpet. One more glance around the room before her eyes settled on me; the disappointment in hers was a thousand times worse than Caden's. A million times worse.

That was my best friend. Someone I'd confided in for four years—someone whose lap I'd slept in, whose hair I'd held back when she thought she could handle her drinks better than Riley Roberts (no one could). Someone who'd spent two weeks in my hometown with me because my sister had only been sixteen, and Mom had disappeared for a week—to where, I still didn't know.

Iris was everything to me, and she'd just fled the room because of something *I'd* done. Because I couldn't get it together and be honest with her. Because I'd been so scared of losing her, any sign of reason had been thrown out the window.

I wanted to follow, but Anni pressed me back onto the couch. Gently, she argued, "You should give her a minute. Talk to her in a little bit." And she was probably right, so I deflated below her touch. My face disappeared in my hands, accompanied by a loud groan.

"You're not mad at me?" I muffled the words into my skin, but she must've still heard.

"Confused," Anni corrected. "Most of all about how Alfie managed to keep a secret for"—she checked the time on her phone—"longer than eight hours."

I huffed, actual amusement in the sound despite my dire situation. Alfie, sitting on the floor, complained, "Hey!"

Anni ignored him, ran a hand through my hair—reassuringly and sweet. "She's not going to hate you." Thinking, she added, "At least not forever."

I knocked on the door to Iris's bedroom ten minutes later. I'd never been very patient, and this wasn't the situation to start practicing. Though I did wait until she beckoned me in with a curt, "Yes."

Her bed had the same blue sheets, and it stood below a round window overlooking the ocean. Iris always lived out of her suitcase on Oakport, which meant its contents were scattered all across the floor, and you could barely see the wood.

And I assumed she'd known it would be me as effortlessly as I'd known I'd find her like this: lying in between the mess of clothes, looking up at the ceiling, arms sprawled out. Her thinking pose.

I didn't wait until she looked at me, just started explaining, justifying, apologizing. All in one big jumble of words, messy and incoherent—and yet I was sure she understood every single word.

"Listen, look. *Iris.* I wanted to tell you—every single day I wanted to tell you, and then I thought of exactly this happening, and I couldn't. I tried once, and then Jason happened, and I just wanted to be there for you. Not hurt you *more.* I don't want to lose you over some stupid guy I—" *Don't even care about*, I wanted to say.

But I think it would've been a lie, and Iris could probably smell those on me right now. "Over some stupid guy," I repeated and settled on. "And I was trying so hard to stay away from him, you've got to believe me. I was mean and unaccommodating. And when he insisted on helping me with my bucket list, I just—"

She interrupted. "What bucket list?" While she hadn't graced me with a single look, she sat up, elbows behind her, to look at me now.

"My—" I shook my head, waving her off. "It doesn't matter. That's not the point." And I'd wanted to steer back to my apology and my explanation, but she wouldn't let me.

"It's exactly the point!" she roared as loudly and unapologetically as she usually laughed. "Valentina. If you honestly think I'm going to be mad at you for breaking some rule I made up when I was angry and heartbroken four years ago, there's something wrong with you." *There probably is.* "The problem isn't that you broke the NFR. It's not even that you lied to me. And we're not going to put Jason into that equation; he was just a convenient excuse not to tell me—"

I wanted to argue, then realized there was no point. She was right, wasn't she? I knew she'd been upset about Jason, but at the end of the day, was he that important to her? No.

Iris went on. "The problem is that I just found out my best friend likes a guy through some wordy, messy apology thing. Not because she wanted to tell me about it. Not because she thought I'd want to know. Only because she felt guilty and thought I was mad at her. You don't tell me—*us*—anything. What fucking list, huh? Why do you know everything about our lives but we know nothing about yours?"

I blinked at her. By now, she was standing in front of me. The look of disappointment on her face had morphed into hurt and anger—none of it, I realized, thanks to Caden but simply because *I* hadn't told her about him. For good reason, though. Right?

"Because no one cares!" I hadn't meant to shout the words. I hadn't wanted to raise my voice at all. "Why on earth would anyone care about some stupid bucket list I made because I was angry at my family? I was fine doing it by myself."

"You shouldn't be," Iris snapped. "You shouldn't be friends with people who don't care about your stuff, Valentina. We do, though. We care so much that whenever you suggest something, even though it doesn't happen often, there's always a loud, collective *Yes!* heard across campus. Because finally we can do or eat or see something Valentina Rhodes wants. We love you, dude. We want to be a part of your life because we like *you*, not because you say yes to everything we do."

Caden had said the exact same thing, and I didn't like that one bit.

Something glimmered in Iris's brown eyes, and I didn't want it to be tears—so I looked away and convinced myself it wasn't. "Sometimes it just doesn't feel like we're even friends, you know? If someone were to ask what your favorite food is or what you like to do in your free time, I'm not sure I'd have an answer."

And the way she looked at me was devastating. Any anger from earlier had evaporated to make space for the hurt in her tone and features. For the way her voice wobbled, her lower lip trembled, and her brows had drawn together.

I swallowed thickly. "I don't think I'd have one either."

What would you like to eat? *I don't mind.*

What do you want to do? *I don't mind.*

Where should we go? *I don't mind.*

Do you want—? *I don't mind.*

By accommodating everyone else around me, I'd forgotten about someone much more important: myself.

By not wanting to be a burden, I'd burdened myself. Denying myself things I didn't even know I'd wanted to do—all manifested in that small, messy bucket list hidden in my notebook. I didn't even know why I'd been hiding it.

Iris fell around my neck, squeezing me in a tight hug and with a single sniffle against my shoulder. And I'd never been more relieved in my life.

As an olive branch, I said, "After graduation, when Mom didn't care and Lisa barely acknowledged it, I was so angry, I made this list with things I wanted to do this summer. For myself, you know? Because I don't think I've ever done anything for myself. But I don't know why I didn't tell you guys. I'm sorry."

She huffed, bringing some distance between us to look at me. Her eyes were dry again—or at least drier. The smile on her lips was faint and pitying, but at least she wasn't frowning anymore. "It's just sad." Iris sighed. "That you think you have to do anything by yourself. We would've loved to be part of whatever you want to do."

"Well . . ." I hesitated, only for a second and out of sheer habit. "There's still one thing left."

CHAPTER 31

CADEN

Mike had stormed off, and I couldn't even tell you in which direction. All I knew was that he didn't go back inside, so that's where I headed.

His words still floated around my head. *You're off the fucking team, by the way.* I should be panicking. I should call Coach Hepburn before Mike got the chance, explain the situation, and beg to keep my designated spot. I should be on the phone right now, pleading and crying if I had to.

It's what Alison would've wanted, right? *Be the best soccer player the world has ever seen. Or at least your school.* Those had been her words, and didn't I have a duty to honor them?

Don't you think if she had to choose between success or happiness for you, she'd choose the latter?

Valentina—and her words of fucking wisdom—snuck back into my brain, flying around, wreaking havoc and destruction in what had been a neatly aligned code of conduct: If Alison would want me to do it, I'd do it.

And now, kicked off the team, captain spot basically gone, I wasn't even panicking at the thought of disappointing her. Because maybe she wouldn't be all that disappointed. Maybe she'd be proud that I'd finally managed to get out and finally got to do what I wanted.

When I slid the door shut behind me, the house was silent and, apart from the living room lights, dark. I couldn't hear arguing through the walls, yearlong friendships destroyed over some No-Fraternization Rule that had been broken, and I didn't *want* to be relieved.

I wasn't sure if the silence was worse, though. That not knowing what was going on—where Valentina was, if she was fine—was more unbearable than knowing she'd never look at me again. That once I'd get back to our room, I'd find her having moved into the detached unit above the garage. If I'd just insisted on sleeping there a few weeks ago, maybe none of this would've happened. Then again, I wouldn't have gotten to know her the way I had either. Wouldn't have touched her or kissed her or made her laugh.

Our room was actually empty, and a sense of dread formed low in my stomach. But at least her things were still there—pillow and blanket, suitcase and her clothes in the top drawer (I'd just peeked inside, really, to make sure she hadn't actually left for good).

If she wasn't here, though—and by the sound of it, her friends weren't either—then where the fuck was she? And why the fuck did I care? Instead of worrying about my future, I was worried about *her* again.

Of course I would be.

Standing in the middle of our room, I went through the worst-case scenarios and got stuck on the one: She'd run off, left her friends clueless and confused, and they'd gone after her. It was way past my theoretical Valentina-could-still-walk-around-alone-without-the-risk-of-being-kidnapped-or-worse curfew—close to midnight, for sure. And if she was out there by herself, frantically running around or hiding in secluded spaces to avoid having to explain this ... *thing* between us to her friends ...

I shouldn't worry, though. She wasn't my concern anymore, and it wasn't my responsibility to make sure she was safe. A grown adult could take care of herself. A grown adult who, apparently, had spilled my biggest secret to the one guy she wasn't supposed to tell. I kept trying to remember that.

Valentina Rhodes sold you out. Valentina Rhodes is the reason you just got kicked off the team. Valentina Rhodes pretended to care and listen, only to run to Mike and tell him everything.

But she was also the only person who'd ever encouraged doing what *I* wanted instead of blindly focusing on my could-be soccer career, which would most likely end the day I'd graduate from Hall Beck University. The only person who'd rightfully told me Alison wouldn't want me to play if it didn't make me happy as well.

I shouldn't worry about her, but I did—and I think I was starting to realize why.

I think I'd known for a while.

CHAPTER 32

VALENTINA

"Something touched my foot!"

"I can't see anything!"

"This is so scary! I want to go home. *Please.*"

There was crying and screaming and laughing, water splashing while my friends paddled for their life like they might've forgotten how to swim properly. All I could do was laugh, floating on my back, our clothes all scattered by the shore of the small lake (the open sea seemed a bit too dangerous at night).

During the day, it was beautiful here. White, sandy shore, calm, relatively clear water, and hidden from view by rows of trees. At night, all it really seemed was scary.

The water was dark. The trees didn't feel comforting anymore, like someone with bad intentions was hiding behind one of them, ready to drag our naked selves out of the water one by one.

Naked because we'd gone skinny-dipping. Naked because—after Iris told them about the bucket list, scandalized as if it had been a hit list—my friends insisted on being part of at least one of the items. Then made me promise to go through most with them again. *"We can skip the sex part,"* Alfie had joked. *"You've got Caden for that,"* Iris had added, giggling.

And my heart was so full, knowing I'd messed up and knowing they were still there. Realizing I didn't need to be perfect to be loved by the right people.

"So everything else—" Anni interrupted herself with a squeal, paddling a few feet away from where she'd probably touched some algae or a slimy stone. "*Ugh*! So everything else on this secret list, Caden did with you?" she tried again.

I nodded before realizing they couldn't see. Stood upright, felt something slimy touch my foot, then screamed just like Anni had. "Yes," I hissed, still attempting to get away from whatever had grazed my ankle.

One of the first nights, he'd slept outside because he hadn't wanted to leave me by myself. We went for a run—my last, for obvious reasons. He'd invited himself to join me on my full-moon walk. He'd tried to show me how to play pool. I'd watched the sunrise while he'd still been asleep beside me, after we'd had sex on the beach. He was the law I'd broken, so technically, he'd been there for that one, too.

"How did I not realize how much time you were spending with him?" Anni sounded genuinely disappointed in herself. "I literally thought the only time you two interacted was when you slipped into your respective beds and said good night."

"Turns out, it wasn't always their *respective* beds," Alfie threw in, and I knew if we could see him, he'd wink. Maybe he did regardless.

I snickered, half amused, half annoyed that he kept bringing up his accidental walk-in. "Probably because I was very focused on *not* having you guys realize."

"How do you think he felt about the fact that he was your dirty little secret?" *Iris.* "Can't imagine it was nice. Did you ever talk about that?"

"No," I said even before thinking about it. He didn't seem like the type of guy it would be an issue for, seeing as he didn't do the whole serious dating thing anyway. Why would he care about things like that if he didn't care about me in the first place?

"Why would he just tell everyone now, though?" *Anni.*

"He thinks I told Mike about the job," I guessed. It was the only explanation I could think of. He'd warned me a few weeks ago.

You tell anyone about this, and I'm arts-and-crafting a banner that says Valentina Rhodes slept with Caden Callahan *and hanging it in the living room.*

A collective *Oh* echoed across the water's surface. Then, "No, that was Finnick."

"*Finnick*?!" Literally the last name I would've thought of.

"We went to the boardwalk a few days ago, remember? You and Caden stayed home, and—" A loud groan from

Anni. "Oh my God. It was *so* obvious. Anyway, we ran into Finnick, talked a little. He asked where you are, if you're okay because he hadn't heard from you. Then if *that* guy was your boyfriend and if he ended up taking the Anova offer because he knew someone who worked there or something. Mike exploded the second we were by ourselves. He was *so* angry. I wouldn't be surprised if they're currently fist-fighting in your backyard, Alfie."

"It's a shame we're missing it," I grumbled and slowly but surely made my way out of the water. It was getting cold, and I could not deal with another fish that was probably just a piece of algae touching my skin. My friends followed. "I'd love to see him suffer, just a little bit."

Anni gasped. "Valentina! I don't think you've wished harm on anyone before. Who *are* you?"

"No one has ever spilled my deepest, darkest secret—"

Iris tried to interrupt. "Because you—"

"Never have any secrets, I know. But *still*."

"Well, he kind of thinks you spilled his biggest secret. And in comparison, his seems a little more . . . serious?" Alfie winced, towel around his waist as he pulled a sweater over his head. "Sorry. But it's true."

"Oh, shut up." I dried myself off, keeping an eye on the suspiciously dark trees lining the lake. Just in case—of what, I didn't know. "Are you guys on his side or mine?!"

Silence.

"Okay, ouch," I added. "Got it."

"Well, it's just—" But Iris took it upon herself to finish Alfie's thought for him.

"You hooked up with the guy months ago. When you see him again, you're—these are your own words—rude and unaccommodating. Then you hook up anyway but make him promise not to tell anyone. He doesn't know if it's because you're embarrassed or what, but he goes along with it because he clearly likes you—"

"He doesn't *like* me."

Iris ignored my objection. "You spend time together outside of just the physical aspects of your relationship."

"Not a relationship either." But I got ignored again.

"Then, when he thinks he can trust you, you stab him in the back. Or, well, he thinks you stabbed him in the back. I love you, Valentina, but you were kind of the dick in this situation. And," she added, quickly, "I never thought I'd get to say that."

"Honestly, I'm kind of proud of you," Anni muttered in amusement. "In a weird, morally gray way."

So I slipped into not only my shirt and shorts but a thirty-pound suit worth of guilt.

I *had* been the asshole, hadn't I? I'm sure if I'd asked Reddit, they'd lay all the reasons out for me, in more detail than Iris just had.

All the way back to Iris's beloved Bronco (she was already talking about how she had to let her go in two weeks). I couldn't shake the feeling. Something in my stomach curled and uncurled approximately every thirty seconds, which were the intervals of remembering another awful thing I'd done to Caden.

Hypothetically, if he did like me more than a . . . platonic bunkmate/fuckbuddy, I'd used him shamelessly, acted like I'd been embarrassed by whatever thing there was between us, and made him swear not to tell a single soul. Like Iris had said: my dirty little secret. Since when did *I* have dirty little secrets? In my twenty-three years of life, the possibility had never even occurred to me.

So on the way home, I'd tried to make sense of that. As the only one who didn't drink tonight, Anni drove, and Iris sat next to her. Alfie and I shared the back seat. Their conversations were animated, laughs and gasps flew through the otherwise silent night as we rushed back home.

Meanwhile, I'd been silently preparing for the inevitable conversation with Caden, apparent dirty little secret of mine and the guy I obviously liked. At least more than I'd wanted to admit for the past few weeks. It was a weird combination, I knew that: You didn't usually want to keep the guys you liked secret. And you wouldn't usually describe them as dirty either.

But here we were.

CHAPTER 33

CADEN

Although today had been a lazy day in, I'd probably reach my ten-thousand-step goal if I didn't stop pacing around our room soon regardless. It was almost three in the morning and neither Valentina nor her friends were back. If I'd been worried before, I was officially losing my mind now.

I'd tried to keep myself busy—mostly to (1) not stalk through the night trying to find a girl who probably never wanted to talk to me again and (2) not mourn whatever loss that last realization could bring with it.

So I'd read through that Anova offer another thousand times—on top of the two thousand times I'd already done—only to make a decision I'd most likely regret. Very soon, on top of that.

I'd paced the room after that and hadn't stopped until now. When the door creaked open, a familiar face and cherry-red hair peeked through the crack. I immediately stopped dead in my tracks, like prey noticing its predator—unsure whether to run or hide. Whatever she decided, I realized, I'd be completely and utterly at her mercy. There was no running or hiding, just accepting. Whether she'd spare me or tear me to pieces. By the look on her face, I couldn't tell which was more likely.

Only that she was beautiful, even when I was supposed to be mad at her, and especially when her red hair was wet and streaky and parts of her white shirt had turned damp and see-through.

"Hi," she said, closing the door behind her cautiously to lean against it for support. The way her eyes bore into mine, I might need that support to stay upright, too. My toes were tingling and my knees felt weak, and I didn't know why—she was *just* looking at me.

My voice was more hoarse than I'd anticipated when I replied, "Hey." I cleared my throat, diverted my eyes only for a moment to feel like I could actually breathe again. The anticipation might seriously kill me. Not knowing what was going through her head and not knowing what I wanted to go through mine.

I *should* be mad at her. I should be furious at the way she'd broken my trust. And I should at least try to channel that, right? No matter how much I just wanted to fall into her arms and pretend the past three hours had never happened.

So I cut her off. Her puffy lips had parted, and she'd been about to say something. I'd never find out what.

"You fucked me," I burst out, and I hadn't been all that sure what I'd say until the words hung in the air between us. She blinked at me, a little perplexed and a lot . . . *understanding*, which, arguably, made it worse. If I was supposed to be mad at her, she couldn't be understanding. She couldn't show even a shred of decency because I'd fall for it. The second she apologetically batted her eyes at me, I'd be done.

"Caden—"

"No." I shook my head, maybe in the hope it would blur my view, make her disappear from the forefront of my mind. "You fucked me, Valentina. I trusted you, and you ran to—"

"I didn't tell anyone!"

Unsurprisingly, it was easier to lean into my shred of anger than come to terms with that other emotion taking up the rest of my heart and body and soul.

"Bullshit," I snapped, taking a few steps toward her. She did not back away—didn't press farther into the door or shrink into herself. "I didn't tell anyone else, and Mike said it was you." Or at least hadn't denied it when I'd mentioned her. That's worth about as much. "You got me kicked off the team, all because you couldn't keep your mouth shut—"

Valentina's eyes narrowed, and whatever compassion had been in her features slowly turned into something else. Anger, maybe. Annoyance or exasperation. *Good*, I thought. Justifying anger was much easier when the other person was fighting back.

"You did the same thing, you know?" she muttered, voice low but firm. "You almost cost me every single person I care about, Callahan. Where's your apology for that?"

I didn't like the second wave of relief that washed through me at hearing the word *almost.*

"Oh, come on," I huffed, steering away from the feeling. Stepping closer again, until it was inches separating us, not feet. Until my body cast a shadow over hers, and she had to look up to meet my eyes. "You can't honestly be surprised. I warned—"

"Threatened," she corrected. "You threatened to tell on me if I tell on you. Only that I. Didn't. Tell," she spat. "But you did."

"Come on!" I repeated, exasperated, angry, tired of hearing the same stupid excuse. "No one else knew. McCarthy sure as shit didn't tell Mike because he would've done it three months ago, not now. You were the only other person I told. You were the only person I trusted enough to tell—"

Something rattled her stoic expression. Her brows twitched, drew up—only for a moment, in surprise, maybe, and something else entirely. She swallowed thickly, like she didn't expect the admission and wasn't quite sure what to do with it.

"What, are you surprised?" I snorted in fake amusement. "Yes, Valentina. What a shocker: I trusted you!" I repeated, the anger I'd tried so hard to summon coming easier now. "Every time I told you about Alison. Every time I listened to your advice and stupidly thought, *Hey, it seems like she might care about my well-being after all.* I didn't talk to you about my sister and childhood because I thought it might get me laid, you know."

She fiddled with her necklace, and her eyes diverted from me for the first time. Probably because playing the dead-sister card was as uncomfortable for her as it was for me. But it was valid—wasn't it? I'd confided in her, trusted and stupidly cared for her. How dare she throw all of that back in my face?

"Why, then?" she asked, and her voice was only half as loud and fierce. Barely a whisper, really. "Why'd you tell me?"

And for some reason, she slipped right back through the Valentina-sized crack in my walls. After I'd just managed to get her back in front of them—for five minutes, but still. Her tone had been so soft, her question so hesitant. Her round eyes flicked back to mine, lashes batting against her cheek.

And it disarmed me, plain and simple.

"You know why." *She must.*

I hadn't exactly been subtle about wanting her, about the spell she must've cast on me. From the very minute she'd stepped into this room, I'd been enchanted. Honestly, since I'd woken up in my bed without her months ago, I hadn't been able to stop thinking about her.

Valentina shook her head, like she was putting two and two together as well and couldn't quite come to terms with it. Couldn't quite believe it, no matter how reasonable it seemed.

"I don't—" She cut herself off. "What's your endgame, Callahan? *What* do you want from me?"

I barely had to think about the answer. "The truth, an apology," I began listing, and she wanted to cut me off, I could tell. I didn't let her. "Then you."

Somewhere in the past five minutes, I'd come to terms with it. Staying mad at Valentina, looking at her and not wanting her, was unrealistic. She had me so thoroughly wrapped around her little finger, and she didn't even know it. The way she blinked at me, perplexed, and her lips parted in that same way, I could tell she was oblivious to the power she clearly wielded over me.

"Caden," she said, and my hand moved all on its own. I tugged a wet strand of hair behind her ear, then couldn't get myself to pull back. Her face in my hand, her chest unevenly rising and falling just inches away. "I'm being serious, I didn't tell Mike," she said, voice low. My brows furrowed. I'd opened up again, and she still—"Finnick did."

My mouth shut. I'd been ready to argue and immediately reeled back that instinct. And I didn't like the way it sounded when I asked, confused, "Your Finnick?" I grimaced, then corrected, "Finnick Maxwell?"

Her lip twitched, despite the situation. "Not my Finnick, no. But yes, Finnick Maxwell." I hated how much I liked her clarifying the former. "He overheard us talking at Blitz, remember? Some sister who worked at Anova?"

It was like the lightbulb above my head lit up.

I *did* remember. He *had* overheard. Valentina never opened her goddamn mouth, and I still—

My gaze shot to hers, eyes wide, a million things in them that I couldn't interpret myself. "Fuck," I cursed. What else was there to say? She hadn't fucked me; I'd fucked her. "Fuck, I'm—"

"I know. I'm sorry, we shouldn't have talked about it so close to him, but I—"

I blinked at her, rapidly. "What? Why are you apologizing?"

Now *her* brows furrowed, confusion replacing what had definitely been guilt in her features. *For what?*

"He was there because of me. He heard because of me. He told the rest about Anova because he was asking about—"

"You," I figured, and she nodded, looked away. Shamefully? "That still doesn't mean it's your fault," I explained, tilted her head back up to look at me. "*I'm* sorry," I finally said. "I should've fucking talked to you before just telling your friends about us." I realized that now—about four hours too late. Jumping to conclusions had always been my thing, though. "I shouldn't have—"

"You're not blaming me?" she asked, perplexed, cutting me off.

"You didn't say anything, did you?"

"No, but—"

"No, then. If you didn't say anything, it's obviously not your fault."

She blinked at me. The past fifteen minutes seemed like a roller coaster of emotions for her. From guilty, to confused, to angry, to perplexed—back to guilty, then perplexed again. "And I am sorry," I repeated, just to add to it. Exaggerating, I said, "I hope you can find it in your heart to forgive me."

And thank God, it made her laugh. Like a burst bubble, the sound catapulted past her lips. She giggled, and I knew she didn't mean to when her hands shot up to cover her mouth and her head fell against my chest to hide it.

"I'm sorry, this is not a laughing matter," she said, but I could still hear her smile.

"Val"—my hands wrapped around hers, guiding them away from her face, making her look at me again—"there's no need to apologize for laughing. It's the most beautiful sound in the world."

Her lips pursed, brown eyes wide. *Caden*, she mouthed, almost like a warning. And I wasn't sure if she'd meant to actually say my name and the words had simply died on her lips. She looked at me like that might've been the case.

"What?" I tilted my head, couldn't help the hint of a smile on my face, given the same thing happening on hers.

Instead of answering, she got onto her tiptoes, wrapped her arms around my neck. Her body was almost flush with mine, and her back hit the door behind her. She placed a single kiss on my cheek, and that innocent touch from her did more than any much-less-innocent touch from another woman could have. Shot blood into my cheeks, made my skin tingle and my heart skip a beat. "You need to stop," she whispered against my skin before kissing my jaw, then my neck.

My head fell back, eyes closed, all my senses focused on the way her lips felt against me. Distractedly, I asked, "Stop what?"

"Saying things like that if you don't mean them."

My gaze snapped back to hers. Lids heavy, breath heavier. "You can't possibly still think I don't."

She shrugged, letting her eyes trail the room behind me. Behind my neck, I could feel her hands fidgeting. "You're not exactly known to care about the girls you sleep with."

"You're not just a girl I slept with though."

And just like that, her attention was on me again. Gaze flicking from my eyes, to my lips, and across the rest of my face. Restlessly, she took me in, tried to figure me out. Her breath hitched, just lightly, but I was attuned to her quirks better than my own.

"No?" she asked. "What am I, then?"

Technically, she wasn't anything to me. The question shouldn't be what she was but what could she be? What did I want her to be?

Fuck holding back. Fuck my fear of opening up and losing her.

"Everything," I breathed onto her lips. "You're everything, Valentina."

And she looked at me like she might feel the same way.

CHAPTER 34

VALENTINA

Mild afternoon sun. Green grass so vibrant, it seemed painted. Ocean glittering a beautiful blue. A bench by the edge of a cliff, overlooking it all—and my friends, panting and gasping for air and, for once, not laughing.

Exercising had never been a laughing matter to them.

From all possible directions, complaints flew my way. Demonstratively, I shook my head. "Don't even start." I snickered loudly. "*You* guys insisted on doing the entire list with me."

Alfie, still slumped forward, hands on his knees, was wheezing. "We could've skipped the run."

"We *should've* skipped the run," Iris agreed. She hadn't even made it to the bench, just collapsed onto the dusty ground, where she'd stayed.

The only thing keeping me from suffering as much as they had was my own amusement. I couldn't miss this moment of victory because I was so exhausted that my legs were about to give in. *Priorities.*

"I've killed your friends," Caden noted from behind me, amusement in his tone. A second later, his arms wrapped around me, and his chin rested on top of my head. He kissed my hair once, quickly, and none of my friends even batted an eye at it.

Less than a week ago, I thought they'd go into cardiac arrest. I thought I'd be kicked off this island, never to be allowed back, thanks to the pull Alfie's family had.

But nothing.

Just Caden, touching me sweetly—for once, appropriately—and my friends, still glaring and swearing and breathing very heavily like he wasn't even there, focused only on their previous run. "I'll need at least half an hour to recover!" Alfie muttered, and the rest agreed enthusiastically before he threw himself onto the bench, taking up the entire thing.

"I think you might have," I agreed with Caden, laughed, and turned in his grip until his blue eyes connected with mine and I could see the corners of his lips turn upward. "I thought the worst you could do was drive them away from me. But you just killed them straightaway."

He shrugged. "I'm efficient like that."

I hummed as I swallowed another laugh. I think he knew exactly where my eyes went, even without turning to follow my gaze. I watched Mike a few feet away, doing burpees, for some reason. "How'd you get him to join without plotting to kill you?"

In the past week, they'd still kept their distance. When Caden entered a room, Mike left it. When Mike suggested doing something, Caden knew better than to give his opinion. It was like watching two twelve-year-olds' petty fighting, only that they were stuck in the—very well-trained—bodies of two mid-twenties guys.

Like I'd guessed, Caden knew exactly who I was talking about. "Oh." He waved me off. "We hashed things out."

My gaze snapped back to his, eyes narrowing. "When?!"

Because I hadn't noticed any hashing out, only petty behavior from both of them.

"This morning." And he couldn't help his laugh, probably because my face told him I didn't believe a word he said. I kind of had to, though—Mike was here, wasn't he? And not as a favor to Anni. "He offered me my spot back. As team captain."

His words hung between us, breeze ringing in my ears. Last week, right before we'd made up, Caden had accepted the Anova offer in Boston. When he'd told me, there'd been tears in my eyes, and I think there might have been a single one in his—not that he'd ever admit to that. But it had been a big deal, deciding against what he thought Alison would've wanted. Taking a step toward his own happiness and putting himself first, for real this time.

Abandoning the soccer team and letting Coach Hepburn know that he wasn't coming back. He made me promise not to tell anyone, but he'd asked me to hold his hand throughout that call. After he'd hung up, he'd kissed each of my fingers and muttered thank-yous into my skin, until—unsurprisingly—we'd ended up naked.

In the past week, we'd been boyfriend-girlfriend-ing a little too close to the sun, and sometimes I'd forget we weren't. He wasn't my boyfriend, and I wasn't his girlfriend.

"And?" I asked, trying to get away from my spiraling thoughts, hoping to lead them somewhere other than the status of our relationship. So back to soccer, and Mike, and that captain thing. "What did you say?"

My heart hammering loudly in my chest hoped it was *no.*

"I thought about it," he admitted, then slowly walked us closer to the edge of the cliff, presumably to get some privacy. Below us, waves crashed against the sharp edges of stone protruding out of the water. Loud and rough and unapologetically cruel to whatever got caught in them. "*Really* thought about it, you know?"

"Like you haven't really thought about it for the past three months?" I tried to sound amused, but the attempt fell flat.

There was no need to pretend I didn't care about whether he did or didn't go back. He knew I wanted him to take the job almost as much as I knew it.

He shrugged. "Well, you'd be at HBU now," he said. "That's a plus I didn't need to consider before."

"Caden—" I warned, but he held up his hand, effectively cutting me off.

"I know, I know. I was supposed to make this decision for myself." Because if Caden Callahan—self-proclaimed *most selfish asshole in the world*—wasn't putting himself first, how could I be expected to? *Me*, Valentina-has-never-once-made-a-decision-for-herself-and-doesn't-even-know-what-being-selfish-feels-like-Rhodes. "But you can't expect me to not at least consider it, Val."

I pouted. It was so sweet, I couldn't be mad. Still, I whispered, "I hope that's all you did. *Considered*."

His lips quirked. He let my words hang between us, and I think it was deliberate, the way he made me wait. The way he was letting my anticipation build, almost until my patience snapped in two. Another minute, and I might've slapped him whether he went back to HBU or not. "Don't worry, I'm still employed," he finally said.

My entire body sagged in relief. If Caden could do it, I could, too.

If Caden could make that decision for himself and not for his sister, I could start saying no, too. I could start suggesting my preferences without being scared of everyone else hating them. And even if they did, it would be fine. That's how it worked, right?

People didn't just abandon you because you suggested pasta for dinner when they wanted sushi.

"It's just," he continued, sitting in the grass and beckoning me to join him, "you said she'd want me to be happy above all else, right?"

His mouth twisted, and he was probably reconsidering his choice for the ten thousandth time. "Soccer just doesn't do that for me anymore. I don't want to go pro, so what's the point of staying just to play another two years? Once

I'd finish grad school, I'd have to make the same decision, anyway. Get a PhD—continue playing for HBU—or start working and finally stop running away from my actual life to live one for my sister. One she doesn't even *want*?" He sighed, exasperated, probably exhausted by the thoughts that had been haunting him for . . . a while, at least.

His head fell on my shoulder, and I couldn't help but smile at the familiar scent of his shampoo. His hair was much longer by now, blond dye slowly growing out. "But I still feel terrible."

I leaned against him, played with his fingers in my lap, when he added, "Plus, I'm leaving you."

My hand froze in his, and my gaze stayed ahead to not accidentally make eye contact.

Beautiful view, really. Behind me, I could hear Alfie's, Iris's, and Anni's faint chatter and Mike's heavy breathing—all louder than the wind howling.

"I shouldn't be part of that equation," I huffed, basically whispered. I wasn't nearly important enough to influence a decision like that. And I definitely shouldn't be the reason Caden stayed when he so vehemently wanted to leave.

At that, he sat up. "Why not?" he asked, and I could feel his eyes on me, studying my profile. Then, out of the corner of my eye, I could see his nose twitch before he huffed, half amused. "Because this is a summer-fling thing? Because you thought you'd go back to HBU and never see me again?" His head shook. "Is that why you wanted me to take the job so badly? Because it meant I'd be gone—"

"No!" Finally, I did turn toward him. "I wanted you to take that job because you clearly want it. And because if you can choose for yourself, then maybe I can, too."

His features softened, and relief spread through every bone in my body. The last thing I needed him to think was that I *wanted* him gone—when there was nothing I wanted more than locking him into my room and never letting him out again. (Who needed daylight and fresh air, anyway?)

"Val, baby," he cooed, and his brows rose in understanding, "you're already doing that."

"What?"

"You're already making decisions for yourself, and you started way before I could've had anything to do with that," he clarified. "When you did your bucket list. Then again when you decided hooking up with me was worth the potential wrath of your friends—although I guess I did have *something* to do with that one." I hit his arm playfully, but all he did was laugh. "And now," he continued, "not worrying about keeping your friends busy and entertained but just sitting here, with me."

And I guessed he was right, in a way.

"Look at us," I huffed, unsure how to react without the tinge of irony in my tone. "Finally adult enough to look out for ourselves."

The corner of his lip twitched upward, but he sobered up quickly, looked at me with so much appreciation in his gaze, I didn't know where to put it all. "I'm proud of you.

Really." Then he did laugh. "And I'm not just saying that because I know it turns you on."

"Caden!" I gasped—and laughed and blushed and hid my face in his chest.

His hands shot up in playful innocence. "What? I know you inside out, sweetheart. And it only took me two months."

"A month and two weeks," I corrected, because the time before going back to HBU for grad school was holy to me.

"A month and two weeks," he corrected himself, nodding. "Imagine the things I can find out if you give me six months. Or a year—*ten*."

I looked back at him slowly, not quite sure what to expect behind those words. Amusement in his features? Genuineness? I wasn't sure what was worse either—but I did know what I'd hate more. And it brought me back to where our conversation had started.

"You're going to Boston soon," I noted, like it was reason enough not to get both of our hopes up. "I'll be at HBU, and you'll be about a hundred and fifty miles away."

"And?"

"It's very far, Caden." I felt like I was talking to a toddler then. Explaining very slowly and very patiently why we couldn't get fast food on the way home.

"It's not even a three-hour trip," he said. "Two hours and forty-one minutes."

I knew where he was going with this, and I—"No." I shook my head. "You can't actually be considering—"

"I am." His voice was even, like it wasn't even a question. Like there was no room for arguments and no matter which one I'd bring up, he'd have at least three rebuttals, anyway. And then, like he'd heard my thoughts, he said, "Unless you tell me you don't want me, I'm not arguing about this."

I blinked at him, dumbstruck and speechless. He smiled, satisfied. "So?" he asked. "Do you want me?"

Of course I did. My body had known before my mind had been able to catch up. I wanted Caden in every way possible—whispering filthy nothings into my ear, tickling my back until I fell asleep, making us smoothies for breakfast, knowing I'd hate them.

But that wasn't the point.

"You can't drive a hundred and fifty miles God knows how many times a week," I argued instead of answering.

"I can."

I shook my head. "I don't want to be a burden—"

"You've never been a burden, and you never could be. I'd drive across the entire country for you, Valentina. HBU is a stone's throw away. An easy commute."

"Caden—"

His smile alone cut me off. "Do. You. Want. Me?"

And it burst out before I could stop it. "Yes."

"Great." He nodded, smile wider than I'd seen it before. "Then we'll figure the rest out. Together."

CHAPTER 35

CADEN

August slipped away. Those last two weeks on Oakport felt like a good soccer game: fun, exciting, then suddenly hearing the final whistle telling you it was all over—when you felt it hadn't even really begun. When you had another good couple of minutes in you.

And I couldn't make use of them.

Valentina attempted to heave her suitcase out of the house—until I took it from her with a scolding look that immediately died when she smiled at me. "Didn't I tell you I'd take care of it?"

She rolled her eyes, handed it over, then kissed me on the cheek before we moved toward her car—or the thing that would hopefully get us from point A to point B (I still wasn't sure if it could be classified as a *car*). "You did," she admitted. "But I thought—"

"You thought you didn't want to bother me," I guessed. Correctly, by the way she hit my arm playfully.

Valentina opened the trunk for me, and it made a loud, squeaky noise before I maneuvered her suitcase inside. The . . . *car* bounced a little on impact. "But *I* thought," I began, pretending to think long and hard—only my smile gave me away—"I told you you'd never be able to do that."

"Bother you?"

"Mhm," I hummed, then pulled her closer and leaned against the car, carefully, in case it decided to break under my weight. I wouldn't be surprised. "You're capable of a lot, but annoying me isn't one of those things, Valentina."

She pressed her lips to mine, short and sweet. "Not even if I'd start being mean to you again?"

"I kind of liked it," I argued, only to hear and see the laugh that tumbled out of her a second later. Her arms wrapped around my neck, and my hands automatically slipped into the back pockets of her jeans.

"Oh yeah," she remembered. "The degradation kink."

The next words, thank God, were neither mine nor hers: "I'm going to be sick!" Iris announced, pretending to gag as she waltzed out of the door into the front yard. "Can we go back to two weeks ago, and I'll just pretend to be really mad about this?" Her finger flicked back and forth between Valentina and me. "Only so I don't have to be reminded of how painfully single I am every time I see you two together."

Valentina laughed when she turned in my grip, pressing her back against me. My arms easily wrapped around her stomach, pulling her closer again. Maybe because I knew I'd be gone in three days. Because I was starting a job in a different city and it would be the first time we'd be apart. Because I already missed her, when she was literally in my arms—ass nestling against my crotch.

She knew exactly what she was doing, but instead of acknowledging it, she shouted back at Iris across the yard. "You never say anything when it's Anni and Mike!" she cried, outraged and amused—and still wiggling against my lap. My hands around her tightened, and she swallowed a yelp.

"Because I'm used to it from them." Iris leaned against the same car, finally making Valentina stop moving.

Too late, though. I was hard as a rock, and I knew she knew. The triumphant look she sent me over her shoulder said enough.

"I'm—" Valentina stopped herself, then went on to say, "Not sorry."

Iris gasped, my hands fell away from Val's waist to clap ironically, and she pretended to bow for us. "Thank you, thank you," she repeated over and over again.

The clapping grew louder when the rest of the group appeared in the yard, one by one leaving the house. Alfie was last, locking it behind them. "What are we clapping for?" Anni asked despite all three of them having joined in by now.

"Valentina is *not* sorry!"

Two more gasps, identical to Iris's. A second later, they all burst out laughing. Three seconds later, they were in each other's arms. Like they'd planned it, Valentina and Iris broke into a sprint at the exact same time, running the few yards until Alfie and Anni met them in the middle.

Their group hug was a mess. Limbs entangled, screeching and "Ouch, my hair!" audible every now and then. Cries of "I'll miss you so much!" when they'd see each other in exactly five hours back on campus.

Alfie and Iris.

Valentina and me.

Anni and Mike.

The latter leaned against the car next to me now. "If you don't say goodbye to me like that when you leave for Boston, I'll be pissed, dude."

"I'll kiss you goodbye, and I'll make it sweeter than the farewell party the team threw you a few months ago." Mike was done studying, which meant everyone had known he'd leave the team. He had his master's, and he was moving to New York at the end of fall. Still a few weeks left, but he wouldn't be on campus all that much—to pick up Anni, if at all. So the party had happened right after graduation.

"We'll throw you one even sweeter." He laughed, nudging my side.

"And I'll actually be able to drink at this one." I sighed wistfully. "No captain making me feel bad for *letting down an entire team* because I wanted to have *one* beer."

Mike only shrugged, the same nostalgic expression on his face that must've been on mine. Despite the stress and the headache and the fact that I didn't like soccer all that much anymore, the past four years on the team had been great. The past four years with the boys even greater. Winning and losing alongside them, learning and growing into the men we were today—it had been an honor, and I'd miss them.

Until now, I hadn't really thought about that at all. I'd been so focused on how little I liked the sport and how much I wanted to get away from HBU, I'd stopped appreciating it. Even if something wasn't for me anymore, that didn't mean I couldn't appreciate the time I'd spent with it. And one thing ending only meant something else was just beginning.

Valentina fell around my neck, buried her head in my chest, and let her hand run through the hair at my nape that had gotten way too long in comparison to its usual neat trim. She sighed against me, let herself go limp, and wasn't at all surprised when I picked her up. Her legs simply wrapped around me, and she clung to my neck a little harder.

"All done?" I asked lowly, right into her ear. She nodded before emerging from the depths of my neck.

"All done. Shall we?"

In response, I carried her all the way to the passenger side, opened the door with one hand, and let her gently slip into the seat. "Are you sure you don't want me to drive?"

"Very."

"And are you sure you know *how* to drive? She's . . . special." *She* being the car.

"Less sure," I admitted. "But I'll figure it out."

And I only stalled the car once before we drove home.

Home. Not the place you grew up in or an overpriced apartment you rented but where your heart felt full and your smiles were wide and you knew, no matter what, the people around you would never leave.

I let my eyes drift off the road just once, very quickly, to look at *my* Home, in the passenger seat, smiling back at me.

EPILOGUE

VALENTINA

Four months later

Last year, I'd spent New Year's Eve at the Pressley mansion in the Hamptons. I'd made the mistake of posting an Instagram story about it, and my sister had been hounding me to take her there ever since. I didn't hear from her often, but about that, she'd remind me once a month: *It looks so pretty! I need to go! When was the last time you did anything for me? Come on!*

Not like I'd been doing everything for her since before she could remember. Cooking, cleaning, keeping us alive when Mom couldn't.

And we pulled up to the faintly familiar house exactly a year later regardless. Because I wasn't great at saying no anyway, and it got damn near impossible when it came to my sister. Besides, Caden wouldn't have let me. The second

I'd mentioned her desperate need to go to a Pressley party, he'd been on board. Like Lisa had briefed him before, he'd turned into her biggest advocate in a matter of seconds. Now I understood why.

After I'd been moved into the back seat and they'd been talking about the latest trends in hair, makeup, and clothes for the past . . . I honestly don't know how long it'd been. After I'd seen the way he looked at her and I'd remembered Alison would be about Lisa's age now.

He'd gotten my sister out of her shell faster than I'd ever seen before. Her judgy looks had been directed exclusively at me, she laughed at his jokes, and she hadn't yet told him how *weird* something he'd said had been.

All things I'd been having to deal with for years.

Lisa—blonde hair in a high, sleek ponytail, black, tight dress ending just above the floor—started making her way to the adjacent room, where the bar was.

"She loves you," I noted casually, a flute of champagne in one hand, the other resting on Caden's arm.

"No." He shook his head. "She doesn't even know me," he reminded, gaze trailing back to her. "She's just so much like—"

"Alison," I guessed, and he nodded, swallowed thickly. "Hopefully, your sister was a little more grateful than mine." I snickered. "She loves you so much, she's completely forgotten about me. The reason she's here, by the way."

Caden huffed a laugh, and his arm curled around my side before he pressed a kiss on the top of my head. "I tend to have that effect on the people close to you, don't I?" he said jokingly.

I rolled my eyes, but I couldn't deny it. He added distractedly, placing another kiss against my hair, "You still smell like fresh dye. Or the aftertreatment." Which must've been a leftover from yesterday's last-minute attempt to freshen up the color. Not every day were you invited to a billionaire's estate—even if your boyfriend's best friend was dating said billionaire.

"So do you, then," I countered, because we'd thought, *If we're already dyeing my hair, we might as well do his.*

Our hair-dyeing fit had resulted in a freshly blond buzzcut at three in the morning, when we'd finally been done. My cherry-red hair had already been dry when we'd collapsed into bed, only to be woken up five hours later by our alarm to pick Lisa up from the airport.

I snuck a quick kiss to his lips before turning back, watching my sister hesitantly parting the crowd. I nodded toward the glass in her hand. "Hopefully that's sparkling water?"

Which got me the sixth judgy look of the night before she added, "Don't be weird, Valentina."

Of course, I thought, but I couldn't help but feel good when she decided to lean against the wall beside me regardless. I eyed her carefully, watched her smack her lips in disgust, grimacing as she wiped the champagne taste from her lips. I didn't comment.

Caden excused himself with an apologetic glance, then hurried over to Dylan and Athalia on the other side of the room, presumably to thank them for letting us stay the night in one of the approximately one thousand guest rooms.

Alfie's summerhouse was nothing compared to this.

Sofas and tables had been moved (to God knows where), and the large entrance, connected with the living room, served as the main space of the entire party. Marble floors, shiny chandeliers, a front of windows overlooking the garden, the pool, the rosebushes.

Dylan and Athalia stood by the glass front, chatting and laughing with her brother, Henry, his arm around a beautiful brunette, curly hair in an updo. The ring on her finger, diamond probably visible all the way from the moon, shimmered in the low light whenever she scratched her neck or tugged a strand of hair behind her ear or generally just gestured.

With everything I'd heard about Henry Pressley, that was probably the point.

Lisa sighed beside me, and the sound immediately drew my gaze to her—usually a sigh meant bored or disappointed or unhappy, and I couldn't have her be any of those. I was supposed to be *cool* sister right now. Cool sister who took her to cool parties. Parties that were fun, not boring.

But her eyes flicked across the space, and she didn't look bored at all. "This is disgusting." She raised her glass in emphasis. "How do you manage to keep it down at all?"

It was stupid, I knew that. But this was the first time my sister had asked for advice on anything. The first time she'd voluntarily engaged with me without necessarily wanting something. I'd always chalked it up to age, puberty, and our not-quite-usual upbringing and hoped she might grow out of her dislike for me. Maybe I'd been right—and maybe hoping hadn't been completely . . . hopeless.

I huffed in amusement. "Anni always says, 'Muss nicht schmecken, muss wirken.' Or something like that." I was sure I'd butchered the German pronunciation horribly. "Which roughly translates to, *It doesn't have to taste good; it just has to work*. Meaning—"

"As long as you get buzzed, it's worth it."

"Exactly. Just don't tell anyone I'm giving an underaged girl drinking advice."

She laughed—*actually laughed*—then held out her pinky for a promise. I was almost too stunned to reciprocate and probably caught it a second before she would've pulled back.

"Promise." This time, when she sighed, my alarm bells didn't go off. As furiously, at least.

Lisa's lips thinned, and despite herself, she took another sip of champagne. She tried to hide her first reaction, which would've probably been a disgusted shiver. "I wish we'd always been like this," she said after a while.

Although her tone was casual, the rest of her screamed the opposite. She was stiff, absentmindedly played with her earring, took another sip to seem busy. Identical to my telltale signs of nerves and anxiety. "Like what?"

"Close." The clarification shot out of her. "Closer, at least."

"Seriously?" And I couldn't help the tinge of annoyance in my tone. "You've been pushing me away since you learned how to push, Lisa."

My sister rolled her eyes, let one hand glide across her sleek hair. "Because you never acted like a sister. Because it was always *Do your dishes. Clean your room. Have you done your homework? When are you coming home? Have you heard from colleges?*"

"Come on," I tried to argue. "That's not fair, and you know it."

With Mom being at least emotionally absent, Dad being physically absent, too. "What was I supposed to do? Run the whole thing by myself? Not expect you to do the bare minimum?" Now I took another sip of champagne for comfort—and accidentally drained the whole glass. "Not give a shit about you or your future?"

"No. I don't know." Lisa sighed again. "I guess I just wish I'd known earlier that I had this cool sister who gets invited to amazing parties, has a perfect boyfriend, and lets me drink underaged. Not just a second mom."

Cool sister. Perfect boyfriend, too—but *cool sister* had come first, so that must've meant something.

"Don't tell anyone about the drinking," I repeated, my warning draped in amusement. "I'm serious." I wagged a finger at her, and she giggled.

Giggled like she had back when Dad had still been there and Mom had still been fine. Back when Lisa had still liked me. Back when I was still allowed to be a kid.

Before I'd become that second mom to Lisa and she'd kind of lost her big sister in the process. It had been necessary, yes, but that didn't mean it had been fair for either of us.

"I'm sorry," I said, but to my surprise, Lisa shook her head, rolled her eyes in amusement and sincerity alike.

"You're always sorry, Valentina. Maybe it's time to demand some apologies, for a change."

Which I'd take as her own stubborn way of apologizing. Reaching the height of puberty, I probably wouldn't get more out of her.

Before I thanked her, or—God forbid—started crying, two strong, familiar arms wrapped around my waist, pulled me into an even more familiar body behind me, accompanied by the faint smell of hair dye and conditioner. Caden placed a kiss on my cheek, and Lisa, demonstratively, turned back to the crowd.

"I agree with her," he whispered into my ear, lips grazing my skin. "Demand apologies for a change, Sweetheart. Also," he added, "you said you guys don't really get along, but . . ." Caden trailed off, and I shrugged, turned until his blue eyes met mine.

"Apparently, she realized I'm cool," I pretend-bragged. "She didn't know her sister gets invited to cool parties and has a *perfect* boyfriend."

"Perfect, huh?"

My eyes rolled at the way he wiggled his brows, but I couldn't help my laugh. I never could when Caden was involved. The past four months had been giggles and smiles and giggles again. Even though we didn't see each other nearly as often as we'd like.

There were FaceTime dates every Wednesday, where we'd cook the same meal and eat it watching the same show—and we weren't allowed to watch it without the other. Fridays he'd get to HBU around ten, and he'd always bring me a new book to read the following week while he was gone; it's dramatically upped my reading game, and I might actually hit my goal by the end of the year, even if I'd been much less productive on Oakport.

Some weekends, we'd watch an HBU game or go out with Iris, Alfie, and Anni—all doing a graduate program—others, we'd only move out of my bed to get the food we'd ordered. Balanced, cozy, *perfect*.

"Perfect," I repeated. "Or so she says."

Caden snickered, kissed me, then pulled me into his chest, like he might never want to let go again. Despite the crowd around us, despite the loud music and chatter and drunken yells, for a moment, it felt like there was no one else. Just us.

And although I knew perfect people didn't exist and perfect moments were rare, any moment spent with him felt a little like one of them. Every time our eyes connected and he smiled and called me *Val*, or *baby*, or *sweetheart*, I had to remind myself that I *did* deserve this.

Caden had taught me how to let go, fall, and trust that someone was there to catch me, no matter what. That I was worthy of love, and from him, I could demand it—take what I needed and more, without the fear of losing him.

That I loved him just as much as he loved me and that we both deserved exactly that kind of love. Not perfect but special.

Calm, fun—and one of a kind.

EXCLUSIVE BONUS CHAPTER

VALENTINA

Three years later

There was something oddly educational about your graduating class coming back together years later. You found out that the guy you knew in passing from a beer pong championship crowning was a teacher now. The straight-A student with bright career prospects went back for another undergrad degree. And a random guy on your school's soccer team was playing the World Cup.

Granted, Henry Pressley wasn't just a *random guy*, but he was still a guy my boyfriend had played with for years. A guy my boyfriend had probably scored against.

I shifted on Caden's lap, turning over my shoulder to ask, "Have you fouled Henry Pressley before?"

His attention went right past me, glued to the screen where the opposing team's national anthem was ringing out. For a guy who, two years ago, never wanted to hear the word *soccer* again, he seemed mighty interested now. There wasn't even a ball on the field, but every single pair of eyes in the room was locked in on a game that hadn't even started yet.

Out of HBU's twenty-eight-strong roster, twenty-seven of Caden's former teammates were sitting in Athalia Pressley's living room for a watch party she'd planned. The twenty-eighth was the reason for said watch party.

Athalia had planned this since her brother had first been scouted for a potential addition to our national team. So Dylan had added her to their group chat, and the rest, apparently, was history: fifteen months later, and here we were. In her apartment, watching her brother in the starting 11 of the most important soccer game of his career. His international debut, just two years after graduation.

"Did you say something, sweetheart?" Caden muttered, eyes still not on me. One glance around the room, and every single guy looked just like him.

The white of Athalia's designer couch was barely visible below the piles of bodies on top of it. A space that was designed for six people, max, was being occupied by at least twelve. Caden and I were squished in tightly between Blake, in the corner, and Dylan, who Athalia sat on top of. The ring on her finger seemed new and expensive. It must've been subconscious, the way she held her Solo cup perfectly to show it off.

Mike had thrown himself onto the corner piece the second he'd arrived, hours before the game even started, but his dedication and determination were paying off now. With the most space for himself—which still wasn't a lot—Anni benefited on top of him.

How they'd managed to fit five more people between us wasn't my business. I was comfortable enough on Caden's lap, and he seemed comfortable enough with me on top. So comfortable, he kept forgetting I was there to begin with.

"Yes, I did say something," I muttered sweetly. "But it seems like you're never going to hear it."

Finally, and it had felt like hours since the last time it happened, Caden's eyes snapped to me. He pouted, amusement and apology on his face. "I'm sorry, I'm sorry. It's just—"

"Soccer," I finished for him, then sighed a kiss to the tip of his nose.

"One of my best friends playing the World Cup," he corrected.

"You were *not* best friends." I couldn't hold back a laugh. "I bet you barely talked!"

"Val," and Caden sounded earnest, shifting below me to properly look me in the eyes when he continued, "everyone on the team is best friends. We're a family."

Athalia leaned over, and since we were sitting so close, it must've barely been five inches. "Objection," she deadpanned. "I know of at least two guys who weren't family." A not-so-subtle glance at Dylan, who was watching just as intently as the rest, probably trying to spot his ex-nemesis. "Funnily enough, they're the only two people forced to be actual family now." And again, she raised her hand in our direction, wiggling her ring finger.

"You guys are missing the point." Caden again. I wasn't sure if he was embarrassed or just *really* convinced of his relationship status with Henry Pressley, whom the camera had just focused on during the national anthem. The entire room erupted into cheers.

It was sweet, honestly, to see a group of mid-twenties guys so unapologetically enthusiastic about one of their friends. Athalia agreed when she said, with a smile on her lips, "I've never seen them this happy. Not even after winning the championship."

"This is a lot bigger than the NCAA," Dylan muttered in her direction.

Which let Athalia point at her fiancé in emphasis. "See!" she said to underline her point. "Even he's excited, and they despise each other."

"The World Cup isn't just bigger than the NCAA, princess. It's most definitely bigger than some petty feud between your brother and me."

The two broke out into a whispered argument full of giggles and eye rolls and what I assumed to be flirty teasing, judging by the way both of their cheeks reddened with time. Caden was locked in on the TV again, eyes as wide as a little kid's on Christmas morning spotting his presents for the first time.

Objectively, it might have been the cutest he'd looked in the two years I'd known him. His blond buzzcut freshly cut and dyed for the occasion, blue eyes twinkling, skin glowing. All because he was watching someone he knew play soccer on the big screen.

I couldn't help the kiss to his cheek, and the appreciative hum in the back of his throat warmed my belly *and* my face.

"You proud of your best friend?" My undertone was teasing, but he didn't seem to catch it.

"Very." The camera panned across the field, showed the two teams getting to their positions as the stadium cheers bellowed through the speakers, almost as loud as the boys' chatter around us.

They were clearly nervous, all twenty-seven of them. It was contagious; otherwise, my hands wouldn't be fidgeting in my lap, too.

"I mean, look at that," Caden continued as his head nestled onto my shoulder. His embrace around my middle tightened. "That guy used to lose against Harvard with us, and now he's playing the Netherlands in the World Cup. Same position and everything."

The commentator on screen was saying close to the same thing: "It's incredible to see Henry Pressley on the field already. Just three years after his MLS debut for the New York Blue Eagles, he's quickly filling his father's shoes. Or should I say jersey?"

"Same name and number on his back, you're right. He might actually fill them out quicker than we think," the other added, excited. Or as excited as commentators got. In comparison to the people in this room, he sounded monotone. "He's good."

"Fast."

"Really smart with his attacks and passes. Incredible pass ratio. Damn near identical to Felix Pressley in his prime."

The two on TV went on, but the second Caden pressed a kiss to my neck, it became really hard to focus on what they were saying. Or care about it in the slightest.

"Are you having a good time? I feel like you're not having a good time. I'm distracted—"

"Don't worry about me." I cut him off, turned just enough to look at him over my shoulder. "I'm a big girl. If I'm not having fun, I'll get up and do something else. And honestly . . ." I hesitated, not sure whether I should go on. Three years ago, I wouldn't have even played with the thought.

So much honesty, so little room to hide behind lies and deceit to make the people around me happy. "It's nice. To see you like this," I went on. "You haven't been excited about soccer in a while. It's nice to see you remember why you loved it so much."

His mouth quirked, and the small part of me that would've lied and said *Of course I'm enjoying myself. How could I not?* was relieved nonetheless. That I could be honest with him, say what was on my mind without worrying about saying the wrong thing.

People-pleaser Valentina wouldn't have dared to bring up the fact that she'd noticed his forced aversion to the sport that had meant so much to him and his sister years ago. She wouldn't have dared to let him know that she wasn't a fan of the development either.

Not here, at least. In the middle of a crowded room, on his lap—where the risk of a public fight was much higher.

But Caden just huffed against my skin, nodded in agreement. "We're all still in town for a few more days. We were thinking of playing tomorrow . . ." He trailed off, then picked up another thought. "I haven't really—" He shook his head. "Since I quit the team. I think I might want to give it a try, now that . . ."

Now that he was settled. Now that he had a job that he liked and dealt with the guilt his sister's death had left behind. Now that he'd gotten professional help and his therapist had been successful in finally convincing him of what I'd been telling him all along:

Your sister loved you much more than she loved soccer. Your happiness would be much more important than what sport you play. And, most importantly, *You need to live your life for yourself.*

I think the reality of that was slowly sinking in—and the possibility of enjoying both soccer and his life outside of it was, too. The team definitely helped. Seeing Henry living his dream did, too. I think.

He didn't want to finish his sentence, and I never forced him to. Mostly because, after thirty minutes of pretalks and anthem singing, the game finally started with Henry Pressley in our national team's starting 11.

*

Through the entire first half, everyone on the couch was so tense, I'd almost fallen off Caden's lap, and he barely managed to catch me. Whatever girlfriends were still left had decided to move into the open kitchen behind them after that.

We were not allowed to talk above a loud whisper, as per Mike's instructions. At which Anni shook her head vehemently, then continued speaking *louder* than she usually would.

"Personally," I muttered, hopping onto the kitchen island just as they went into halftime, "I would've just kicked the ball into the net."

No idea why every single head shot in my direction. Or why they were all scowling.

Anni laughed but kept an eye on the guys behind me in case they took my controversial statement to heart. So far, she seemed relaxed enough to say, "Can't be all that hard. Run. Receive. Score."

"Twelve-year-olds play that game! So—"

But Caden wouldn't let me finish the sentence, and I was still trying to get over Anni's betrayal of not warning me when he slid between my legs and got comfortable there with a playful glare. "Be careful what you say next, sweetheart."

"Why?" My voice lowered, my smile widened. "You going to punish me for it?"

It was always so easy, switching between loving-kindness and cruel teasing with him. Half an hour ago, I couldn't believe I got to watch him enjoy soccer again, and now, I couldn't imagine anything better than teasing him about it.

But the glare on Caden's face blew away as easily as Henry's goal opportunity in the twentieth minute, when he lost the ball to a fast guy in an orange jersey and an unpronounceable name on the back of it. Caden's eyes widened instead, the teasing frown on his lips turned into a smirk. He came closer, leveling our faces and leaving barely five inches between them. "I could."

My head tilted. "Yeah?" I asked. "Right here?"

"The bathroom," came his rebuttal. Way faster than expected. "Wouldn't be the first time—"

"Or the second. Or third."

At the memories, blood shot into my cheeks and, by the looks of it, into a different region for him altogether. His hands found themselves on my waist, squeezing, massaging, making me wonder whether the bathroom really was a viable option.

Two years down the line, and still, all it took was one little touch of his to get me going. That was one of the million things that had never changed between us.

Just like my heart still skipped a beat when he entered a room I was in. Like every *I love you* still felt like the word *home*. And every kiss left butterflies behind.

Caden still did that to me, easily and unavoidably.

So while we didn't escape into the privacy of one of Athalia's many bathrooms—"Fifteen minutes is not enough for what I want to do to you, baby"—watching him jump off the couch, screaming and cheering as our national team scored their 1–0 against the Netherlands, was probably even nicer.

Seeing him happy. Enjoying a thing he used to love, then force himself to like, then avoid completely. Watching him celebrate with friends he hadn't seen in a while and completely fucking losing it when we got to the ninety-minute mark and Henry had officially won his first match.

Beside me in the kitchen, Athalia had tears in her eyes.

On the screen, Paula did, too. Holding her very pregnant belly and screaming louder than any fan in the stadium until her husband ran all the way across the field, into her arms.

I wondered whether I looked at Caden the same way she did and very quickly decided yes. Full of love, adoration, pride.

And although my boyfriend hadn't won his first international championship game, I was just as proud of him for choosing not to pursue a career that hadn't been for him—and now finding his way back to a hobby he used to love.

The little things. It had always been the little things with us.

Just the way we loved it.

ACKNOWLEDGMENTS

When I started writing this book, I was on the verge of falling in love—so close, I could practically taste it. I was convinced this would be my most romantic novel to date. Instead, Valentina and Caden turned messy and disagreeable and not quite right for each other (while somehow still being exactly what they both needed?), and you can probably guess why!

Oakport, Calentina, their perfectly imperfect group of friends, and everyone's cameos seemed perfect to say goodbye to Hall Beck University (for now), and I'm so immensely grateful for every single person who's come along for the ride. I look back on the past year at HBU with a heart so full, I don't know where to put all the love and gratitude I feel.

Thank you to my publisher for letting me write these books, feeling like home, and generally being the greatest. For letting me throw ideas at them until one sticks and being the most enthusiastic cheerleader for those that do.

I couldn't have written *Lessons in Falling*, a book about friendship and authenticity above all else, without the inspiration that my friends grace me with every single time we hang out. Fiona, Anna, Celina, Anastasia, thank you for being as unapologetically yourself as Iris, as generous as Alfie, and as unintentionally funny as Anni.

To my grandparents, thank you for giving me my first taste of Girl Trips at the ripe age of eight—taking me and my friends on holiday every year since. I'm sure that incessant need to write about friends on holiday wouldn't exist without you.

Linda, thank you for telling me about that time you shared a bunk bed with your crush. Valentina and Caden will forever be in your debt because they wouldn't exist without you.

Thank you to every single person who has picked up this book, perhaps those that came before it—and maybe even the ones I have yet to write. Doing this is a dream come true, and I am so grateful I could burst.

Lastly, if you were able to relate to Valentina's need to be as small as she possibly could be or Caden's tendency to put his loved ones before himself: You can be yourself, and you can choose yourself. People will only love you more for it.

ABOUT THE AUTHOR

Selina Mae is a writer of romance and reader of (you guessed it!) romance and has been compensating for her lack of meet-cutes by writing them into her rom-coms. When she's not writing, you will find her rereading her comfort books or crying at happy endings.

Keep reading for an excerpt from
Ashwood Anthology* #1: *Ruled by Rivalry
by Selina Mae

THE NEW YORK GOSS
ELLIOT ASHWOOD: THE COMMON MAN

When you hear the name Ashwood, you think luxury. What started as designer fashion has, over the years, grown into an empire that's almost impossible to keep track of.

But we don't have to tell you about the hotels, the champagne, the galas, or the dozen industries that make Hunter Ashwood one of the wealthiest men alive. Only that their evergreen share prices are dropping—and fast.

In a recently resurfaced video, Elliot Ashwood, youngest of the Ashwood boys, is seen incoherently babbling about their designs: "I wouldn't touch anything coming out of Adeline Ashwood with a ten-foot pole."

Pair that with the underage drinking on display, the beautiful brunette with her head on his lap, and the fact that he took a shot at the Ashwood legacy college as well—"That's why I'm . . . not in Bumfuck Nowhere, Connecticut. I didn't want to go to Yale because fuck Ashwood. Fuck everything we've built."—and you can see why investors aren't exactly thrilled.

While we care less about stock prices, market share, and whatever else our finance friends at *The New York Goss* love to obsess over, we can't help but wonder what the fallout from such behavior will be.

Elliot has since issued a formal apology (damage control, anyone?), but the numbers haven't bounced back just yet. And maybe that's why a source close to the family told *The New York Goss*, in an exclusive, that the Ashwood heir has now been made to take an unpaid internship at Adeline Ashwood. Not just to win back investor trust, but to show the public he's a changed man.

We certainly want to believe it! But will his good looks and charming smile work as well on Wall Street as they do on social media? That remains to be seen. One thing we are sure of? The public is going to love watching the smug heir fall from grace—straight into the life of an unpaid intern.

CHAPTER 1

Even now, my mother remains the most organized person I know. She's the reason I wake up at six every morning to go for a run. She's why I'm determined (almost to a fault) and don't give up. She loved fashion, so I studied it. Graduated with honors and got the internship opportunity of a lifetime.

Whenever I got to visit home, I made sure to tell her headstone how far we'd come.

While I was in the city, my best friend would have to do. Pressing my phone tighter against my ear, I dodged another rogue local with a face that told me he *would* become physical if I got in his way. "I don't think an intern gets to—no, I don't think so. If I get to style your boyfriend, Paula, I will let you know!" I added with an airy laugh.

"If you're styling my boyfriend, I expect to be consulted."

"*Right.* The girl who can't make a decision to save her life and almost showed up to a first date in sweatpants . . . wants to consult me on fashion choices."

"Hey!" I could hear the amusement in what she tried to sell as outrage. "Technically, that was not a first date."

"No, it was worse. You were already in love with the guy," I deadpanned.

Finally, her laugh rang through the speaker, mixing with police sirens and honking cabs and one angry Italian accent yelling, "Stop pissing on my sidewalk!"

Around me, people frowned at their screens, squeezed through the dense rush hour crowd, and loudly complained about tourists stopping a foot short of them to take photos of a particularly tall building. My smile seemed out of place.

But this was all I'd ever wanted, so I couldn't help it.

"So, if you're not *styling Henry*," Paula mocked, "what do you have to do?"

"Run-of-the-mill intern stuff, I suppose." I stopped at a red light and watched at least twenty more people cross against the light. One of them rammed their elbow into my side for *not* breaking the law. "*Ouch*. Get coffee, write emails. Observe. Assist."

"Maeve Peterson: a glorified servant. Can't say I haven't been there." She sighed wistfully and, in sync with the light turning green, asked, "Nervous?"

To avoid getting trampled on my first day, I basically ran across the street. "Excited," I corrected as soon as I could focus on something other than my basic survival. "I just left my Ashwood-provided apartment"—that I was lucky enough not to share with another intern as originally intended—"in *New York*. I'm on my way to the biggest luxury designer in *New York*. Get to be a glorified servant."

A pause for dramatic effect. "In *New York*. Me and my best friend live in the same city again."

Paula was currently writing a profile on a Blue Eagles player. The team was on a training trip, which meant so was she. Couldn't say I envied her week full of soccer and sweaty men, but she was coming home tonight.

"You and your best friend will live in *New York*," she clarified. "That seems to be a common theme here."

"In New York!" Not a single person glanced my way when I happily skipped over the next crosswalk. I'm sure they're used to much worse. "You're starting to get it. I'm on my way to my dream job, in my dream city, living in my dream apartment."

With two bedrooms, a large window in the kitchen, plus a fire escape I'd definitely be using as a balcony. "And no roommates!"

The line crackled at her loud exhale, not quite a laugh yet. "I was a great roommate."

I tossed my empty coffee cup and rounded the last corner when I spotted it. My stomach dropped in anticipation and excitement. *This is really happening*, I realized, looking up at the giant signature Adeline Ashwood bow engraved on the four-story building in the heart of SoHo.

"You were a great roommate. Listen, babe, I just got to the office—"

"The office," Paula hummed in approval. "Sounds so official. Let me know when you've taken the place over!"

The certainty in her tone before she hung up should've been intimidating. *Let me know when you've taken the place over.* High expectations hid behind that statement, but I'd grown up with those, and there was no need to keep them low. I'd been daydreaming about this day in some form or another since I was six years old and started picking out my own clothes.

Granted, they weren't anything as fancy as Adeline Ashwood, but it's the thought that counted.

I fiddled with the collar of Pop's old button-up, straightened the sleeveless knit vest layered on top, and made sure both were tucked into the tailored pants I'd been lucky enough to find in the back of Mom's closet when we'd finally gone through her stuff years ago.

Donate. Toss. Maeve.

It didn't take a genius to figure out which pile had been the biggest.

With a deep breath, I banned the little flutter of nerves and rush of nostalgia. Then pushed the door into the best day of my life open.

Straight into a security guard's face.

"Oh my God." I took a step back just to make sure I wasn't about to get tackled by the guy. The black sunglasses on his nose sat crooked after the accidental attack, and he lifted them to really look at me.

With small eyes scanning and a crease between his brows, he realized I wasn't a threat and relaxed. "That's one way to make an entrance." Still rubbing his nose, the gruff voice contrasted the quirk of his lips. Not a smile but not *not* a smile either. "How can I help you, Miss—?"

"Peterson. Sorry, it's my first day. Internship. Are you alright, honey?" Realizing my first impression at Adeline Ashwood was nearly committing aggravated assault, my cheeks flushed. The emotional-support nickname slipped out in Mimi's southern drawl. (My grandma was very proud of her accent, and when I visited after my first year of college, she was horrified to discover I'd been almost completely East Coast–ified.)

He waved me off casually, and his brown eyes disappeared behind the sunglasses again. "Been through worse than a door in my face. Just scan your badge at the gate over there. Elevator to the second floor, then right, right again, left—and you should find Rachel Roland's office."

It was abundantly clear that he was no longer open to questions after that. Not for a *What?* or *Sorry, could you repeat that?* He'd spoken so fast and I'd been so focused on not being nervous, it was over before I could even grasp he was giving me directions.

First step: Badge. Then gate. I got that much.

I'd packed my leather tote meticulously. Laptop, notebook, lunch. Pens and badge in the extra pocket inside. So I wasn't sure why on earth I couldn't find the latter. I stopped short of the gate, a forced smile on my lips when I made brief eye contact with the lady behind the counter.

"Can I help you?" she asked, only making me search more desperately. Her blonde ponytail screamed *no bullshit.*

Fuck. Where was that damn badge?

I shook my head. "No, I'm sorry. Just—there it is!" Although it left the inside of my bag in a state of unprecedented chaos, relief flooded my veins. Ponytail couldn't possibly begin to understand just how much of it when she gave me a polite smile and turned back to her computer.

Meanwhile, my heart still sounded like it was beating in sync to an EDM song when I scanned my badge and got to the elevators. Not tripping in the lobby wasn't really an accomplishment, but it felt like one.

I pressed the button for the second floor (that much I still remembered) and tried not to marvel at the inside of the elevator too much. Textured light panels, marbled floor with the signature Ashwood bow engraved in the middle. The mirror opposite the doors made me aware of something else that didn't usually happen: I looked a mess.

Yes, my cheeks had gone back to their normal color and no longer resembled the natural red of my hair, but the latter was a mess. Ginger strands stood in every possible direction, got caught in the buttons of my shirt, and no longer screamed, *Wow, she's got her life together!* even though I'd wielded that blow-dryer like a wand this morning. Unfortunately, my curtain bangs no longer had that perfect wave in them either.

Note to self: More hairspray.

I tried to salvage what I could, brushed the front pieces behind my ear, and scurried out of the elevator. Everything—from the logo on the opposite wall to the couch below it, the gleaming white floors and the light-pink accents, the bouquets on pillars lining the hallways in both directions—screamed luxury. Expensive and better than you in every sense. If I remembered my onboarding sheet correctly (and I did), the second floor held meeting rooms and personal offices, while the floors above housed the archives, atelier, and spaces to welcome clients and models and whatever other external stakeholders might come in.

My gaze swept through the hallway one last time. What had he said? Right, left, right again? I usually had no problem recounting directions, but I was more nervous than I'd like to be when I set off.

I passed offices with a single glass panel through which you could see inside, and behind each one was at least one person hunched over a computer, sketching, or pacing with a phone to their ear. Small golden name plaques decorated the doors, with a bow engraved above familiar names like Sheffield, Rodriguez, and Laurent: the heads of Adeline Ashwood's design team and the brains behind every new collection. I tried not to screech.

Another wall held framed black-and-white prints of their most iconic pieces, presented on models at fashion shows or celebrities at galas. I couldn't help but slow down and soak up the fact that I was really here, working for the people who had created these. Iconic dresses, staple bags, and accessories that were worn by anyone who's anyone. One day, hopefully, designed by yours truly.

Adeline Ashwood by Maeve Peterson.

It had a nice ring to it that eventually lured me farther down the hall, around corners, until there was just one door at the end of the hallway without a name plaque or glass panel to see through.

One look at my phone cemented a decision I'd made the second I'd seen the room. It was almost nine. Which left me basically on time—almost too late for my first day—and there was no need to wait until I really was.

I knocked.

Nothing. It took so long, I'd already raised my hand again when the door finally flew open and a small woman with tortoise-rimmed glasses blinked back at me. Her black ponytail was sleek, not a single strand out of place. My eyes just grazed the top of her head, focused on something else entirely.

Not an office.

A meeting room, every single chair except for hers occupied with men in suits and women in blazers and pencil skirts. Authority and power oozed out of every single one of their pores. My gaze snapped back to Rimmed Glasses, her eyes as wide as mine, like she could just about imagine my horror.

"Yes?" she squeaked. My hand lowered all on its own, and if it wasn't for every single pair of eyes on us, I would've probably tried to pinch myself out of this very realistic nightmare scenario.

Because one of those pairs belonged to Hunter Ashwood, piercing blue eyes more intimidating than they should've been from a distance. It wasn't just the look on his face though. It was the way he sat, pin straight, hands folded on the table. The crisp four-piece suit without a wrinkle in it.

And, yes, that expression too. Unwavering, relentless, still looking at me.

It took everything in me not to stutter when I said, "Sorry. I'm looking for the intern . . . welcoming?"

Totally made-up name, but what was I supposed to do?

Behind Rimmed Glasses, some lips quirked. Mouths went to ears, and whispers floated through the room until a single shift of Hunter Ashwood in his seat shut every single one of them up again. If possible, I got even smaller in the doorway, but the woman in front of me was too tiny to hide behind.

She blinked back at me like she couldn't quite believe I was here either. "To the left, straight ahead, left again."

I nodded—vigorously—and didn't even manage to say *Thanks!* before the door closed between us.

Left, straight, left again.

This time, the directions burned straight into my brain. In five years, I'd still be able to recount them in my sleep. A trauma response, maybe. Something that would forever remind me of what my first meeting with Hunter Ashwood had been: a complete disaster.

I found the Roland name plaque exactly two minutes before nine, right where both the security guard and Rimmed Glasses had promised it'd be. The coffee vending machine in front of it was a sign, I think. A gift from the universe that said, *Things will get better now.*

They *had* to get better, starting with that coffee. The past thirty minutes hadn't just shaved twenty years off my life, but the caffeine already in my system had immediately given way to panic and adrenaline and shame, leaving space for the next fix currently trickling into a to-go cup.

I was tired. I needed a minute to collect myself, preferably with this cup of black coffee and some breathing exercises. Before Rachel could swoop me up into what would turn into . . . the best day of my life?

The coal-black liquid (that seemed to be complimentary, thank God) filled the cup to the rim, and I took a deep breath to mark a new beginning. The last thirty minutes hadn't happened.

I'd walked into Adeline Ashwood without incident, immediately found my way, and had been so early, I still had time to get a coffee.

I took a long sip, and it washed the embarrassment straight out of my body. I was probably first-degree burning the inside of my throat, but the wake-up call was needed.

Stop fucking around, Maeve.

When I opened my eyes, I almost felt normal again. Like I could go in there and finally nail at least one of my first impressions of the day—never mind that it was the fourth one. Just in time, the clock read nine on the dot, and a door opened behind me.

And it all happened so fast, there was nothing I could've done.

I turned, ran straight into a chest, and the cup slipped out of my grasp. Trying to catch it only resulted in its contents spilling directly onto the stranger's crisp white shirt. And shoes.

Fuuuuuck. Hot liquid dripped off him, and I was very aware that this might be my second attempted assault of a stranger in the span of minutes. Screw trying to be positive, today literally couldn't get any worse.

He cursed like a sailor, shook his arms out, and tried to keep the drenched shirt from burning his skin. Judging by his pained hisses, he was quite unsuccessful.

"I'm so sorry—" I said, reaching for the enormous stain, but attempting to rub it out only made it worse, so I finally looked up at the guy whose day I'd just ruined.

And . . . fuck again. Apparently, it *could* get worse.

CONTENT WARNING

(AND SPOILER WARNING!)

This book contains potentially triggering content. This includes

Mention of substance abuse, death of family member, loss, toxic family dynamics

LYX

Ready for your next romance obsession?
Visit us at LYXBooks.com and follow us online @LYXBooks.